Caribbean WHISPERS

Caroline Bell Foster

© 2009 Caroline Bell Foster
First Edition
10 9 8 7 6 5 4 3 2 1

All rights reserved. No part of this book may be reproduced, stored in a retrieval system, or transmitted, in any form or by any means, electronic, mechanical, photocopying, recording, or otherwise, without the prior written permission of the publishers or author.

If you have bought this book without a cover you should be aware that it is "stolen" property. The publishers and author have not received any payment for the "stripped" book, if it is printed without their authorization.

All LMH titles, imprints and distributed lines are available at special quantity discounts for bulk purchases for sales promotion, premiums, fund-raising, educational or institutional use.

Editor: Nicola Brown
Cover design: Sanya Dockery
Book design, layout & typesetting: Sanya Dockery
Cover picture: www.freedigitalphotos.net

Published by LMH Publishing Limited
Suite 10-11
LOJ Industrial Complex
7 Norman Road
Kingston C.S.O., Jamaica
Tel.: (876) 938-0005; 938-0712
Fax: (876) 759-8752
Email: lmhbookpublishing@cwjamaica.com
Website: www.lmhpublishing.com

Printed in the U. S. A.   ISBN:978-976-8202-62-8

For Victoria

Chapter One

A thunderous roar made Jonas Evans suddenly jack-knife into an upright position with startling speed. The small boat rocked violently from side to side as he tried to steady himself before he fell into the dark, turbulent waters of the Caribbean Sea.

It was only after several long panicky seconds had passed that he realised the loud noise wasn't in his throbbing drunken head. In fact, it was the crashing waves, as they aggressively tried to demolish the grey craggy rocks which protected this small stretch of private beach owned by his family.

Luckily, he had woken in time to avoid the looming rocks. He rowed a short distance to where the sea became the calm turquoise blue that made Jamaica famous and towed the decaying wood of the twenty-foot *Rum Runner* towards the beach, bracing himself to find a little strength to anchor it. He completed the task and then wiped the sweat from his forehead with a small, dirty red rag he always carried, shoving it into the back pocket of his filthy jeans when he'd finished.

He searched under the unstable wooden seat of the boat for the ever present bottle of overproof white rum. The clear fiery liquid soothed his frazzled nerves as he gulped thirstily as though drinking a glass of lemonade.

"Dats more like it," he murmured, as he bent to stash his treasure under the seat once more.

Feeling better, he stretched languorously, arching his back deeply and lifting his arms over his head, allowing his green mesh vest to ride up over his heavy rounded belly. He then lit a thin roll of ganja. He'd enjoyed the long deep sleep out at sea today where nobody was around to disturb him and demand anything from him.

He breathed in the drug, whilst he watched the steady rise and fall of his huge stomach. He chuckled and it jiggled. He laughed out loud and patted it lovingly, resting his arms on top of the fleshy mound. Jonas was proud of the huge rolls of fat which hung over his belt. His other brothers were skinny, but not him. No, he ate and drank well and he didn't care if the rest of his family starved to death as long as he wasn't inconvenienced.

Jonas hated fishing, yet it was preferable to farming the land, at least this way he was his own boss, nobody watching over his shoulder. Besides, he liked hearing the big explosive booms as the dynamite tore the reef apart. He found it intensely gratifying to watch the dead fish float to the surface all blood and guts. He chuckled.

The secret patch of ganja he cultivated further inland took care of his needs – food, liquor and women. He sold it to a man who required a regular supply to sell to the tourists down in Negril.

Flicking the tiny stub of ganja away, he started to walk a little unsteadily up the craggy slope of rocks which separated the beach from the main road. A thick unruly curtain of mangrove trees hid the entrance of the beach so only a few people in the community even remembered it. Anyhow, it wasn't a popular swimming spot as the sand was coarse and the current too strong for a leisurely swim.

He spotted one of his brothers talking to a school girl. He called him over.

"Hey bwoy! Yuh nuh ave nutten betta fi do?" he asked Tally, the second youngest boy, who fancied himself as the village Casanova.

"Cho man," Tally complained, "yuh jus' come an' mess up mi lyrics," Tally accused sulkily.

Of the two men, Tally topped Jonas' five feet by several inches. But apart from that difference they were identical, even though at thirty-four, Jonas was much older.

Both had the chilling beady eyed look of a mongoose, dark, muddy complexions, wide snout-like noses, chins that were short and weak, and lips that were large, thick and constantly wet like rotting logs on the beach below them.

Jonas' body was almost comical in its appearance. His brothers jokingly called him "The head" with his huge rounded stomach and a large fat head which squatted on his thick shoulders.

"Go tek dis uppa yard." Jonas shoved the cooler at his brother before he could protest and pointed to the pink and brown concrete house with a rusty zinc roof. The house sat precariously on four crumbling concrete stilts on a small hill across the street.

Tally scowled and hissed his teeth loudly but turned away anyway. Jonas was known for his quick slaps.

Jonas, free for the rest of the evening, walked in the opposite direction towards Jack's, the local bar. Jack's was the only place around where he could get good food and entertainment. Every night and any other time he wasn't out at sea or sleeping, he could be found at Jack's.

Chapter Two

The midday sun scorched down on his head with a vicious intensity that made his head pound. Jonas groaned, as again he damned himself for leaving his straw fishing hat at the house. It was that coolie gal's fault! If she hadn't woken earlier than usual and gone out to take a bath he wouldn't have this blinding headache.

He had been so busy sneaking around and trying to get a glimpse of her lovely young body as she poured water over herself, that he'd forgotten most of his gear. Again! She was a sight. The best looking gal he'd ever seen, and her body! Well, she'd started sprouting breasts now and he couldn't wait to get his hands on them.

As Jonas felt his body swell, he looked around for a distraction. Whenever he thought of his young stepsister his blood gushed into that part of his body and he'd have to adjust his pants.

He turned on the engine and motored out for another half mile. He then cut the engine and rummaged around for several sticks of dynamite he'd already prepared. He pull-started the engine, motored out for another half mile or so, lit a fuse and threw the dynamite as far as he could. Seconds later, there was a satisfying boom and a huge underwater bulge disrupted the natural movements of the water. He motored over to the site and cursed. Nothing, not even seaweed.

Shrugging, he cut the engine, spread the fishing net out on the vessel's floor and lay down. He lit a spliff and inhaled. It wasn't his fault he couldn't bring in any fish today, he thought. He was having ackee and salt fish at Jack's tonight so he was alright. The others would have to fend for themselves.

Drifting off to sleep, thoughts of his stepsister came into sharp focus once more. At eight years old, when they had moved into her house, she had been a pretty little bony thing. At thirteen she was growing nicely into her bones – beautiful, long jet black hair down to her waist, large dark eyes and a nice straight nose. She reminded him of an exotic dancer he'd once seen in a club down in Negril. He'd wanted her, and almost got locked up for touching her. He'd get his little stepsister. He licked his fleshy lips, picturing himself deep inside her. His hand moved into his pants.

Chapter Three

The warm sand felt heavenly beneath her feet.

Miriam Robinson sat as close to the shore as she could possibly get without getting her toes wet. She was tired and hungry and would have loved to fall asleep in her bed, but the tiny house was overflowing. All of her stepbrothers were home so she came to the only place where she could be alone. Almost every evening she tried to come down to the cove. It was the only time she had to herself and she would stay out as long as she dared. Not that she would be missed, she mused sadly. As long as dinner was cooked, the plates washed and the yard swept, nobody cared what she did.

She missed Pappy, her real father.

Miriam hugged her knees to her chest and relaxed. The sun began to set taking with it the remaining warmth for the day. She was shivering and so took off her worn, faded dress knowing she'd be warmer in the water. She enjoyed swimming at this time of the evening.

She smiled sadly as she swam out, kicking her slim but strong legs against the tugging current. Pappy had been dead for almost seven years now and she missed him with each passing second. If he was still alive, her life would be so different.

He had worked hard to realise his dream of building a small hotel on his land. Unfortunately, one day the mule he'd been riding into the field had thrown him, killing him instantly.

Miriam lost two people that day, her father and her mother, Elsa, had lost her sparkle and became a fragile, timid woman whose spirit had died along with her husband. In a moment of sheer madness she had remarried and regretted the union ever since. On her wedding night she was raped and brutally beaten, the first of many.

Tears swam and trailed miserably down Miriam's face, mixing with the salty sea water. She tried not to cry when thinking about her mother, crying was so futile, so childish.

She hated the house, especially now that she was getting older; her stepbrothers leering at her every move, walking into her bedroom without knocking, knowing she'd be alone inside, and on several occasions she'd seen the worst one, Jonas, watching her take her baths in the mornings. There had even been a time when he'd backed her against a wall and touched her breasts and since then she'd begun to tie them down so they wouldn't be so noticeable.

Her younger stepsister wasn't so bad but she had a nasty habit of stealing and lying; and every chance Rosie got she blamed Miriam for something. This always resulted in Miriam getting her face slapped by her stepfather – who never bothered to ask questions.

None of it bothered her anymore. She had stopped having and showing her feelings long ago. She lived each day as it came, remembering her father and the happier times to get her through each day.

Miriam could remember the happy smiling faces of her parents as they picnicked on the beach, her father's dark handsome face and straight black hair always flopping into his eyes. It was her father who'd shown her the cove.

Her mother, Elsa, was once a beautiful woman, small and delicate like a daisy, with a gentle smile and loving ways. She was envied by all the other black women in the village for catching a landowner and a half white, half Indian man – a man who could give her 'pretty' children. Elsa was now timid, dependent and weepy; her hair completely white with sadness and despair. She had given up on life and looked old and worn.

Miriam knew she was on her own. Her mother wouldn't be able to get them out of this situation, it depended on her. She had to be strong. It was going to be a long hard road. That's why she studied so hard and did what she was told; quietly waiting for the time when she could reclaim what was rightfully hers, this beach and all the acres of land across the main road. She wouldn't be rich and maybe she'd have to sell an acre or two but she would survive. They would survive. She was sure of that.

The stars had begun to twinkle in the early darkness of the night sky. She pushed all memories away, both good and bad, and made a game of counting the stars as she floated on her back.

Jonas woke in a spluttering fright to inky darkness. He rubbed his eyes and blinked rapidly. Bloodclaat! A wha dis, he thought, seeing nothing but miles of spooky water and pitch black sky.

The quietness was chilling, the water eerie, so he quickly started *The Rum Runner's* engine, breaking the never ending silence. He turned the boat in what he thought was the right direction. Then he took out his half empty rum bottle, drained it and threw it overboard. He belched loudly, grabbed another bottle and motored on.

What seemed like hours later, Jonas saw a light in the distance. He rubbed his eyes and peered at it, hoping it wasn't in his drunken mind. As fast as he could, he sailed in the direction of it and chuckled. He felt very much like one of the Three Wise Men.

Chapter Four

Miriam was swimming lazily when a faint buzzing sound caught her attention. She stared into the darkness, straining her ears. It sounded like a boat engine, but there wasn't a light and anyone who lived in the area knew it was a dangerous part of the coastline. The rocks under the water's surface made entry virtually impossible.

The boat was coming closer and she swam hurriedly to shore, took off her underwear, squeezed them out and put them on again. She pulled on her dress and braided her thick long hair.

She thought about leaving – as it was getting late anyway – or staying in case the fisherman might need help. She decided to stay. A slap was nothing when compared to helping to save a life.

Miriam waited nervously at the shoreline biting her bottom lip and praying that the boat would get in safely. It was getting cold and she could feel goose bumps spreading along her arms. With an old kerosene lamp in her hand, she moved to where she remembered fewer rocks were and hoped the boat would be able to get through unharmed. She had kept the old lamp tucked away in the rocks in case she ever managed to sneak away at night.

Minutes later, Miriam was able to see a small fishing boat. It was a miracle, it had escaped the deathly rocks. She felt relieved and excited.

The excitement soon died. It was her stepbrother, Jonas.

Miriam slumped unhappily. It was too late to leave. She'd probably get a beating for leaving him out here alone, and if she stayed, he might be grateful and keep her place a secret.

Jonas couldn't believe his luck. He'd followed the light and made it to shore, but he didn't recognise which beach he was on, not that he minded, he just wanted to get off this raas boat and head over to Jack's.

Jonas jumped into the cool water and was hurriedly tugging the boat to shore, when he looked up and saw his stepsister Miriam looking at him nervously.

"Well gal yuh nah 'elp mi wid dis?" he slurred sarcastically.

"Yes sir," Miriam replied quickly.

All she wanted was to get out of the secluded cove as soon as possible. She didn't want to be alone with him. She helped him haul the boat onto the sand, desperately wishing she could blend into the darkness.

"Go tek di cooler out, an' hide it by dem rocks," Jonas ordered.

His gaze travelled over her slim body and settled on her bare legs. He watched her drag the cooler along the sand, getting a glimpse of her young breasts when she leaned over. His body grew warm.

※ ※ ※

Jonas watched Miriam as she sat on a rock to pull her flip flops on. Her long braid brushed the sand as she bent down. He could tell she was nervous and he felt something like satisfaction race through his veins. Miriam stood and looked at him, unaware of the effect she was having on him, standing in the shadow of the lamp light wearing a thin cotton dress she'd outgrown long ago and which clung to her damp skin.

Jonas' throat dried up.

"Come ere gal," he ordered softly, his throat tight with lust.

With her heart pounding at the base of her throat, Miriam stood before him wondering if he was going to slap her for being out late at night. She looked down at her feet expecting to feel the stinging contact of his hand against her cheek.

"T'anks," he said suddenly and pulled her into his embrace.

Miriam was taken aback. Never had any of them embraced her; much less thank her for something. Her arms hung limply at her sides and she held her breath, hating the smell of raw fish, rum, sweat and urine that clung to him.

Jonas squeezed her tighter and splayed his fingers over her bottom, hauling her against him. Miriam panicked. She pushed at his chest but he held her tighter and began to bite her neck, whilst one hand groped the front of her body.

She screamed. A scream anyone could hear but no one did. Her screams bounced off the cliffs and went out to sea unheard. She pushed at him, kicked at him and raised her knee to his groin. For a second, Jonas let her go, a stunned expression on his face as he growled in a mixture of disbelief, anger and pain.

She grasped at the precious seconds and scrambled frantically over the rocks towards the cliff but he caught up with her, grabbed her braid and hauled her down to the beach. He used his free hand to punch her on the jaw and her body went limp. He lay across her and tore open her dress, ripping it from the front of her body and taking the bra with it in one vicious movement.

Miriam's body hurt and she felt waves of nausea crawl up her throat. The vomit erupted, choking her as she gasped for air and tried to twist free of the thick fists which were pummelling down on her body.

Jonas cursed and moved her away from the sticky mess. He ripped her panties and spread her legs apart. With the last of her strength she fought him and he attacked with renewed eagerness. His hands and teeth were everywhere. Her screams caught in her throat. Salty tears blinded her and she closed her eyes trying to block out the sight of his devilish face twisted with craziness. She willed herself to die.

Suddenly, she was free. Her eyes flew open. Jonas was taking his pants off! She sprang to her feet but was flat on her back again before she could take a step. He'd punched her with such hatred, such force, the night sky blurred.

Biting into her shoulder, Jonas pushed her legs apart and rammed himself into her, piercing her flesh with one vicious stab. He tasted the sweetness of blood on his tongue where she'd bit her own lips. It drove him wilder. His only thought was that he had her. He finally had her.

Jonas flopped tiredly beside her lifeless body. She was whimpering a tiny sound which lodged in her throat. Her face was bloody and swollen; crusts of vomit had dried in her hair.

He paced back and forth, the cold sand kicking up with each step he made. Plan, he thought frantically, he had to plan! The bloodclaat gal would tell on him! He kneeled beside her and pressed his big hand into her throat. Die! Die! Her breath faded away.

He took a deep breath, put his clothes on, drank some liquor and took his clothes off again. He went for a swim. He was now composed.

He walked over to the body and felt for a pulse again. She was still alive! Raas! Why won't she die?

Without thought he picked up a rock and slammed it down on her head. Blood squirted from her temple. He dragged her lifeless body into the water and pushed it out, knowing the current would pull it under.

In the distance he could see the pale light of a passing yacht. He dismissed it, knowing it was on its way to Negril. He leisurely pulled on his clothes, blew out the lamp and looked at his watch. It was after one in the morning.

He carefully picked his way over the sharp rocks, cursing himself for not having any shoes as the stones cut into his feet. When he reached the road, he looked back and smiled before heading for Jack's. He needed a drink.

Chapter Five

Thomas Davis Walters III was supposed to be a happy man. Yesterday he'd won the coveted Montego Bay Marlin Tournament – the second year in a row – yet he'd only felt a moment of happiness. His usually cheerful blue eyes remained pale with despondency. He couldn't understand the way he was feeling. He normally enjoyed the second city and even owned a luxurious apartment up in the Montego Bay hills. But since waking, he'd been unable to relax and enjoy himself with all the other revellers who'd come out on their expensive yachts to enjoy a few days of fishing and merry making. He just couldn't shake the daunting feeling that his life was about to change – a change he couldn't control.

"Joseph! Joseph!" Thomas called, climbing the steps to the bridge.

"You bellowed?" Joseph asked smiling. An unlit pipe was dancing at the corner of his mouth. He'd stopped smoking years ago but he still needed the familiarity of the pipe in his mouth to keep it that way.

"Yeah, let's head home."

"Now?" Joseph asked surprised, raising a slightly grey eyebrow.

"Yeah. Let's take the Negril route so we can stop in Black River." Thomas smiled fondly at his best friend and first mate of forty-odd years.

Joseph grinned, switched on the powerful engine and looked over the side waiting for Thomas to untie the rope and step onto the boat. This meant, Joseph thought happily, that he'd be seeing Mrs. Dobbson a day early. He couldn't wait.

※ ※ ※

Joseph stopped breathing. He'd heard a noise, or thought he heard a noise. He relaxed and began to read his thriller, only to hear the sound seconds later. He looked at his watch, nine thirty-one, then he reached for his map to pinpoint their exact location. They were half a mile off the coastline, nearest port being the fishing village off Cousins Cove.

He heard the sound again, this time a little fainter. He switched off the engine and went downstairs to ask Thomas if he'd heard the eerie noise.

"Thomas," Joseph whispered, in case his friend was sleeping. He knocked on the door of the master suite and slipped inside.

"Thomas?" he said again, going over to pick up the thick book which had slipped from the other man's sleeping fingers.

"Hey Thomas," Joseph said much louder and shook Thomas' shoulders. "Wake up!"

"Mmm...Wha-what is it, Josey?" Thomas muttered drowsily.

"Did you hear that noise?"

"Obviously not," he drawled sarcastically. "What noise?"

"A while ago."

"What kind of noise?" Thomas asked sleepily, struggling to sit up and blinking rapidly when Joseph switched on the overhead light.

"A terrible sound. Heard it two or three times."

"Josey, it could have been anything. There's plenty of seagulls around here...where are we anyway?"

"Just off Cousins Cove, a fishing Village about thirteen miles from Negril. I've…"

Just then, a long painful sound split into the silence.

"Jesus Christ! What in God's name was that?" exclaimed Thomas. He stood and used both hands to push his thick silver hair from his forehead.

"Don't know, but it sounds scary," Joseph replied faintly.

Thomas reached over and lowered the radio, waiting for the sound again.

"What do you think it was? Sounded more like a scream really," Thomas said, more to himself. "What time is it?"

"Almost ten."

"How far are we from the coastline again? Can we pull into port?"

"We're too far to tell yet. I'll go a little nearer and see what the scanner picks up." Joseph left, leaving Thomas with a fearful feeling in his stomach.

He pulled on a pair of crumpled white shorts and a faded blue T-shirt before going on deck. It was cold and windy. The sound came again, only fainter, almost like a moan. It sounded as though someone was being tortured. He shivered.

A few minutes passed, Joseph yelled out.

"Thomas! Tommy! Come up here. Quick!"

Thomas leapt up the steps and Joseph handed him a pair of powerful binoculars. He moved it along the dark coastal shore. The only lights were miles away and he could barely make out dark jagged rocks and a small beach, which looked completely cut off from the rest of the shoreline. That's when he saw a faint light.

As they approached land, it became clear it was a girl crying out.

"Can we get any nearer Josey?" Thomas asked worriedly.

"This is about as far as we can go. If we had a smaller vessel, maybe, but from the scanner, it'll be impossible to pass through without ripping the bottom out from under us," Joseph explained bleakly.

"What about the dinghy?"

"I already thought about that, but there are rocks just below the surface. We'd never get ten yards. We'll just have to wait until light."

Thomas didn't like it, but everything Joseph said was true. It was just too dangerous and too dark; there wasn't even a moon out for Christ's sake!

"Can we radio the police or something?"

"I did." Joseph pursed his full lips together in annoyance. "I couldn't get through."

"Waste of bloody time they are," Thomas muttered, echoing Joseph's thoughts. "Ok. Let's drop anchor and wait here until daybreak. Something terrible is happening out there Josey."

Thomas turned to look into his friend's deep brown eyes, both men feeling completely helpless and utterly defeated. To not get involved didn't enter into either of their minds.

Joseph had dropped off to sleep on a bench, but Thomas had his ears straining for any sound of life. His eyes never left the dull light, until, sometime after midnight, the light went out and all he saw was ghostly darkness.

Dread clenched his heart.

⁂

Thomas' eyes were burning and his whole body was stiff and aching from looking out at the beach for so long. It was almost five and the gentle whispers of first light had just touched the night sky. He swiftly went over to Joseph and shook him awake.

"Josey it's morning," Thomas said urgently.

Joseph rubbed his eyes and stood, looking around as though not quite sure of his surroundings. He went to the bathroom and splashed cold water on his face, drying it impatiently with a towel, before heading outside. It was a little past five.

Thomas was already preparing to launch the small, bright yellow dinghy. He had inflated it at record speed, gathered three life jackets and was looking around impatiently for the first aid kit.

"Where's the bloody first aid box?" he demanded roughly.

"I'll get it. You get a bottle of brandy. We might need it," stated Joseph, his brown eyes solemn.

They looked at each other for a few seconds, mentally preparing themselves for what they might find.

It took a good twenty minutes to reach the beach. They pulled the dinghy onto the sand and looked around. The beach was tiny, nothing more than twenty-five meters and completely enclosed. Crops of jagged rocks protected the cove from the open sea, and high, craggy, grey cliffs stood guard over and around it, forming a tight letter C.

Nothing was out of the ordinary, a tired old fishing boat called *The Rum Runner*, and a bright blue cooler which was stashed awkwardly in a far corner. Joseph headed for the cooler, whilst Thomas walked around for some sort of clue.

"Nothing in here, just a couple of empty bottles," Joseph shouted over to Thomas.

Thomas stood still, looking about the steep cliffs, a million questions running through his mind. Then he looked down and his heart stopped, an icy chill skittered up his spine making the tiny hairs at the back of his neck stand on end.

"Joseph! Over here."

Joseph ran over and looked down to see where Thomas was pointing. Blood stains, footprints and what looked like something being dragged, trailed into the sea. Both men followed the path until their feet got wet. They stood still and gazed out. Shifting his gaze, Thomas scrutinized all the rocks. He caught a glimpse of colour and squinted at the sight, trying to make out what it was.

"Joseph? What's that over there?"

"Over where?" Joseph asked, looking in the direction of Thomas' pointing finger.

"By that flat rock, just left of the boat."

"Let's go and look."

They climbed back into the dinghy, paddling as fast as they could against the current, until they were upon the rock. A girl, naked with cuts and bruises all over her, lay face down on a slab of wide rock. The rock was splattered with dried blood from higher up as though she had crawled up there to save herself. The girl's left hand was gripping the rock tightly, her knuckles white, her fingertips blue. Her lower body had slid into the water.

"Steady the boat Josey, while I climb onto the rock."

Thomas stood and jumped onto the rock, his bare feet fiercely gripping the slippery stone.

He was almost afraid to touch her. She looked so pale, so still, so lifeless. . .so dead. Tentatively, he reached out and touched her neck. She was cold and he pulled back as though burned.

"Feel her pulse," encouraged Joseph in a hushed voice.

Thomas leaned over her again and pushed her hair aside. His fingers moved under her jaw and for a few terrible seconds he felt nothing and then the faint pulsating feelings of life leapt into his fingers.

"She's alive! Thank you God! Thank you Jesus!" Thomas exclaimed with relief. "Joseph, try and bring the boat around to this side of the rock then we can slide her into the dinghy without too much movement. But first, pass the blanket, she's freezing!"

All this was done as quickly and carefully as they could. They got her onto the yacht and Joseph put a long shirt on her and tucked her under a pile of fleecy blankets.

It was obvious that the girl had been raped. Dried, crusted blood and purple and black bruises covered her inner thighs. Thomas passed a little brandy between her cold stiff lips.

"Where's the nearest hospital?" he asked Joseph.

"Most likely in Savanna-la-mar, but there has to be a doctor's office in Negril."

"Ok. We'll stop in Negril. Oh Yes! My old friend Dr. Jenkins lives in Negril. I'll call ahead and get him to meet us."

Thomas left to do just that, leaving Joseph to rub more brandy over the child's lips again. She was a beautiful little thing, couldn't be more than thirteen or fourteen. Her face was swollen, her lips bruised and cut and her jaw was almost the size of a grapefruit. Her left eye must have received a vicious blow, as it was a deep shade of purple and blue, and probably wouldn't be able to open for another few days.

He gently felt through her hair looking for further injuries. The lump above her temple was deep and maybe needed stitches. The bastard must have used something to hit her, probably tried to kill her. How could someone do such a thing?

He felt the engine die and he moved to look out of the window. The famous white sand beach of Negril stretched before him in miles and miles of startling splendour. Lines of hotels and villas dotted the beach tastefully. There were scores of happy tourists sunbathing on white plastic lounges, or playing volleyball and swimming; all oblivious to the horror only a few meters away from them.

Thomas dropped anchor and they changed places. Joseph took the little dinghy to shore to collect the short, balding doctor who was waiting impatiently under the scanty shade of a tall palm tree. Ten minutes later, the flustered doctor walked into the bedroom, thankful for its coolness. After thirty-two years in Jamaica, he still couldn't get used to the heat and at the moment, looked and felt as red and sweaty as a lobster. It was days like these he wished he was back in England.

"Good to see you man! Golly. What's it been, three years?" said the doctor pleasantly as he pumped Thomas' hand enthusiastically then moved pass him to remove the blanket from the girl's body.

"You can leave now Thomas," he said with sudden seriousness.

"I'm staying right here, Jenkins," Thomas replied stubbornly.

Suddenly Dr. Jerkins sucked in his breath sharply, dropped the blankets and immediately spun round.

"What in God's name have you done to this poor child? There are very few decent people in this crazy world Thomas Walters, but at least I thought you were one of them! By golly!" His face was twisted in disgust and his pale watery eyes were full of stabbing accusations.

"What are you saying…that I did this?" Thomas' eyes almost bulged out of his head. "Jenkins, what kind of man do you think I am?" he roared incredulously.

"I don't care about your sexual style, but I will not tolerate beating upon young girls, nor will I help clean up your mess!" The doctor pulled off his surgical gloves. "I'm calling the police." He turned to go.

"Wait!" Thomas grabbed his arm. "I didn't do this to the poor girl. I swear it to you…"

"Then how did she get this way?"

Thomas launched into a brief explanation of how they had come by the battered child.

"Does this mean you do not have an intimate knowledge of this child's body?"

"Yes it bloody well does!" Thomas exploded loudly as he pulled himself up to his full height.

"Well in that case kindly leave the room, my patient deserves a little privacy."

Thomas left the bedroom, closing the door softly behind him and went to sit next to Joseph on the small sofa. Both men sat in silence, their eyes locked on the teak coloured door.

Half an hour later, Dr. Jenkins emerged and sat facing the two men.

"Well gentlemen the animal who did this to her should be charged with rape and attempted murder. On the surface her wounds will heal in a few days; but the knock on her head I think was meant to kill her. She's quite strong, she responds to things I tell her and she may be sleeping on and off for a while." He shrugged. "I left some antibiotics by the bed with instructions, some eye drops, and a morning-after-pill."

He instructed, "Make sure you put an ice pack on her eye and on the bruise on her face."

The two other men sighed in relief, their bodies slumping in synchronism.

"What can we do now? Does she need to go to the hospital?" Thomas asked.

"When she wakes – which should be shortly – ask her some basic questions like her name, address, age and so on? If she doesn't know, she may definitely need to go to the hospital. That blow..." He shook his head. "Treat her gently; she's had a terrible scare."

"Jenkins, we can't thank you enough," Thomas said, willing to give the man a million dollars if he asked.

"You can thank me by getting this child well again and letting me see her every now and again. When are you taking her home?" he asked casually as he put his instruments into his black medical bag.

Thomas and Joseph looked at each other. They had been so concerned with getting her help that thoughts of her family hadn't even entered their minds.

"When she wakes up, we'll get her address and send a message," Joseph said, sending Thomas a probing look.

"Ok, that'll do for now. Are you going to report it to the police?"

Thomas and Joseph looked at each other again. "We'll have to ask her."

Dr. Jenkins, curiosity satisfied, stood to take his leave.

"Good to see you again Thomas. Take good care of her now."

Joseph escorted the doctor back to land.

Thomas got up, peeped on the girl, who was sleeping peacefully, and left the door ajar. His stomach growled and he patted it, remembering he hadn't eaten since yesterday afternoon. He walked towards the kitchen, feeling the dark lingering weight slowly lift from his shoulders. His life had reached a turning point. He was looking forward to whatever tomorrow held.

Chapter Six

Jonas was making his way slowly back to the beach. He couldn't see or think straight and the only thing he kept telling himself was that he had things to do. He hadn't slept yet, not after going to Jack's so late and when he did leave, it was the time in which he normally left the house. He had to act normal in case anything went wrong.

As he entered the Cove, he looked about double checking that absolutely no one was around. With unaccustomed nervousness he looked over the cliff face, his whole body swayed. Stepping back quickly he fished into his pocket for his rag and mopped his face. He was soaking wet with sweat. He slowly descended, refusing to look down onto the beach. Upon reaching the sand, he looked around. The boat was where he remembered leaving it; the cooler was over in the corner, but the girl was gone.

All night, whilst he got himself drunk, he kept wondering whether her body would wash up on shore or maybe she was still alive. Minutes later, he happily dashed his doubts aside as he finished looking around. There was no trace of the night before. He put the cooler into the boat and pushed the old vessel into the water and went back to rub the boat marks out of the sand with his bare feet. It was then he noticed a dark red blood stain on the sand. He retched violently but nothing came up. His stomach rocked and heaved. He staggered away and splashed sea water onto his face, then got a paddle and covered the stain with wet sand.

Before climbing into *The Rum Runner,* he looked around one more time scanning the top of the cliffs. No one was around. He'd gotten away with it.

He chuckled happily. That little half breed coolie gal got exactly what she deserved.

Something wasn't right. Her bed didn't feel like her bed and she could sense that something was different. Miriam opened her eyes and looked up. This was not her ceiling. The roof of her bedroom was rust covered zinc. This roof was expensive looking highly polished wood.

Panicked, she moved her head. This was not her room or her house even! Where was she? And where was her mother? She tried to move, but every muscle, bone and vein protested and she fell back against the sheets.

Something was terribly wrong. She closed her eyes again in case she was dreaming, but when she reopened them she was in the same place. Taking a deep breath she slowly sat up. She stayed still for a moment and waited for her head to stop spinning before swinging her legs over the side of the bed and standing up with shaky legs. She didn't move a step before she started to vomit violently into a basin which was placed strategically beside the bed.

Miriam was on her knees when two men came into the room to help her. One was dark and short with soothing dark eyes. The other was tall and white with a shock of silver hair.

"It's ok," Thomas said to the girl, bending down beside her and rubbing her shoulders. He had been surprised to find the poor child awake and out of bed.

Miriam let the man hold her. She felt weak, tired and slightly dazed. It was as though she was on the outside looking in with no control over her body. When she finally stopped retching, she rocked back and sat on the floor, waiting for her stomach to settle. The dark man who had been standing near the door came forward and handed her a damp towel.

"Thanks."

"Are you alright now?" the white man asked.

Miriam looked at him; her first thought was 'What lovely eyes!' She had never seen eyes that colour. They were so vivid, so blue, that neither the sea nor the sky could match their intensity.

"I think so," she said to him, looking at him closely. *And what thick hair!* "Where's my mother?"

She made the question sound more like an accusation, Thomas noticed and gave Joseph an enquiring look.

"We were hoping you could tell us that," he answered softly.

"I don't understand," she said in a small voice, confusion etched all over her pretty face.

"Ok, we'll talk later, but first get into bed and we'll bring you some soup. Are you hungry?" Thomas asked gently, as he tucked her into bed again, propping several pillows behind her head.

"Oh, yes!" Miriam said, just as her stomach made a loud unfeminine sound. "Sorry," she said, embarrassed.

Joseph went to warm the soup.

"My name is Thomas Davis Walters III," Thomas introduced, "and this is my best friend, Joseph Harper."

He waved a hand indicating Joseph who'd returned and was seated beside him. Joseph smiled shyly at the girl, who smiled back weakly.

"What's your name?" Thomas went on to ask.

"My name?" She looked blankly at the two men, trying to remember. "Miriam! ...Miriam Robinson!"

"Well Miriam, where do you live?" Thomas went on.

"Paradise Pass, with my Mother and *them*."

Thomas and Joseph both noticed how her voice had hardened.

"How old are you Miriam?"

"Fourteen, almost fifteen. How old are you?" She asked in return, taking him by surprise.

Thomas chuckled before answering. "Forty-nine almost Fifty. Joseph and I are the same age."

"Oh," she said, digesting this. "What happened to my other eye?" she asked them both, realizing for the first time that one was shut and throbbing.

"Well…you we…I mean…you were in a kind of accident," Thomas stuttered out awkwardly.

"Oh." She bit her bottom lip, whilst her brain tried to remember the accident. "Oh."

Joseph, having gotten over his acute shyness, leaned forward and took her hand. "We won't talk about that right now. First we have to get you fed with some of my famous chicken soup!" He smiled fondly at the child.

"Mmm, I'm starving. What time is it Mr. Thomas? You have all last names!" she exclaimed, laughing some more.

Her laugh made such a beautiful sound, Thomas wanted to hear more. "Yes I suppose I do," he answered lightly, "it's eight fifty-six."

He stood, pushed his chair back and pointed to a door.

"That's the bathroom through there. . .and the closet in here." Miriam's one eye followed him. "But don't go walking all over the place. You need to rest," he warned. "And if you need anything, ring this little bell. Ok?" He smiled broadly down at her, she was such a beautiful little thing.

"Ok." She smiled back at him, a heart stopping smile that made his heart grind to a halt, before stumbling rapidly into the tunnel of paternal love for the very first time in his life.

"Are we on a boat?" she asked when she noticed the tiny windows.

"Yep," he answered, moving towards the door.

"It must be a very big boat to have such a big room. Do you sleep in here too?" she asked innocently.

Thomas chuckled. "No." He opened her door and stood in the doorway. "This is Joseph's room," he showed a door to the right. "And this is my room." He touched a door on the left.

"Wow," was all she managed to say.

Thomas left, smiling to himself. What a darling child and what a sad tragedy. He didn't know whether to be thankful she didn't seem to remember any of it or not. He passed Joseph, who was heading in the direction of her room, carrying a tray laden with soup, rolls, water and fruit.

"She's a nice kid Tommy, very bright. Should we tell her?"

"I think we should wait a little, she might remember on her own. Besides, all we know is how we found her anyway," he pointed out.

Joseph knocked on her door.

"Come in."

"Hi Miss Miriam," Joseph greeted cheerily, placing the tray on her lap.

"Hi Mr. Joseph." She was looking at the tray. "Is that all for me?" she asked incredulously.

"Yep, every single bit of it," Joseph told her happily. "Now I want you to eat slowly, you haven't eaten all morning."

She was biting into a roll as though it was the last piece of bread in the universe. Then she put the bowl of soup to her head and drank. Joseph was astonished.

"How did I get here?" she asked when she finished her meal.

"You knocked your head," Joseph stated awkwardly. Thomas was always better at this type of thing.

"How?" she asked.

"Well I don't know how. . .you have to tell us that."

"Oh," she whispered, scrunching up her face. "I don't remember!" Tears trickled down her face.

"There now, don't you cry. Get some rest and we'll talk later."

Thomas walked in carrying a TV.

"Look what I brought you Miriam!" He grinned at her but not before giving Joseph an annoyed look for making the poor child cry.

"That's for me?" she asked astonished.

"Yes, all yours." He put the TV on top of the dresser facing her bed and handed her the remote.

"Wow, my own TV to watch. Can I watch anything I want?" she asked eagerly.

"Sure," Thomas replied.

"Thanks. Thank you both," she grinned, already flipping through the channels.

That was the very moment Thomas knew he would give this girl the world. "You're welcome," he replied gruffly, his heart melting.

Chapter Seven

The two men were quietly talking on deck, each holding a glass of Irish whiskey. After every evening meal they would go off together to talk and drink. This had been a ritual since they'd been boys, first with soda – stolen out of the pantry late at night – then graduating to beer and then finally to the finest brandies and whiskies in the world. They'd been together from the very day Thomas' father had caught Joseph stealing mangoes at the tender age of six. He'd had no family and Thomas II had taken him in and cared for him as if he was his own. Thomas and Joseph were as close as any natural brothers, had even slit their fingers when they were eight to seal their brotherhood by sharing their blood.

"Well, what do you think?" Thomas asked his best friend.

"I don't know what to think really. . .she's such a nice kid, so lively and happy, it's hard to imagine anyone doing what they did to such a precious child." Joseph shook his head gravely.

"Yeah, I know what you mean. She doesn't remember, does she?" He didn't wait for Joseph to answer. "I don't know whether I'm relieved or not."

"And what about her family, what about her mother?" Joseph went on. "We'll have to talk to her later. We need to get in touch with them. They must know that she's missing," Joseph pointed out.

"I don't want to give her back," Thomas admitted quietly.

"What do you mean. . .you don't want to give her back?" Joseph spluttered. "She's not ours – or should I say *yours* – to keep! We need to report this. Can you imagine what could happen if the press ever got a hold of this?"

Thomas shrugged and turned to his lifelong friend.

"Josey, she's what I've missed all these years. I want to give her everything, I want to make her happy, take care of her, and watch her grow into a woman, get married. Have…

Joseph cut him off.

"Alright, I get the picture! But that little girl may just have a family who wants to see the same things. She has a mother who must be frantic with worry as we speak! We can't – I correct myself – you can't just keep her. She's a human being."

"I know…I would never take her away from her family Joseph, if she didn't want to, that is…" he remarked pointedly, a small smile playing mischievously at the corner of his mouth.

"How can I adopt her?" he said aloud to himself when Joseph had excused himself. He was already thinking of the ways.

꽃꽃꽃

Miriam woke an hour later. She opened her eye and looked around. For the life of her she couldn't remember any accident. The last thing she remembered was floating on her back down at her cove. Whatever happened after that was a complete blank.

She slipped out of bed and walked into the bathroom. She moved to the sink and stopped dead. Her face! What had happened to her face? It wasn't her, it couldn't be! The face staring back at her was covered in bruises and scratches as though she'd been in a fight.

Panicked, she removed the long shirt she was wearing and looked down at her body. With a burst of energy she turned the shower on full blast, the hot water stinging her body. She felt dirty, very, very dirty as the rush of memories of that night came back to her in vivid technicolor. She scrubbed herself with soap again and again, trying to wash his filthy hands from her body. She used the back brush and scrubbed at her legs, not caring about the pain she was causing herself. She had to cleanse herself, had to remove every memory of him from her skin!

Gulfs of tears fell and she let them fall unchecked. She scrubbed for what seemed like hours. Finally, she calmed down and stepped out of the unit wrapping a large white towel turban–like around her hair, and secured another larger towel around herself, before sitting on the toilet seat.

"I'll kill him! I'll go back and kill that bastard," she vowed darkly.

She was rocking back and forth, her arms wrapped about her as though she might be cold, only she wasn't. She was steaming hot, burning with hatred. She stayed like that for almost an hour before getting up to wash her face again with cold water. She then dried her hair roughly with the towel, before going into the bedroom to peer into the closet. It was all men's clothes but she didn't care. She rummaged through them and found a reasonably sized striped T-shirt and a pair of shorts, which she had to tie with a piece of cord she'd found.

She felt much better and made her bed before venturing outside.

"I'm not going back," she told them abruptly a few days later when they'd finished questioning her about her life in Paradise Pass.

"I want to stay with you two," she outlined into the astonished silence. "I can wash, cook and clean, all I ask is for you to let me go to school. Deal?" She looked at them seriously, her chin proudly raised.

Thomas and Joseph looked at each other astonished. This little slip of a girl was standing before them with her hands on her narrow hips, still battered and bruised, wearing their clothes and bargaining with them!

"We have someone to do all those household things Miriam," Thomas said. He watched the child slump forward defeated. "But…" he added quickly.

Joseph nodded to him, not needing to say the words. Thomas cleared his suddenly tight throat. "We do like having you around, so yes Miriam, it's a deal."

Miriam gasped then flung her arms around their necks, squeezing them tight.

"Just tell us how we can get your mother alone," Thomas urged moments later.

Chapter Eight

Thomas drove the white Toyota rent-a-car with a smile on his face. Whatever it took, he would make sure that Miriam would continue to be a part of their lives. He was not going to let her go and live the life she had been living. He even had a briefcase full of money to offer her mother as a last resort. He wasn't taking any chances. Thomas loved that little girl with all his heart.

Joseph and Miriam were in an identical car behind him. Miriam had insisted she was well enough to come. He was glad she was in the other car. He didn't want her to witness what he was about to do. It could get ugly. He would buy her if he had to. Anything, but she *would* be leaving with them for Kingston tonight. That he was sure of!

Fifteen minutes later, Joseph flashed his lights and dropped back. That was the prearranged signal to tell him Miriam's mother was near. He slowed and looked about. All he saw was a fragile looking woman dressed in a threadbare red skirt, dark green blouse and a long blue faded apron. Her feet were bare and she was carrying a large basket laden with breadfruit, sweet potatoes and yams on her head.

Driving cautiously beside the woman, he slowed and came to a stop just ahead of her, leaning across the passenger seat to wind down the window.

"Excuse me, ma'am?"

She looked at him and Thomas quickly hid the shock from his eyes by lowering his head and focusing on the ground until he could get himself together.

She looked so old. . .so ill, so-so haunted! Her eyes were sunken and glazed and she was full of deep wrinkles. Her eyebrows were sprinkled with grey. She was of a dark complexion, yet the tone looked dull grey and ash like – the skin, thin and papery. Her eyes were a deep, mysterious cherry brown. She looked older than the thirty-odd years Miriam told him she was.

Recovering quickly before she moved on, he started again.

"Excuse me? Are you Mrs. Evans?" he asked, hoping she wasn't.

She looked at him and Thomas felt his very soul being ripped apart, leaving him open and vulnerable to her reading. The sensation was downright spooky!

She nodded, but began to walk away again. He felt exposed and immediately became defensive.

"Look I need to find Mrs. Evans," he bit out harshly.

She kept on walking and he drove a short distance away, around a shallow corner and parked under the huge shade of a large Royal Poinciana tree. He leaned against the fender and waited for her impatiently. He wanted to get this meeting over and done with. When Mrs. Evans reached him, she put her basket down in the bushes and looked around. Without speaking she quickly got into the car and waited. Surprised, Thomas went around to the driver's side and sat down. Thank God he'd rented a car with darkly tinted windows, he thought as he turned the air conditioning on.

"It's a pleasure to meet you Mrs. Evans," he began.

"Drive," she said looking anxiously about.

After fifteen long minutes she indicated for him to pull over.

"Where is my daughter?" she asked bluntly.

Thomas was surprised that she spoke such clear English. He wasn't prepared for an intelligent woman and quickly disregarded the idea of offering cash. And how did she know that he wanted to speak to her about Miriam?

"How did you know I'm here about Miriam?" he probed cautiously. A small smile appeared on her face, before disappearing as quickly as it came.

"You're a white man looking for me. I don't know any white people. It is obvious you know my Miriam. Now where is she?"

"She's safe."

Mrs. Evans turned fully in her seat and looked at him, pinning him to his seat. He couldn't move or breathe. She was looking into his soul again.

"Will you stop that?" he snapped. She was scaring him.

"What do you want with me Mr.-?"

"Walters. Thomas Walters," Thomas supplied apologetically. "I'm a rich man Mrs. Evans and I think it would be better if Miriam were to live with me in Kingston," he blurted. This was not going the way he wanted it to go.

Mrs. Evans looked ahead. A car passed. She flinched.

"You are welcome to come of course," he offered, praying she wouldn't take him up on the offer. She was much too intimidating and he wasn't used to the feeling, especially coming from a woman.

"How do I know you will look after my child? What promise will you give me?" Her voice was soft.

Thomas cleared his throat. He didn't know what to say, this wasn't an ignorant country woman he was dealing with here. He wasn't prepared for this type of interrogation.

"In the short time I've known her, I feel as though I'm the person who must help her. . .as though –" he searched for the right words, and finding none said exactly how he felt. "I was chosen to be her father, to love her and bring her up the way you would have liked."

Mrs. Evans digested this then asked, "What happened to her at the beach? How did you find her?"

Thomas told her the story, holding nothing back. She looked straight ahead, silent, until he'd finished.

"Everyone thinks she's dead. I thought it best to let them think that. I knew she hadn't died, Thomas. I knew she was safe." She thumped her flat chest. "I knew in here," she added passionately. "I want what's best for her. I want her to have a chance in life, a chance she would never get if she stayed here. I failed her and I failed her father. But I will give her the chance to grow. . .be a lady," she smiled as a lonesome tear trailed down her cheek. She touched his hand and turned his palm up. For several seconds she said nothing, reading the intricate lines on his palm.

"It says here that I can trust you." She looked into his blue eyes again and Thomas shifted uneasily. "Your eyes tell me that you're a man of honour, with powerful means."

"I am, Mrs. Evans." He wasn't about to argue with that.

Her eyes narrowed.

"But you are not married."

"I was, a long time ago. She died."

She looked at him once more, hard and deep.

"I will die soon for my heart is bad. I can rest knowing that she will be away from them. Promise me you will look after her and that she will never know I am sick."

She pushed her hands deep into the pockets of her apron and brought out a bulky white envelope.

"Take this. It's hers."

"What is it?" Thomas asked as he unfolded several official looking documents. One was Miriam's birth certificate, the other a land title.

"That is the original and only copy of the land title."

"You trust me with this?" Thomas asked astonished.

"It is Miriam's. Don't let them take it from her. This is all I can give to my daughter. Tell me your address," she ordered.

"I can write it down…"

"No my memory is good. I will send you her death certificate," she paused and looked up suddenly. "She is near, bring her to me."

Chapter Nine

Thomas got out of the car and waved to Joseph to drive up. Mrs. Evans also got out and waited with open arms for Miriam to reach her. They embraced lovingly.

"It's alright my child. You'll be safe now," she whispered.

"Will you come Mama?" Miriam asked hopefully as tears fell.

Her mother smiled and wiped the tears away from Miriam's cheek with calloused thumbs.

"No my precious. But don't you fret over me. I'll be fine. You just study hard and don't give them any trouble. I'm sorry I failed you Miriam. So very sorry," her mother told her sadly.

"You didn't…"

"Shush." She placed a finger on her daughter's lips. "Now listen. You are to give up on your life here. You no longer exist. I will bury Miriam Robinson. You must go and start a new life."

"But I…"

"Let me finish." She shook her gently but firmly. "Tomorrow you will wake up in a new home with a new name. I want you to be strong, I want you to be happy and I want you to reach your dreams and make me and your pappy proud."

Her mother hugged her hard, then looked at Joseph.

"You are the gentle one," she said to him. "Don't be too soft on her now," she told him smiling.

Joseph shifted nervously under her intense brown gaze. This woman seemed to have special powers.

"I'll try not to spoil her."

"You'll find it hard not to."

Joseph didn't like Obeah – the Jamaican equivalent to Haitian voodoo – but Mrs. Evans seemed to be one of the gentle good spirited ones.

"Do you practise?" he asked her.

Both Miriam and Thomas stood wondering what he was talking about.

"Only when it comes to my daughter," Mrs. Evans confessed passionately, holding her daughter's hand tightly.

"Is there anything we can do for you before we leave?" Thomas asked, not wanting to leave the woman in this dreadful situation. "I have some money..." Thomas offered awkwardly.

She smiled weakly.

"No thank you. I must go now. You will rise to great things Miriam. I love you." She turned to go, her small frame erect as she walked away.

"We can drop you close to your home," Thomas called out.

"It's best if I walk," she replied without turning around.

Thomas looked at Joseph and then Miriam. Her mother was nice and obviously loved her daughter; but she was a little strange.

"You'll have to think of a new name now Miriam," Joseph said as he looked at Miriam's tear stained face.

She smiled sadly, looked around as though committing the scenic views to memory and took a very deep breath.

"I already have, it's Merissa."

Chapter Ten

Merissa, with her friend Cymone, sat beneath the heavy thick-leaved branches of an Almond tree, nibbling on the bittersweet fruit. They were near the crumbling Aqueduct which ran through the University campus and up into the University Hospital. Textile and Design final exam had just finished and they were busy comparing answers.

"What about question three?" Merissa asked Cymone.

"I think I got that right. I said the cloth was made in India, but the dye was actually brought in China. What did you put?"

Merissa grinned, "Same thing." They laughed. "Come on. Let's go. I'm starved."

"You're always starved; I can't understand how a person who eats as much as you never gains any weight. It's not fair!" Cymone grumbled as she stood and brushed off her shorts.

"Thomas says I have a high metabolism."

Cymone, a native of Trinidad, was only five feet two with a tendency to get fat if she wasn't careful with what she ate. Her complexion was almost blue black, smooth and so cool that she never used makeup. Three weeks ago she'd cut all her chemically processed hair off, and was now wearing it so low it didn't even need brushing. The cut complimented her high cheekbones, large coal-dark eyes and round podgy nose.

Merissa was tall, almost five-eight, with long shapely legs which she rarely showed, favouring the comfort of jeans. Her hair was almost always worn up in a pony tail, as the curls were so tight it was hard to manage otherwise.

Merissa with her striking beauty – which she never bothered about – could easily become a Miss Jamaica contestant, but she wasn't interested in modelling at all. As they walked across the dry grass, Toby Chase watched her. She was easily the most hard working woman he'd ever come across. She possessed such drive and determination he knew she would be a success.

Not as successful as he intended to be, he thought confidently, but successful none-the-less. He was also a Design student, as well as majoring in Creative Art. He enjoyed the best of both worlds. Designing patterns for his cloth and then making his flamboyant creations.

He remembered the time when he and Merissa had met. He'd seen her putting up a notice on the bulletin board about two years ago. He'd taken down the notice and applied for the job. She'd been looking for a tutor in pattern cutting. He didn't need the money as his parents lived in Canada and sent money to him, nor did he have any virtuous intentions in mind. He'd wanted her, along with every other man on campus. But after several weeks of being constantly brushed off, they settled into a deep easy friendship. She was easily his best friend. She even had her own keys to his house.

Cymone was another story. He loved her. She hated him. Most of the time she barely acknowledged his presence and when she did, it was to look at him with such hostility he wanted to bury his head. He'd never made a pass, or proclaimed his love but yet she seemed to hate him from the day they'd been introduced a year or so ago. He couldn't understand it.

Toby waved to them as they approached. He could tell by the way Cymone caught hold of Merissa's T-shirt that they were arguing about sitting with him.

"Must we sit over there?" Cymone asked, desperately looking around the crowded canteen.

"Do you see anywhere else to sit?" Merissa asked. "Besides I haven't seen Toby in days."

Merissa walked off leaving her friend to decide whether or not she wanted to follow. The animosity Cymone surrounded herself in whenever Toby was around was puzzling and extremely annoying. It was difficult for her to balance their friendship when the three of them were together. She always ended up playing referee and she didn't like it. The two of them were her friends yet if things didn't calm down she knew she'd have to choose between them. She didn't want that.

Merissa sat beside Toby and kissed his cheek. Toby Chase was a handsome brute, Merissa thought – not for the first time. Grey eyes that changed with his emotions and blonde hair that was presently worn in jaw length dread locks and tied down with a red bandana. He was hot, likable and extremely popular.

She noticed he'd pierced another hole in his left ear.

"Another one Toby?" He already had three silver hoops dangling from his left ear and two in his other.

"A man of my celebrated means must always be different," he replied with a toothy grin. "Hello Cymone."

Cymone smiled tightly.

"I can see this is going to be a lovely lunch," drawled Merissa sarcastically.

"What would you both like for lunch? My treat," Toby offered brightly.

"Well in that case mister money bags, how about some jerk chicken and make sure the festivals are fresh," Merissa ordered without hesitation.

"You're a bottomless pit," Toby teased, his grey eyes crinkling at the corners. "What for you Cym?"

"Chef's Salad," Cymone said simply.

"And?" encouraged Toby, his palms faced upwards questioningly.

"That's it. Chef's Salad."

"That can't be all you're going to be eating, surely?" Toby enquired, his grey eyes darkening.

"Have you got a problem with that?" Cymone demanded, her temper rising.

"Yes I damn well have! You're starving yourself!"

"I'm not. And what I eat, or don't eat, is none of your damn business." Cymone was fuming. "Merissa I'll call you later. Enjoy your lunch…although I don't see that happening." She slanted a derisive look at Toby then turned and left.

"Well that was fun," Merissa teased lightly.

"It's not fu-"

"Don't you say it Toby!" Merissa quickly warned. She hated profanity.

"It's not funny. She always sets me off," he groaned miserably as he rubbed his face with both hands.

"You're always trying too hard to make her like you," soothed Merissa. "Why don't you just tell her how you feel?"

Toby's mouth twisted into a sarcastic smirk. "Yeah sure Meri. She'll probably run a mile in the other direction!"

"Maybe two miles."

"How can you joke about something as serious as this?" he demanded coolly. "This is my life we're talking about here."

"Ok, I'm sorry," Merissa apologised. "Look, forget lunch. You can take me out for dinner later tonight."

Toby nodded miserably.

"I'm going to go home and get some sleep, before Tommy and Josey get home from the office. Tommy is thinking of starting a regional airline. American Airlines fed him peanuts on his last trip to San Juan. I've been hearing complaints ever since!" she laughed.

"See you about eight?" Toby asked.

She nodded and kissed his cheek affectionately. "Chin up Toby. She'll come round."

Chapter Eleven

Merissa drove with lazy expertise up the steep winding road of Red Hills passing the architectural delights of huge mansions which dotted the many hills and valleys on either side of the road. Turning off Red Hills Road, she drove uphill for another two minutes until she reached the high iron gates of Empire Estate.

The Estate was only three years old and built with the very rich in mind. Three storied houses fashioned to resemble early Spanish designs graced the acreage. Expensive cars, many with yellow license plates signifying diplomatic status, stood discreetly on long winding driveways. Acres of lush green manicured gardens surrounded the estate.

Merissa drove even higher until the spectacular view of Kingston and the harbour came into view. The scenic splendour of hazy blue-green mountains, the criss-cross of Kingston City and the sparkling water of the Caribbean Sea could all be seen in one sweeping glance.

Merissa parked her ice white four wheeled drive beside Thomas' car and frowned when she checked the time on her watch. Thomas was never home at this hour being the workaholic that he was. Something was wrong. Quickly she let herself into the house. She flung her keys down on the mahogany and marble centre table and walked quickly into the spacious living room.

"Thomas?" she called out, as she slipped off her sandals and walked bare footed through the living room.

She peeped into the breakfast room and kitchen. They were empty. She walked quickly up the stairs to the second floor which housed both Thomas' and Joseph's bedrooms, a library and two bathrooms.

"Thomas?" she called out again.

His bedroom door was slightly ajar and she pushed it open, stepping into the blue and cream room with trepidation.

"Thomas?"

He was in bed with his eyes closed. His hands were clutching the striped comforter. Alarmed, Merissa quickly felt for a pulse. His skin was cold and clammy.

"Thomas?" she whispered.

"Princess is that you?" he murmured. His voice was hoarse and slurred.

"It's me," she confirmed, "What's wrong?"

"Got the flu."

She knew it wasn't. His neck was swollen and he was sweating profusely, yet shivering at the same time. His face was grey and clenched tight with pain, his lips blue.

"I'll be right back," Merissa told him and rushed out of the room to call Joseph, who would probably be over at Mrs. Dobson's house.

She was right.

"Josey, it's me," she said and went on quickly to explain.

"I'll be right there," Joseph assured her.

Minutes later, she heard his car and rushed to open the front door. She was crying.

"He's all blue! He said he's got the flu, but it's not. I know it's not!"

"Calm down Merissa," he said as he held her shoulders and watched as she struggled to take several deep breaths. "It'll be alright," he soothed, as he dashed up the stairs with the agility of a much younger man.

Joseph stood in shock when he saw his lifelong friend lying there all pale and swollen. Thomas never got sick.

"Merissa!" Joseph called out, as she entered the room. "Get some things together; I'm taking him to the hospital."

"Ok. Which one?"

"General."

"Josey, you go ahead. I'll meet you with his things."

He smiled at her gently. "Good girl." Then he bent towards Thomas. "Tommy? Can you hear me?" he whispered in his friend's ear.

"Course I can," Thomas grumbled weakly. "I'm not dead yet," came the sarcastic reply.

Joseph grinned, that sounded like the Thomas he knew.

"I'm taking you to the hospital and I need you to get up. Can you move?"

"I'm not going," Thomas said with a stronger voice.

"Yes you are."

"I'm not going."

Joseph sighed loudly. "Merissa, go get him a glass of cold water please."

As she reluctantly left the room Joseph spoke to Thomas.

"You're not well Tommy, and if you want to fight about it, we will, but either way you're coming with me. So either help me and sit up, or would you rather I hurt my back by lifting you?"

Thomas looked at him with dull, shallow blue eyes and gave him a very dry look. But he sat up and slowly moved to the side of the bed.

Joseph silently noted that Thomas still had on his office clothes.

"Ok, let's walk slowly down to the car," Joseph said as he supported Thomas' much larger frame.

Thomas tried to control the groans of pain which tumbled from his stiff lips and hot sweat broke out on his forehead as they slowly descended the staircase. This morning he'd woken with several large boil-like things around his groin area each one about the size of a golf ball. He'd tried to go into office but couldn't make it. He'd felt worse as the day progressed. He went to bed believing he could sleep it off.

"Thanks Meri," Joseph said, putting the glass of water to Thomas' lips; he watched him grimace as he tried to swallow.

Merissa stood on the bottom step with tears in her eyes.

"Princess, why are you looking at me like that?" Thomas asked hoarsely. "I'll be fine. Now give me a kiss and I'll see you later."

She kissed his cold, clammy cheek. They left and Merissa sprung into action. She packed and made her way down the hill into the city.

"Oh God, please let nothing happen to Thomas," she prayed reverently.

As she sped down the hill, memories of the past years crowded into her thoughts. The three of them were virtually inseparable, they did everything together. She could remember the way Thomas and Joseph had laughed as they showed her how to ski, when they took her to Colorado, so she could experience a white Christmas. She remembered the way they would stay in her room those first terrifying months when her sleep was disturbed by the horrors of her past. She remembered the comfort, his strength and his mischievous eyes as they looked at her lovingly. Thomas and Joseph were her whole world. Nothing was going to happen to either of them. They were a team.

The next few hours passed in a haze. Thomas was admitted and whisked away to have some tests done. All they could do was wait. A long time later, a tall, bald doctor came out and asked them to come into his office. The office was dark, all browns and blacks. It wasn't comforting.

Merissa read the brass name plate and title on his desk, Dr. Francis, Oncologist. What's an oncologist? she thought.

"My name is Dr. Francis." Merissa noted he seemed a little nervous and a dark shadow of dread numbed her senses. "What I'm about to say won't be easy." The doctor swallowed loudly.

Merissa watched the jumping movement of his Adam's apple. He was very nervous. She watched the way he tapped his yellow pencil on his desk. Tap, tap, tap. Both Joseph and Merissa looked at each other and held hands.

"We've done a lot of tests on Mr. Walters and it seems he's on the advance stages of Non-Hodgkin Lymphoma." He waited for this to sink in and shifted in his leather chair.

"What exactly is that?" Joseph asked quietly.

The doctor cleared his throat.

"It's a type of cancer that runs through the blood stream and attacks the Lymph nodes in the body."

Merissa felt her whole world crash down around her.

"Oh dear God no," she whispered. Tears pooled in her eyes then slowly ran down her cheeks.

"How. . .how far gone is it?" Joseph asked, his hands beginning to shake.

"I'm sorry sir." The doctor cleared his throat again and ran his hands over his non-existent hair. "But I think he has about six months to live," he finished quietly.

Merissa went hot then cold. She felt faint.

"No!" she shouted. "You're wrong! You're wrong! Joseph tell him, te-tell him he's wrong! Oh God!" She glared at the doctor and leaned over his desk accusingly. "I want another doctor," she demanded. "Thomas can't be dying, I won't let him! Joseph tell him. Please tell him. Tell him Josey! Not our Tommy. Not our Tommy. Tell him! Tell him!"

Dr. Francis called a nurse.

"Miss Walters?" Merissa glared at him reprovingly as though he was the one to blame.

"I'm going to give you a sedative, ok? Just so you can sleep tonight." He felt for the poor child.

"No, leave me alone. Stay away from me!" She paced the room, and then suddenly looked at Joseph who was pale and shaking. She fell to her knees beside him and held him tightly. "Joseph don't make him die. . .I don't want him to leave us. Josey please."

Dr. Francis left them, unable to watch the emotional scene inside. In all his twenty odd years as a doctor, he still felt the pain of telling loved ones they were about to lose somebody.

Inside, Joseph held Merissa for long minutes trying hopelessly to compose himself for her sake. She needed him.

"Why Joseph? Why our Tommy?" she asked him between gulps.

"Meri darling. I don't know," he whispered in her hair. "I wish to God it wasn't to be so. But we've got to be strong for Tommy's sake. We've got to be strong." The tears he'd been trying to control overflowed and mixed with hers. They held each other tightly.

A nurse came and handed Merissa two small white tablets and a plastic cup of water. Merissa thanked her and waited for her to leave before promptly depositing them on the doctor's desk, untouched.

She went to the door. "Josey, I need to go."

"You'll be alright?" he asked her, knowing she needed to be alone.

She nodded and straightened to her full height before turning to go.

Chapter Twelve

Toby and his neighbour Alex were engrossed in a game of dominoes. Empty Red Stripe bottles and banana chip packets were strewn all over the place. They had been playing for the past four hours, only breaking to go to the bathroom or to the kitchen.

Alex rubbed his tired eyes and stretched.

"Toby you beat me this time. But next week, hell man, I'll mash you up!" He grinned, finished his beer, and then helped Toby clean up the room.

They were good friends, having lived beside each other ever since Toby and his family had moved to Jamaica from Canada several years ago. Toby and Alex were intellectually opposite. Alex was good with figures and liked to watch quizzes and read autobiographies. The brightest colour in his closet was a red tie he never wore. Toby was more artistic and clever with his hands. He never wore grey or brown and had an extensive collection of Archie comics.

Alex was about an inch taller than Toby, with a smooth cinnamon complexion which always looked as though he had just washed his face. Thick silky eyebrows topped warm toasted eyes rimmed with long lashes. He had a strong square jaw with the slightest hint of a cleft. His jaw was shadowed by a day old stubble.

Alex had always been the ladies' man. He was never without a condom in his pocket but his sex life was now almost non-existent. He was tired of all the faceless women who'd passed through his life, who never meant anything more to him than a passionate night or two. He'd never in all of his twenty-nine years had a serious girlfriend.

The TV room looked presentable again and after making arrangements for Friday night, Alex said his goodnights and let himself out.

"Alex! Close di gate for me nuh man," Toby called out.

"Ok," replied Alex, walking down the driveway.

As he began to wind the heavy chain around the gate and was about to padlock it, he felt another presence. There was a car parked a little pass Toby's gate. Alex knitted his brow. With trepidation, he walked cautiously over to it and peered inside. A girl was hunched over, with her head resting on the steering wheel. She was obviously distressed over something as she was crying softly, her shoulders were shaking.

He tapped on the window. "Are you alright?" Alex asked.

She looked up, startled.

"Yeah...yes I'm fine," she answered unsteadily.

Alex, not wanting to leave the girl alone outside, knocked on the window again. "Are you sure you're alright?" he repeated in concern.

Merissa glanced up again and tried to smile. It hardly showed. She blew her nose loudly, and climbed out of her car, all this while ignoring him.

She is lovely, Alex thought, as he watched her lock her car door and move towards Toby's gate. He blocked her path and held onto her arm. She glared at him then shrugged him off.

"You know Toby?" he asked harshly.

He didn't understand the way he was suddenly feeling. He didn't want her to know Toby. He couldn't bare the thought that maybe she was involved with his friend. He wanted her.

"You have a problem with that?" she replied caustically, moving passed him and unwinding the heavy chain.

"Here, let me help you with that," he said quickly, not wanting to be away from her.

As soon as the gate swung open, she unlocked the grill with her own key.

"Toby! Toby!" Merissa shouted walking into the house, forgetting to close the grill.

"Yeah in here!" Toby yelled back.

She went into the TV room, forgetting the stranger who had walked in behind her.

"Oh God Meri...what is it?" Toby flew to his feet and was at her side in a second.

He held her close as she clung to him. He moved to the couch and sat rocking her gently and smoothing her hair. It was then he noticed Alex standing awkwardly in the doorway, watching with a perplexed expression on his face. Toby narrowed his eyes at him.

"Alex? Do me a favour. Get a glass of water for me please."

Merissa moved away so she could talk to Toby.

"Oh Toby, its Thomas!" she sobbed. "I went home and he was home he...he was home Toby! Tommy is nev...never home before me. I found him in bed all blue!" she wailed.

"You mean he was dead?" Toby gasped in shock, his face paling.

"No! Well not yet anyway," she finished sadly.

She stood abruptly to release the clip from her hair, letting the mass of curls spring free before sitting down to curl into his solid familiar strength.

Toby held her to him, hugging her tight. Alex came back and found the two of them like that. He felt a red-hot heat of something he couldn't name spread throughout his body and he didn't understand it.

"Here Toby," he said abruptly, handing Toby the glass.

"Meri, drink this," Toby urged, putting the glass to her trembling lips.

Alex felt like an intruder. He wanted to give them some privacy, but was compelled to stay. He took a chair on the back porch where he was out of earshot yet still able to see what was going on. He was accustomed to being around beautiful women but this girl took his breath away.

His dark brows drew down, almost meeting, as he tried to remember if he'd ever seen her before, not that he and Toby travelled in the same circles. She and Toby seemed to be very close, he mused angrily, almost intimate. She had her own key for Christ's sake! Emotion churned inside him. He peeped inside and saw Toby talking softly to the girl, stroking her hair again.

Merissa was trying her best to pull herself together and after a cup of mint tea felt a little better as she finished telling Toby everything.

"Which hospital is he in?" Toby asked.

"Kingston General."

He nodded. "Are you hungry?"

She smiled a small smile, "I guess. We were supposed to go out to dinner remember?" That conversation felt like a million lifetimes ago!

"You stay here whilst I go make a sandwich and another cup of tea." He leaned over and gave her a quick reassuring hug. "It'll be alright," he whispered, then turned away and looked around for Alex.

"Alex?"

"Yeah." Alex appeared and stood in the centre of the room.

"Meri?" She looked up, her eyes red and puffy.

Alex had never seen such an enchanting face.

"Meri, this is my neighbour Alex. Alex, this is Merissa, a very good friend of mine," introduced Toby.

How good? Alex asked silently.

"Keep her company. I'm making her something to eat," Toby ordered, but his eyes flashed a keep off warning.

Merissa looked at the stranger who seemed ill at ease. He was very good looking, in an intense sort of a way. She was thankful when he moved away and sat down on one of the cushions opposite her.

"I'm sorry if I frightened you earlier in the car," he apologized, giving her a gentle smile.

"That's ok. I didn't know how long I was out there." She smiled back at him weakly, her eyes glistening with unshed tears.

His heart took off when she smiled at him, making him feel funny inside again. For the first time in his life he didn't know what to do or say.

"I'm sorry about whatever happened," he edged, wishing he could say more.

She didn't answer him but curled her feet up in the chair and closed her eyes.

Alex looked at her. He wanted to touch her so badly, but didn't dare, getting up instead and leaving the room to find Toby.

"She's out cold," he told his friend who was busy making a huge corned beef sandwich.

"She's been through a lot today," Toby said, and then his mind seemed to wander. "Let her sleep," he went on, "I'll call the hospital. Poor Joseph must be worried sick. Can you go and park her car behind mine? She may as well stay the night."

Alex didn't like the idea very much, *his* woman spending the night with Toby but he kept his thoughts to himself.

Toby called Joseph in the meantime.

This had been the longest conversation Toby had ever had with the older man. It was all so tragic. He liked Mr. Walters very much and said a silent prayer for him.

Alex was sitting in front of Merissa, watching her tenderly, when Toby walked into the room.

Toby gave him a quizzical look but said nothing.

"You'd better put her to bed Toby," Alex said quietly.

"Yeah."

Toby moved, but Alex beat him to it, lifting her gently from the couch and holding her close to his chest. He smelt her hair and brushed his cheek against it whilst Toby led the way to his sister's old room, Alex noted thankfully. He placed her on the bed, and watched as Toby spread the white mosquito net around it.

In the TV room again, Alex collapsed onto a yellow leather bean bag and watched Toby lie on the couch.

"What happened?" he asked curiously. He wanted to know absolutely everything about her.

"Her father has just been taken to the hospital," Toby explained, sprawling out and yawning widely before going on to explain the night's events.

"Who's her father?"

"Thomas Walters," Toby replied, as though stating the obvious.

"The banker?" Alex said, incredulous.

"That's the one. I can't believe it myself. The last time I saw him was at the gym and that was only three days ago. And now this," Toby mused sadly. "I'm gonna need a favour tomorrow Alex."

"Sure," Alex replied. "I'll be over in the morning." Toby locked the grill behind him.

"Oh and Alex?" Toby said with deadly seriousness.

Alex looked at him with his eyebrows raised.

"Don't even consider it," Toby warned, knowing the direction in which his friend was thinking.

"The thought hadn't even crossed my mind," Alex lied, feigning innocence. "Does she have any friends?" he asked, laughing at the dark look Toby gave him.

In his own house, Alex thought of Merissa. What a lovely name for a very lovely lady. He fell asleep with her on his mind.

Chapter Thirteen

The first thing Alex did the following morning was telephone his secretary informing her that he wouldn't be in office today. He took a quick cold shower, and had a quick breakfast of steamed callaloo and mackerel prepared for him by his helper. He left most of it, eager to go next door. He scaled the fence to Toby's house instead of walking around.

Toby was already up and outside, misting his prized orchids which hung from wired baskets under his mango trees.

"Whata gwaan? You not going in to work today?" Toby asked.

"No. I've decided to take the day off. I need a break," Alex lied.

"I'm just waiting for Merissa to finish whatever it is these women do," said Toby.

"Got any juice?" he asked, wanting to see Merissa again.

"You know the way to the kitchen," Toby replied.

Alex made his way casually inside, his sneaked feet silent on the tiles.

"Good morning," he said and smiled a smile that would make the devil stop and take notice.

Merissa jumped, almost dropping her glass of cold sour sop juice.

"Morning," she smiled weakly whilst rubbing her tired eyes. "Want some of this?"

"No thanks. I came looking for yo…I mean orange juice," he replied awkwardly. God, she was a beauty, he thought.

"Help yourself."

Merissa moved away from the huge American styled fridge and leant against the counter to watch him as she sipped her drink.

He was very good looking, carrying his height well with lazy, almost arrogant confidence. She noted the way his shirt stretched across his back as he removed the carton of orange juice, showing her his well-developed muscles. Her glance moved down. His jeans hugged his long powerful legs and Merissa felt a furnace turn on deep inside of her. A reaction she wasn't expecting or appreciating.

She excused herself hurriedly and went outside.

"I hope you don't mind me borrowing your clothes," she said to Toby who was leaning against her car. She wears his clothes well, Alex noted with amusement.

"As long as you're not wearing my underpants," he teased. "Alex! Come on," he shouted impatiently.

"He's coming with us?" Merissa asked fiercely.

"Yeah."

"Why?" Alex took up too much of her space, and she didn't like it.

"…because Meri darling," Toby went on slowly. "We need someone to drive your car home. Otherwise you'll end up having to park it at the hospital overnight, and poor Joseph running you up and down the hill," he explained as though talking to a petulant child.

"Oh," she said simply.

Alex came out, locked the grill and turned towards them grinning bashfully.

Toby gave him an impatient look and handed Merissa's keys to him. "Kingston General," he ordered, going into his own car. Merissa went with him.

One hour later, Joseph was collected and tucked comfortably in bed having extracted a solemn promise from Merissa to tell Mrs. Dobbson he was now home. Merissa went into her bedroom to change. Pulling her hair away from her face, she looked around for a clip to secure it and then applied a light touch of makeup. She felt so much better.

On the way downstairs she stopped in Thomas' room, and packed a small suitcase with the usual stuff one needed in the hospital. Then, eyeing a brown paper bag on a chair, she opened it, finding several mystery novels he'd obviously just purchased, and threw them in as well. She found Alex and Toby leaning against the wall on the balcony looking at the spectacular view.

"You have a beautiful home Merissa," Alex said, actually wanting to tell her how beautiful she looked.

"Thank you. Can I get you anything?" she asked him softly.

"How about a cold drink?" Toby suggested, somewhat aggressively.

"How about you get it yourself?" she replied sweetly.

Toby came back to see the two of them close. Too close for his liking, and Merissa was laughing at something Alex had said. He didn't like it.

"Ok guys, lets go," he said standing casually in the doorway. Then suddenly paling, he looked around wildly. "What time is it?" he demanded urgently.

"Ten thirty," Merissa answered.

"Rhatiid! I have an exam in an hour!" Toby exclaimed.

"Oh Toby. That's just great! I had you all over the place this morning," Merissa said guiltily. "How could you forget?" she berated him.

"Ok, ok, let me think. It'll take you over an hour to get to school from here," she calculated. "So Alex will have to come with me to the hospital. If you do, you'll lose half an hour dropping the two of us off. I'll just have to take my car back down again."

Alex loved the idea.

Toby hated it, but had no choice.

"Alright. I'll see you later at the hospital." Then walking quickly to the main entrance he stopped and turned. "Don't forget to call Cymone, she must be wondering what's going on by now." He left.

"Who's Cymone?" Alex asked.

"A good friend of mine. We take the same classes."

"Oh, and what class is that?" Alex probed.

"Fashion Design. The three of us are in the rag trade." She smiled and began to move away. "I'd better call her."

Alex watched her walk into the living room. He liked the way she moved.

"She'll meet us at the hospital," Merissa said, coming back to him. "Let's go."

He followed her outside trying not to look at the way her bottom seemed to be seducing him. This girl is going to be the death of me, he mused.

"Alex will you drive?" she asked politely.

"Sure," he croaked, hurrying around to the driver's side and getting in. He did not want her to witness the way his body was signalling to hers – the bulge in his pants.

On the way down the hill they talked, Merissa doing most of the talking.

"Where do you work?" she asked. She was wondering if he was one of Toby's friends who were still trying to 'find' themselves at thirty.

"Kitson and Blake Accounting."

"What do you do?"

"I'm Senior Accounting Manager," he responded.

"At your age?" she smiled at his profile. "You must be a boy genius!" she teased.

He laughed, a deep, rumbling sound that sent waves of delicious pleasure through her body.

"Do you live alone?" she asked after several silent moments.

"Not really. Aggie looks after me. I couldn't manage without her," he replied vaguely.

"Oh," she said, her mind ticking over. She wanted to know who this Aggie person was, but didn't dare ask.

"Can you pull over there a minute please? I need to see someone for Joseph."

Alex drove up the short driveway and stopped near the door. Mrs. Dobbson, a chubby, fifty-something year old widow, came rushing out in a huge floral tent dress just as Merissa was about to knock on the door.

"How is Thomas, child?" Mrs. Dobbson had pulled Merissa into her ample bosom and was hugging her tightly.

"He's doing a lot better than yesterday," Merissa said, not wanting to go into detail. "I'm going back to the hospital now. Josey asked me to tell you he's back at the house. I left him sleeping." Merissa gave her the key, pressing it gently into the lady's soft palm. "He had a little breakfast, but not much," she told her.

"Alright. I'll go up and see to him. You take care now. And Merissa, be brave."

Mrs. Dobbson gave her another long hug before pushing her into the car and giving Alex a cheerful wave.

"Pleasant lady."

"Yes she is," Merissa replied lightly. Then, "Are you married?"

Alex was so surprised by her directness he almost slammed on the brakes.

"No," he laughed. "Well not yet anyway," he added mischievously.

Now what was that supposed to mean, Merissa thought. Did he intend to marry this Aggie person or what?

Alex, knowing what she was thinking, decided not to relieve her mind.

"How old are you?" he asked her instead.

"Twenty-three, almost twenty-four, in three weeks to be exact. I hope Tommy will be around to see it," her voice fell almost to a whisper.

"He will be," he said confidently. "He means a lot to you?"

"He means the world to me. I can't imagine how my life must have been before he came along." She stopped suddenly, realizing what she had been about to say.

"What about your parents?" she asked him, trying to change the subject.

"They died in a car crash twelve years ago," he replied stiffly.

"Oh I'm sorry," Merissa said and unconsciously reached over and touched his leg, wanting to give him a little comfort.

Bolts of electricity flew from his body to hers and back again, stunning both of them into awareness. Never had such an impersonal touch been so sexual. Alex's body was aflame. Merissa pulled her hand away quickly and looked out of the window, all attempts of conversation forgotten as she struggled to compose herself.

Chapter Fourteen

"Don't you want me to drop you home?" Merissa asked Alex as he pulled up into the hospital parking lot.

"No. It's my day off. Plus I promised Toby I would stay with you." Lying was becoming a habit around her he noted with amusement. "But I do like your company." He ran a warm finger down her soft cheek, looking intently into her deep dark eyes.

Merissa's heart warmed and she left him in the waiting room for the second time that day. She was delighted to see Thomas sitting up and eating a pale, watery broth when she entered his room.

"Hey Thomas," she said going into the room, bending and giving him a kiss.

"Hey yourself. Did you bring me some decent food?" he asked immediately.

"No. I hope you're not giving the nurses any trouble?"

"Me? Me? Do such things? All I did was tell that blubber of a nurse that I'm hungry. She brought me this!" He shoved the bowl away and flung the spoon down in disgust. "Bloody hot water for Christ's sake! Now be a good girl and go over to that Chinese place I like for some decent food."

"Doctor's orders are doctor's orders," Merissa scolded. "Now be good and don't forget your manners." She repeated words Thomas had used a thousand times to her.

Thomas grumbled something intangible then looked at the suitcase suspiciously. "What's that for?"

"Oh I just thought you might need a few things from home," she replied cautiously. "Plus," she went on. "I found some books in your bedroom."

He nodded, hating the place. He'd rather go home than have home brought here. "Where's Joseph?"

"I sent him home to sleep. He was here all night."

"So how'd you get back down then?"

"Toby and his friend drove me home in my car, only we had to change arrangements, so I have my own car again. When Joseph comes down I'll drop Alex off."

"So who and where is this Alex then?" Thomas latched onto Alex's name like a strawberry fridge magnet.

"Outside."

Thomas sighed loudly, pursing his lips and closing his eyes. "Merissa where are your manners! Bring the boy in here, I want to meet him."

"Why?" she demanded, alarmed.

Thomas sighed again, only much louder. "Because my dear," he spoke as though talking to a four-year-old. "Anyone who drives up and down the hill, then stays until *you're* ready must really be worth meeting. Go get him and stop asking ridiculous questions!"

Merissa practically leapt off the bed. Well he's in fine form she thought, smiling to herself. This was her Thomas!

"Alex," she said gently.

He was reading an old Time magazine but looked up when she spoke. His face lit up when he saw her.

Gosh, I wish he wouldn't look at me like that, she spoke silently to herself. Her insides shifted when their eyes met.

"Thomas wants to meet you," she said simply, trying to reason with the way she was feeling. They went in together.

Sometime later, an embarrassed Merissa moved to Thomas' side, intending to put a stop to the aggressive interrogation he was subjecting poor Alex to; although Alex was expertly side stepping anything he didn't want to answer with respectful manoeuvring.

Timing her entrance well, Cymone walked in. She went straight to Thomas and kissed him on the cheek.

"Thomas Walters you gave me such a fright," she scolded affectionately as she sat on the other side of him.

"Cymone my dear, if I want to die, I promise you'll be the first to know," he chuckled, patting her hand fondly.

"Cymone, meet Alex York, a friend of Toby's," Merissa said.

"Hi," Cymone said, taking in the good-looking man leaning against the pale wall.

"Hi," Alex replied.

"Why don't you girls go for a walk or something? I'd like to talk to Alex here...alone."

"No one will be talking to anyone for a while," Dr. Francis said as he strode into the room. "Everybody out!"

"Now you look here..." Thomas began to argue.

"Mr. Walters," Dr. Francis said calmly, too calmly. "Would you like to spend a few extra days in here?"

"Course not, you bloody fool."

"Then may I suggest you cooperate with my staff and my orders or you won't have any visitors at all." Then looking at the three people watching the amusing exchange, roared, "Out!"

They quickly left.

Dr. Francis began to check Thomas' vital signs.

"Why did you ignore Dr. Duncan's orders several months ago?" he asked his reluctant patient softly.

"My, oh my," Thomas sneered as a touch of red crept up his neck. "Doesn't word get around fast?" he said acidly. Then exploded. "He's a fool doctor like you! He doesn't know a God damn thing. So may I suggest that you release me today or else I'll..."

"Mr. Walters, please be quiet," the doctor said woodenly. Thomas was temporarily taken aback and snapped his mouth shut with uncharacteristic obedience. "Dr. Duncan told me you knew what you had since last year. He wanted to start Chemotherapy right away then."

"I know," Thomas said quietly, feeling slightly ashamed.

"You know you have cancer don't you?"

"Yes."

"And you want to leave it untreated?" the doctor asked flatly.

"Yes I do."

"Why?"

"Why...why!" Thomas sat up, his face flushed. "Because, I won't be walking around the place without any hair!" came the unexpected reply.

The doctor raised his bushy eyebrows.

"And?"

"And," Thomas was struggling to keep his voice flat and emotionless, "that poor child needs me to look after her, that's why!" he roared, his voice breaking with complex emotion.

"So what will she do when you die Thomas? Or haven't you thought that far ahead?" The doctor shot back brutally.

"I won't die," Thomas said stubbornly.

Dr. Francis felt compassion overwhelm him. Thomas Walters was a stubbornly proud man. The doctor sat on a peeling metal chair, not knowing where to start.

"Look, Mr. Walters, the cancer has spread throughout your body, and it's all over you."

Thomas closed his eyes and sank back against the pillows.

"Can I be frank with you?" the doctor asked.

"I wouldn't respect you if you weren't."

"You have about four months to live. Your whole body has been consumed. Cancer cells are eating you away." He cleared his throat. "You have people outside who love you. I had to watch that poor girl's world fall apart last night. Do you think it was a pretty sight?" He didn't wait for an answer. "How do you think she'll feel when she finds out that you betrayed her? Because that's what you've done, betrayed her, Joseph, your friends and most of all, yourself. You're dying now because you didn't want to disappoint them. But now you've given them no choice, you've…"

"Don't tell them doctor," Thomas whispered urgently. "Please."

"No, I won't tell them. I won't have to face them each and every day. You will."

With that the doctor stood and moved to the bottom of the bed before saying, "I'll release you in a few days, but you do have a choice. You can still start Chemotherapy."

"As you said before doctor, it's a little late for that." For the first time in his life, Thomas was eaten up with shame; he couldn't look the doctor in the eye.

"You won't be having any more visitors until later this afternoon. I'll be giving you something for the pain."

He started to argue, but the doctor raised his hand as if to say 'I've had enough' and left the room.

Thomas buried himself deeper into the pillows, staring at the ceiling. One lonesome tear left his eye. Dear God, what have I done?

Chapter Fifteen

Dr. Francis had given them no option but to leave the hospital.

"What are we going to do?" asked Cymone.

"May as well go over to Toby's," Merissa replied.

The two girls were alone leaning against the car whilst Alex was making a phone call.

"He is fine looking," Cymone said, looking in Alex's direction.

"He sure is," Merissa agreed. Very fine indeed, she added to herself.

Merissa told her about the grilling Thomas had given Alex and that she didn't like it.

Cymone laughed. "Thomas is up to his match making again. Only if I were you, I'd give this one serious, serious thought!" She grinned.

"I already have," Merissa said almost sadly. "He crowds my space. I can't breathe when he's around."

"So what are you telling me?" Cymone asked, knowing the answer.

Merissa never gave any man a chance. And again she wondered why. Something wasn't right. Merissa never talked about past relationships and she had never seen her with a guy except for Toby.

"I'm not interested," Merissa stated flatly, lying to herself.

"Oh yes you are! With the way you look at him and you've only just met him. Meri I'm one of your closest friends I know when you're interested!"

Merissa gave her a dry, annoyed look.

"Where to now, ladies?" he asked as he approached.

Merissa had to take a step back, he was crowding her again.

"I just remembered," Cymone spoke up, smacking her forehead with the palm of her hand dramatically. "I have to check out an apartment this afternoon. So it's just the two of you," Cymone ended, her eyes overflowing with mischief.

"But I thought you had until the end of the month?" Merissa said, eyeing her friend suspiciously and reluctantly admitting she was afraid to be left alone with Alex again.

"I do. But hey," she shrugged. "When it comes to house hunting..." She left the statement hanging in the air. "I'll meet up with you later."

"Where?"

"Here. At about five thirty." She turned and took a step forward before turning back to take Alex's hand. "Nice meeting you Alex." She gave him a brilliant knowing smile and an encouraging wink.

"Thanks," replied Alex. "So what do you want to do now Merissa?" God he loved her name.

"I don't know. I don't have any more exams."

Alex was happy to hear that, he selfishly didn't want anyone or anything to take her away from him.

Merissa decided to run him off.

"But I do need to pick up some things for Thomas in the Half-Way-Tree plazas," she said, smiling up at him.

"Shopping?" He looked a little bewildered as though it was a word he'd never used before.

She nodded, "Yep." Hoping he'd take the hint.

He took a deep breath. "Ok. Where do we start?"

"You want to come?" She couldn't help the amazement from creeping into her voice.

"Sure, why not." He sounded as though he was convincing himself. "Oh."

"One thing though," he said getting into the car. The driver's side, Merissa noticed. "I have to stop by the office for my briefcase."

"Ok," she said and settled in beside him, feeling strangely contented.

After leaving the office, they drove to Half-Way-Tree where the main shopping district was. They walked the entire stretch of shops twice, buying different things. He bought a few shirts and asked Merissa to pick out some colourful ties for him. He liked her taste.

Merissa bought a couple of things for Toby and Cymone, and some pyjamas for Thomas. Alex chose a robe for him.

"I'm starved," Merissa said some time later.

Luckily the normal lunch hour crowd had already gone and the place was relatively empty. Only several harassed mothers with their hyperactive toddlers were around. Merissa got a table in the middle of the food court, and ordered stew peas for herself and peppered steak for him. She didn't know what he liked to drink, so she ordered two large glasses of fruit punch – can't go wrong there.

He came back from stowing their shopping in the car just as the waitress brought the food. He sat opposite her, stretching his long legs out on either side of her chair.

"Do you like peppered steak?" she asked shyly.

He nodded. "But your stew peas sure looks good," he edged, eyeing her loaded plate.

"Oh well, lets go half and half then," she said.

He let her take his plate and watched as she neatly divided the food into two halves. It was at that moment, with her concentrating on sharing his food, that Alex realized he wanted to share his whole world with her.

"Thank you," Alex said when they had finished eating.

Alex had tried to hide his astonishment as she finished her lunch and a large chocolate sundae as well. Then suddenly the air shifted and she looked at him, both of them silently staring into each others eyes. Everything paled into the background.

"You feel it too, don't you Merissa?

She didn't need him to explain. She moved in her chair.

"Yes," Merissa admitted simply.

They sat looking at each other for long seconds, neither one ready to say what it was that they were feeling. Then Alex leaned across the table and kissed her. A whisper of a kiss that brushed her lips in a touch that was almost not.

After a few seconds, Alex murmured huskily, "We'd best get going."

"Alright," Merissa said, moving ahead of him so he wouldn't see the confusion on her face.

They reached the hospital just as Cymone went through the glass doors. Alex switched off the engine and turned to face her.

"Thanks for today," he said, cupping her chin to bring her soft mouth up to meet his.

Thomas saw from his window and was ecstatic.

Toby pulled up beside them.

"Hey Alex," he said.

"Hey Toby," Alex greeted. "How'd the exam go?"

"Cho, me dus that out man," smiled the other man confidently as he watched Merissa closely. She looked flushed, her eyes overly bright. "You ok?" he asked her.

"Of course," she replied, as they entered the hospital.

They spent an enjoyable hour together before the doctor came along and shooed them all out.

In the corridor, with tears in her eyes, Merissa stood motionless. Joseph drew her into his arms.

"You boys, take our Princess home ok," then taking Merissa to one side added, "Merissa, I know this is hard on you, but I don't want you driving up and down that blasted hill alone. Stay with Cymone for a few days or so until Tommy gets out, ok?"

"But Josey, what about you?" she protested.

"I'll be alright; Mrs. Dobbson has offered to look after me so I'm in good hands." He smiled a shallow smile. She hugged him long and hard.

"Be good Josey," she said.

"You too Princess and I'll see you in the morning." He left to find Dr. Francis.

She walked over to her friends trying not to show how thoroughly shattered she felt inside.

"Toby you take Cymone whilst I drive Merissa. She doesn't look like she can drive," Alex said, taking charge.

"Ok," Toby said, over the moon. "We'll meet you at my house."

Cymone gave Alex a withering look before walking out to follow Toby.

"Are you alright Merissa?" Alex asked gently. She was crying silently, her lips trembling and she shook her head at him. She looked completely lost and forlorn so he simply folded her into his arms, holding her close.

After a while, Merissa drew back, and looked up at him.

"Thanks I needed that," she said gratefully, giving him a shaky smile.

He still held her as they walked out to the car.

"Cymone doesn't seem to like Toby very much," Alex said, breaking the silence once they were on their way. He wanted to get her mind off Thomas.

Merissa jumped. "Sorry, what?"

"Cymone doesn't seem to like Toby very much," he repeated.

"Yes she does. Only she doesn't know it yet."

He laughed.

"They need to be alone together," she added, "poor Toby has been in love with her ever since she came to Jamaica."

"Where's she from?" Alex asked, as he manoeuvred around a large mini bus.

"Trinidad."

"I thought I could hear a different accent."

"She's a nice girl but just too damn stubborn for her own good. Everytime Toby is near, she gets all defensive; almost insulting...you'll have to see it."

Five minutes later he witnessed first hand.

Merissa gave him a look that said 'I told you so' as they walked into Toby's house.

"Alright you two. What's the problem now?"

Toby was the first one to attack Merissa.

"She's still looking for an apartment, so I offered to let her stay here until she finds one. Only *she*," he flicked his head in Cymone's direction, "thinks it's a stupid idea!"

"I will not live in the same house with you," Cymone spat out. Alex went to sit on the sofa, enjoying himself.

"I think it's a great idea Cym," Merissa put in softly. "You could save all that rent money!"

"I know that. . .do you think I don't know that!"

"Then what's the problem?" Merissa asked.

"He's the damn problem!" Cymone looked at Toby with an unsavoury expression on her face.

"Ok, ok," Merissa said, smiling at everyone. "I have a solution." She took a deep breath. "Joseph asked me to stay down here until Tommy gets out of the hospital. I was going to stay with you Cym, but it'll make more sense if we all stay here." She shrugged her shoulders. "It just makes sense."

Toby liked the idea. Cymone was still thinking about it. Alex was ecstatic.

"Fine by me," Toby said.

The three of them looked at Cymone.

"Alright," she conceded. "But only for a while until I sort myself out."

They settled down after that, talking about nothing in particular. It was a pleasant evening. Alex fit in well. Laughing and joking with Cymone, until she broke out of her moodiness and started relaxing.

Merissa smiled, watching them. She really liked him. Her mind drifted and she reflected on her time with him. Never before had a man affected her as much as he did. Even the slightest of touches sent her inward calm flying in all directions and thousands of tiny thrills scattering themselves under every pore of her skin. She looked at him under her thick lashes and felt this strong urge to go over and snuggle up to him. The urge was so powerful she had to get up and leave the room in a hurry to splash her face with cold water.

"Got any wine?" Merissa asked Toby minutes later when she felt like herself again.

"I think I'm all out. Alex and I had our annual domino championships last night."

"I've got supplies over at my house," Alex volunteered, getting up.

"You need to take your stuff out of my car, as well," Merissa said, looking around for her keys.

"I forgot about those," Alex said.

He quickly walked ahead leaving her no choice but to follow him outside with the keys.

"Could you help me to choose a bottle of wine?" he asked, when she reached him.

"Ok."

She followed behind him watching the way his jeans caressed his thighs. She felt the now familiar heat spread through her.

His house was bare and plain. All the walls were white, she noticed with a frown. She followed him through the living room, where he deposited his bags and went into the kitchen, switching on the light. A naked bulb hung sadly from the ceiling. His house was starving for attention.

She waited by the doorway whilst he took a six pack of beer from a cupboard and two bottles of white wine from the fridge. He didn't ask her opinion on them, she noticed.

"Can you manage these?" he asked her, indicating the bottles on the peeling vinyl counter.

"Of course. . .you have a nice home," she said, wanting to say something.

"It needs to be redecorated though, it's been like this since Mom and Dad died," he explained.

Merissa couldn't see his face, as he'd already switched off the light and was in the living room stooping down, rummaging through one of his shopping bags.

"Here," he said, standing and holding out a package that was beautifully wrapped.

"What is it?" Merissa asked, surprised.

"Why don't you open it and see?" he said with soft amusement, looking into her eyes.

She put down the two wine bottles and took the present from him, unwrapping it quickly. With delight, she flung her arms around his neck and planted a kiss full on his lips, surprising him; surprising herself, then surprising herself even more, when she kissed him again.

His response was instant, and seconds later, he took control. His tongue teased her mouth gently open, as he pulled her up against him, deepening the kiss. He walked her backwards until her back was against the doorframe of the dark living room. He loved the way her body fit into his with exacting precision as he swept a bold hand down her back and up under her top. She wasn't wearing a bra was his last conscious thought as his mind exploded and all he could do was feel. His tongue moved to the delicate shell of her ear, swirling round and round before sweeping down her neck to suckle softly on the tiny pulse beating frantically there.

She leaned backwards offering him more of herself. He took. He had no choice but to sweep his hands under her top, feeling the silkiness of her skin as he claimed both breasts in his palms. Impatiently he kneaded them together, apart, together, apart, committing their weight and feel to memory, before finally tasting one plump nipple and then the other. His hand swept downwards into her jeans to feel the dewy softness that was all his.

One of them moaned, Merissa didn't know who. Alex moved, going to his knees. He sucked her tiny belly button, swivelling his hot tongue into the dainty circle before moving leisurely on. Merissa tried to tug him back up to her, she wanted his mouth on her breasts again but he chuckled and using his teeth, unsnapped her jeans and nudged at the damp triangle covered by a tiny piece of white lace.

Merissa's hands clutched the door frame above her head as he pushed her panties out of his way with great urgency and explored her feminine folds with his tongue. Within seconds Merissa felt the fires that had been simmering all day explode into a great inferno she wasn't prepared for. She could barely balance as he moved one of her legs over his shoulder, giving him greater access to her secret place, delving in and out of her until she screamed, her body shaking as she collapsed against the door frame and slithered bonelessly to the floor.

He held her, calming her body with the softness of his kisses and the stroke of his hands at the small of her back.

"Lets go upstairs," Alex said huskily into the silence.

Merissa stilled. My God what had she done? How could she have allowed him to do what he did? She pulled away abruptly, stood and straightened her clothes with fingers that were all thumbs.

"That shouldn't have happened," she stated, looking everywhere but at him. "I'm not a tease."

"I know," Alex said as he stood up and fastened his shirt. "It got out of hand Merissa and I'm sorry. Not sorry for what I did because I want to take you upstairs and make love to you now, all night," he stated confidently. "But when you're ready." He touched the tip of her nose and kissed her quickly. "Come on. The others will be wondering what you've been doing to me," he teased. He picked up the beer and sauntered to the front door, leaving Merissa no choice but to follow.

Chapter Sixteen

Four evenings later, Alex and Merissa were finishing a delicious meal of brown stewed fish and steamed bammies at a popular outdoor restaurant in the small fishing village of Port Royal. They'd been seeing each other every night. Meeting at the hospital first, and then going out for long drives.

Alex and Merissa walked around the tiny village taking in the colonial aura of old Port Royal, when it used to be the virtual capital of Jamaica in the days of pirating. Henry Morgan sailed from here and famous Admirals such as Lord Nelson, Benhow, and the chilling Edward Black beard were all residents at one time or another.

They walked pass the police station that used to be the Collector of Taxes in the colonial days and even today, a small section was still used for this purpose. A tall dilapidated lookout tower stood at the back of the building facing the harbour.

"It's sad how the government has let this place run to ruin," Merissa said wistfully, looking at all the beautiful old buildings of colonial design.

Port Royal had once been billed the 'richest and wickedest city in the world' with its pirates and whores. Its raucous history was legendary. The intervention of a higher force put an end to its wicked ways, toppling a third of it into the harbour when the 1692 earthquake struck.

"They've been trying to restore this place for years," Alex told her. "I'm sure I even heard about a foreign grant sometime back."

"Figures."

"Lets go to the museum."

"It'll be closed."

"Doesn't matter." He winked.

Hand in hand they walked the few metres to where the impressive red bricked wall of Fort Charles began. Fort Charles had been built by the English in 1655 after they had invaded and captured Jamaica from the Spaniards in that same year. Huge, oily, black cannons still stood and glistened in the night, their snouts pointing out into the harbour.

"The gates are locked," Merissa stated as she walked towards the iron gate.

"Are you feeling adventurous Miss Walters?" Alex asked with a mischievous glint in his eye.

He was sitting on one of the two anchors that had been salvaged from the sea years ago and had actually been used by the 18th century men-at-war. But now it lay exhausted on either sides of the walkway.

"That depends," she answered cautiously.

"Have a little faith. Follow me," he ordered, leaping to his feet.

Minutes later, she was standing in the middle of Fort Charles, ashamed at having been talked into doing something so juvenile as jumping a wall. But it had been fun.

"Now what?" Merissa asked, now primed for adventure as she climbed the wooden steps to the upper deck and peered over an orange brick wall. The distant elemental throb of the waves and the strong gusts of wind in the trees were tantalizing.

"We go to the beach."

That was not what she was expecting.

"Now?"

"Sure," he replied and captured her hand again to drag her through the old fort and pass the Giddy house – where the old Royal Artillery store had been turned upside down by the earthquake of 1907. They walked around the large rundown emplacement beside it, through thin, thorn filled trees and tall Cactus plants until they reached the beach.

Merissa could hear the roar of the waves and she pushed all of her apprehension aside and ran ahead of Alex, thankful for the half moon that kept the inky blackness at bay. With a twirl, she flung off her sandals and ran down to the water. It had no reef to slow the force of the tide and she could feel the taunting pull of the current on her calves.

"Come on in, Alex. It's beautiful," she called out to him, as she frolicked and kicked at the waves.

He shook his head and sat on the black sand watching her play with an amused, indulgent smile on his face.

During the day, you were able to see small cays in the distance. At night, they were nothing but blobs in the darkness. Suddenly, a gust of wind combined with the dragging of the current sent Merissa over backwards. Alex saw her flap her arms out rapidly, as she tried to regain her balance before she was gobbled up by the dark water. Merissa, swallowing mouthfuls of the salty water, gasped for breath and was very nearly panicking to death when she felt Alex's strong hands lifting her carefully out of the water and placing her gently on the dark sand.

"Are you alright?" he asked, trying unsuccessfully to smother his amusement.

She glared at him, but nodded as he soothed her wet hair out of her eyes. She couldn't see his face as the moon was directly behind him, but she felt his gaze shift and his body still. Looking down, she gasped in horror, seeing her yellow blouse now as transparent as glass.

Her white lacy bra did nothing to hide the darkness of her aureoles and her nipples stood tight and round as pebbles against the chill.

She crossed her arms over her chest trying to cover herself. Alex moved even closer, looking into her eyes, smiling, and then ever so slowly, shook his head. Gently, he unfolded her arms. First one and then the other, with such tenderness she didn't realize what he was doing. He brushed his lips against hers in a feather of a kiss.

She shivered. She wasn't sure if it was from the cold or from the large hands which had gone around her shoulders cradling her body intimately into the hard curve of his.

Then he teased her mouth open and kissed her deeply. The kiss went on and on. The chill of the night disappeared; the heat from his mouth warming her blood. The roughness of his tongue as it delved with complete authority coaxed hers to life and soon she was kissing him back, responding to the sharp points of desire arrowing through her body. He felt so good, his supple body over hers, his mouth storming her senses as it moved over her jaw and down to the damp valley between her breast.

Somehow she was naked, the cool breeze sending goose bumps over her flesh, but immediately disappearing as he ran his tongue and hands over her body. She whimpered, a soft sound that harmonized with the sounds of the waves and the touch of the breeze as it skittered across the sand.

When his lips eventually suckled her breast she was lost, grasping his hair, tugging him up to her mouth or pushing him down, offering herself to his kiss, she didn't know which. She just needed to feel him. Never before had she felt like this, this complete taking over. She loved it. Her back arched into his chest, needing the closeness when she fleetingly opened her eyes. The beach was in darkness, the moon gone. She screamed, unable to differentiate *that* night from this.

"Hey," Alex soothed as he held her whilst she fought him wildly. "Merissa!" he shouted when she kicked out at him. "What's going on?" She was obviously distressed.

"Take me home!" Merissa ordered coldly, struggling to push him away.

He released her suddenly, and lay on his back breathing hard, not understanding. Merissa gathered her clothes and pulled them on, ignoring the wet sand that clung uncomfortably to her damp skin. Alex turned to look at her, his body now under control.

"What's going on?" he asked again.

She looked at him coldly, her eyes narrow and accusing, before picking up her shoes, spinning around and practically running from him.

He caught up with her just as she was about to pass the huge gun emplacement. He grabbed her arm and swung her around, his eyes blazing down into hers.

"Why are you running?" he demanded harshly.

"Look I'm sorry if I'd led you on back there…" she began.

"You didn't…"

"Let's just say it was a mistake never to be repeated," she flung out.

"What are you saying?" he asked, puzzled.

"…that I don't want to see you again," she stated coolly, her eyes firing sparks.

"No!" He grasped her shoulders and shook her roughly as though shaking some sense into her.

"Take your hands off me!" she demanded and glared down at his hands.

Realizing how hard he was holding her, he let her go and she stumbled against the wall. He crowed into her so that she couldn't move.

"We're only just beginning Merissa," he whispered against her mouth in a softly coaxing voice.

She pushed him away violently.

"I don't want to go any further," she spat. "Now please take me home!"

He sighed loudly and ran his fingers over his hair in agitation. He cursed.

"We'll talk about this tomorrow," he muttered arrogantly.

Merissa's temper exploded.

"No we won't. We have nothing to discuss. It's finished."

"Why are you doing this?" he asked in bewilderment. "Things have just started. Everything is right. Perfect."

"I don't want to see you any more Alex," she said tightly, her chest heaving as she turned away.

"The hell you say!" He reached out to grab her again but she evaded his fingers and stormed off, almost running in her haste to get away from him. Suddenly she cried out and stumbled.

"What's wrong?" Alex asked as he hunched down to where she was sitting on the gravel holding her foot.

"I stepped on something," she muttered, fighting the stinging tears that were threatening to overflow.

Muttering something incoherent, Alex picked her up and walked to his car.

Merissa tried not to notice how strong his arms were, or how he wasn't even breathing hard as he carried her rapidly along; or how his jaw looked smooth and inviting to the touch; or how his chest felt against her arm. But she did.

I wonder if he has chest hair, she thought to herself.

Gently, he placed her on the seat and covered her trembling shoulders with a jacket before rummaging through his glove compartment for a flashlight. He shone the small beam onto her foot and grimaced.

"You stepped on a thorn," he stated. And with swift action pulled out the long white spoke before giving her a chance to brace herself. "It's bleeding. Hold on."

In seconds, he had a small first aid kit open and was gently cleaning the wound and placing a plaster on it.

"There you go, as good as new." He smiled up at her, his hand still touching her foot, drawing tiny circles on her delicate ankles.

"Thank you," she snapped, pulling her foot away from him and reaching for her seat belt in one swift move.

Alex frowned.

On the way into the city he broke the simmering silence abruptly.

"I like you Merissa. I like you a lot."

His confession was greeted with insulting silence.

"Are you going to tell me what happened out there at the beach?" More silence. He sighed. "If you don't want to see me again," he ground out between clenched teeth after several taut minutes had passed, "just say so!" he shouted, getting angry and frustrated with her silence.

His pride had been stomped on and wrung out. Enough was enough.

"I say so," she replied quietly.

"No you don't!"

"Don't shout." She took a deep breath. "It's just not a good idea. Leave it at that!"

"Give me a good reason."

"I do not have to explain myself to you. I don't even know you."

"Alright if that's the way you want it."

"It is."

"Fine!"

"Fine!"

They drove the rest of the way home in rigid silence. Alex barely waited for her to get out of his car and close the door, before roaring off, ripping down his driveway and slamming on his brakes, inches from his front door. He didn't know what he was feeling. They hadn't known each other long enough for it to be called anything. Love didn't even enter into it. He swore and stomped out of his car and stormed into his house. The building rattled under the force at which the front door was closed.

He stormed into the kitchen and poured himself a large glass of rum. He felt better once the fiery liquid singed his insides, redirecting his raging thoughts. Feeling calmer, he went to his room, changed out of his wet clothes and lay down on the bed in the darkness trying to reason with himself.

When had he ever been bothered about a woman before? If she didn't want to see him again, it was her loss. Hell, I hadn't even met the woman until the other night, he thought. Women come in packs of six – like beer, when one's finished you simply opened another. To prove it, he reached over and grabbed his telephone.

"Vanessa? It's me. Got any plans for tonight?"

Chapter Seventeen

It wasn't working. Merissa had been sketching new designs for her evening wear collection all morning but nothing inspiring was happening. Feeling frustrated, she decided to pay Thomas an early visit.

"What is wrong with you?" Thomas demanded, as soon as she stepped through the door.

She looked down at her clothes as though they held an answer.

"Nothing," she said.

He looked at her, seeing the dark circles under her eyes, the washed out pallor of her skin and the limpness of her body.

"Merissa baby? Come over here," he ordered softly, patting the space beside him on the bed. She went over and lay down, sharing his pillow, their heads touching. "What is it?"

"It's me," she replied simply.

"What about you?"

"I can't describe it."

"Of course you can. Is this going to be one of those one-sided conversations?" he teased. "Haven't we always been able to talk about anything? Who was the one who told you about your periods?" He laughed, remembering how bewildered and confused she had been when he'd caught her crying in her room, all those years ago. She had thought that she was dying!

"It's not funny," she scolded. Then admitting defeat said, "I'm scared Tommy."

"Scared of what?" Although he already knew.

"Scared of all kinds of things," she admitted vaguely.

He waited for her to continue.

"I've never been so happy before Tommy – not about you of course, but about Alex. He makes me feel all these wonderful things."

"Like what?"

"Things all over. When he kisses me…" she admitted sheepishly. "I feel so-so…" She searched for the right word. "You know what I mean."

"Yes I do. It's what I felt with my Anna, may God bless her soul. I knew she was the love of my life the day we met." Thomas' blue eyes had taken on a faraway look. Anna was his wife, now dead, for well over twenty years, but still very much in his thoughts.

"Were you afraid of her?" Merissa asked.

"All the time," he confessed. "And all I wanted to do was be with her constantly and touch her every minute of every day. It was as though she was a dream. A dream I didn't want to give up or leave, just in case she might disappear."

They were silent for a moment, both lost in their own thoughts.

"Last night was the first time in years that I had that nightmare," she confided softly.

Thomas grimaced. This was not good news.

"Merissa, sit up."

She did, turning slightly, so that she could look at him.

"This is your first love. It might or might not be your last. But only you will know when you've found the right man. Alex is a good lad and I like him. But you're different," he went on. "Circumstances and situations years ago made you so and he may not understand it. When you're more sure of him, and yourself, you'll have to tell…" Merissa cut him off, knowing what he was about to say.

"Oh no Tommy! He'll hate me!" she said panicking.

"If he loves you, he'll understand. He'll understand why he has to tread carefully and not rush you. You have to give him a chance Merissa. You owe him and yourself that much."

Merissa thought about those words for a while. "I don't think I'm ready for this Tommy," she admitted unexpectedly. The very thought of getting involved was petrifying!

Thomas sighed.

"You'll have to let the past go Merissa. You can't keep living like this. You like him and he likes you, although I think he's feeling a lot more than liking you. Give him a chance, for him, for yourself and for me." He finished softly. "I need you to be settled, princess."

They were silent for a moment.

"Not this time Thomas. I'm not ready," she stated adamantly.

Thomas sighed sadly, yet he understood.

"That's ok princess. Whenever you're ready, you'll know."

He patted her cheek.

"I love you."

"I love you too princess. Now go and let me rest, you're wearing me out," he teased lightly, watching as she smiled.

Merissa got up and left him, promising to come back later.

Thomas reached for the phone and dialled home. He and Joseph needed to intervene.

"Mmm, that smells good," Toby said one evening several days later, strolling into his kitchen.

Whenever Merissa had something on her mind, she cooked. There was enough food to feed a small army on his counter much less the three of them.

"Toby, make the salad, I'm going to take a shower," she ordered, smiling at him to soften the request. Toby was not kitchen proud.

"Fine, but call Cymone in here. I'm not doing it alone."

"Ok," she said, as she took off her apron, left the kitchen, knocked on Cymone's door and went inside without waiting.

Cymone was sprawled out on her bed, crying and holding a picture. She looked up with tear stained eyes and dashed them away impatiently as Merissa sat on the bed.

"Who is he, Cym?" Merissa asked, taking the picture from her and looking at the fair skinned toddler, with light brown hair and grey eyes.

"This is my nephew, Nathan," she sniffed. "I guess I'm just missing my family," she admitted, drying her eyes on the pale pink bed sheet.

"He's very cute. Look at that dimple!" Merissa said smiling. "Cheer up Cym. You can go home for a holiday."

"That would be nice, but I can't afford it."

"I could lend..."

"No!" she cut in sharply. She lowered her voice apologetically and smiled. "Thanks for offering Merissa, but I pay my own way."

"You can be so unbelievably proud sometimes," Merissa scolded. "Can you make some juice for us? I made dinner. Toby is doing the salad so..."

"Sure," Cymone put the picture away and tidied the bed.

"She's been cooking up a storm," Toby pointed out when Cymone entered the kitchen.

"So? What does that mean?" She was trying not to look at the naked wings of muscle fanning out on either side of his black tank top.

"It means something's wrong. Anytime Meri gets upset she depletes my food supply."

"Well, it must be this Alex thing then," Cymone pointed out. "Thomas is on the mend and Alex is the only other person she *tries* not to talk about." She raised knowing eyebrows and smiled mischievously. "I think love is in the air."

"Yeah, I guess so. I've never seen her get like this over a man before."

"Me either," Cymone agreed. "Want to play cupid?" she asked conspiringly.

Toby nodded. Anything that would involve getting closer to Cymone he would gladly do.

"Let's invite him over for dinner." She smiled a rare smile at him looking him squarely in the face, something she always tried to avoid. His grey eyes were far too dangerous.

Yeah, just like you and me, Toby thought to himself and watched hungrily as she left the room.

Alex hadn't even taken his tie off before his door bell rang. He swung the door open violently and was surprised to see the diminutive figure of Cymone standing there smiling.

"Hi," she said cheerfully.

"Hi," he replied, looking at her with hostile eyes.

"Aren't you going to invite me in?" she asked sweetly.

Alex opened the door wider without a word.

"Well you're in a fine mood. Toby sent me over to borrow some mayonnaise," she lied. "Look in the kitchen," he replied coldly. His hand was still on the door knob.

"I've never been here before, remember. Where's the kitchen?"

He slammed the door and marched into the kitchen, grabbed the mayonnaise out of the fridge and handed it to her.

"Thanks...why don't you come over and have dinner with us? We..."

"No."

"Why not?"

"Because I damn well don't want any!" He'd already had the front door open again.

She stood a little distance away on his driveway so she could look him in the eye. "She's in a worse state than you," she told him and walked away, her back stiff, her chin raised. "We eat in ten minutes."

Alex stood by his door for several long seconds, closed it, took a quick shower, changed into his shorts and T-shirt and went next door; all done in seven minutes and forty-three seconds.

Merissa had just finished dressing and was sauntering into the TV room, when she stopped dead and stared at Alex with wide eyes and gaping mouth.

"Hello, Merissa," he said, his eyes raking over her slender form.

"Hello," she replied, slamming her mouth shut and trying to stop her heart from demolishing her rib cage with its thumping.

"Well aren't we going to eat? It's getting late!" Cymone said, getting up.

Merissa stared after her a little confused because Cymone headed for the dining room. They never ate in the dining room. Alex followed and passed without looking at her and when Toby made to do the same she stuck out her foot, stopping him.

"I'll kill you for this!" she hissed in his ear.

"Kill me? What have I done?" he asked innocently.

"Who told *him* to come over?" she demanded.

"Alex is my neighbour and if I want him over for dinner, I'll have him!" He took her arm and propelled her into the other room planting her down in the chair opposite Alex before she could blink.

The dining room was just an extension of the kitchen and was only ever used for special occasions.

"Meri, this is really delicious," Toby said much later, devouring his food and mopping up his gravy with a piece of roti. "Don't you think so Alex?"

"It's very nice," Alex told her, his eyes trying to capture hers but she refused to look at him.

"Oh, Cym," Merissa said wanting to wipe the smug look off Alex's face, "can I borrow your white dress? I have a date tomorrow night," she lied. She wanted Alex to know she was no longer available.

"Sure, but which one? I do have several you know," Cymone stated.

"The clingy backless one with the lace at the front," she smiled sweetly.

"You can't wear that! It's practically indecent!" Toby exclaimed. He had a detailed knowledge of both girls' wardrobes.

"It is not," both girls said in unison.

"You'll be looking for trouble if you wear that out alone," Toby informed her unnecessarily.

"Toby darling," Merissa sighed, lightly batting her eyes at him innocently. "You're awfully slow tonight." She paused and licked her lips, looking at the man opposite. "I won't be alone."

Alex's nostrils flared as he watched the play of her tongue against her lips and tried to control the burning rage which was turning his gut inside out.

"Then with whom?" Toby demanded, unaware of the tension radiating around the table.

"Toby, let's get the pudding," suggested Cymone. She began to gather the empty plates. She was the only one who noticed the storm clouds forming on Alex's face.

Toby stood, totally confused, but followed anyway. It wasn't often Cymone asked something from him.

"Do you like my cooking Alex?" Merissa asked, wanting to break the thick, heavy silence which had descended on the room.

"Yes I do. You can cook me dinner tomorrow night."

It was more a statement than a request, she noticed crossly. Merissa clenched her teeth, the utter arrogance of the man.

"I don't think so. I have plans." She pushed back her chair and stood up.

"Cancel it," he told her, his eyes dark and cold.

"No."

"I said, cancel it!" he roared as he stood up also and glared at her across the table.

"No. Why should I?" Before she could move, he was around the table, taking the plate from her, slamming it down.

"I'll show you why," he ground out, lowering his head.

His mouth claimed hers, demanding she kiss him back. She had no choice but to hold on to him, as he was bending her over backwards. If she didn't hold on to his shoulders, she'd fall into the bowl of rice. His hands reached up under her shirt, touching her breasts, playing with her nipples with rough expertise. His lips sought her throat, doing wonderful things to her senses and she loved every minute of it.

She pulled his head back up to hers, and now, she was the one who sought his lips, teasing, seeking, and receiving everything she ever wanted.

It wasn't until Alex heard the laughter of Cymone and Toby coming back into the room that he pulled out of Merissa's arms and went to sit in his chair, his brown eyes blazing with triumph. Merissa grabbed her plate, rushed pass Toby and Cymone and ran into the kitchen, humiliated. She wet a paper towel and patted her face, deciding not to go back in. Instead she went into the TV room and lay on the sofa, it was safer. What a pity her bedroom didn't have a lock on its door, she mused.

A few minutes later the three of them emerged laughing. Toby collapsed onto the love seat and Cymone lay on the cushions on the floor. This left Alex no choice but to sit on the sofa with her. She allowed him to sit at the bottom of the couch.

Alex lifted her legs and put them across his lap. He held them tightly when she tried to move them, squeezing them warningly. She glared at him. He only chuckled and began to draw tiny circles on her silky shin.

"What are we going to do for the summer?" Cymone asked.

"I don't know. I was hoping to go to England, but with Tommy the way he is, I'll be staying here," Merissa said.

"I'll be going to Toronto for a week or two," Toby said, looking at Cymone, who stared at him in surprise.

"You are?" Cymone asked him. She was trying to disguise her interest.

"Yeah?" he answered, suddenly realizing that Cymone wasn't as immune to him as she would like him to believe. Well, well, well he thought, will wonders never cease?

"What about you Alex, got any plans?" Cymone asked the other man.

"Work, work and only more work," he replied. The thought made him tired already.

"How boring!" declared Merissa, watching as he walked two fingers up her leg, stopping at the edge of her satin shorts before walking them back down again. A tremor shot through her and she gritted her teeth, trying to ignore the feeling. But the small smile on his face told her that he'd noticed her reaction.

"I say we put on a fashion show!" Cymone said to them all. "We've got talent and time. We may as well start putting it to good use."

"That's true. Maybe we should give it some serious thought," Toby said, more to himself.

"How about tomorrow? I'm dead beat. All I can think about right now is my bed," Merissa said, yawning and getting up.

Alex stood also and held onto her hand.

"We need to talk," he told her when she tried to move pass him.

"No."

"Well I think we do. Which room is she in Toby?"

"Alison's. . .if you need me Meri, just yell," he added belatedly, after receiving a black look from her.

It was obvious to Merissa that Alex knew Alison.

"Come in here often have you?" she asked dryly.

"Yes. Got a problem with that?"

"Oh no." She moved away from him as soon as he let her go and looked around for the best seat. She chose the chrome vanity stool and faced the mirror.

Alex settled himself down on the bed with his hands tucked behind his head, his ankles crossed. For a long time neither spoke and Merissa, glimpsing at his reflection in the mirror, noticed his eyes were closed and that he was breathing heavily. She got up silently and tiptoed over and peered at him.

Suddenly he grabbed her, yanked her down and immediately flung a well-developed leg on top of her thighs, trapping her body with his.

"Alex York! Let me go right now!" she exclaimed, wriggling under him.

"No."

She struggled for a little while longer then gave up. He was as unmovable as the Blue Mountains.

"We have to talk," he repeated. Sitting up, he pulled her up with him, planting her between his legs and forcing her to lean on his solid chest. He then tucked his hands under her shirt and buried them just below the waistband of her shorts as though they had every right to be there.

"You won't be going out tomorrow night," he stated arrogantly.

"Is that right?" she drawled, sarcasm dripping.

"Yes I'm right!" he hissed. "You will not be going out with anyone but me from now on. Is that clear?"

Merissa drew in an angry breath. The nerve of the man, the utter nerve, she fumed.

"I will see anyone and go anywhere I choose, since I have no commitments with anyone at all, including you. I will continue to do as I please," she told him calmly and confidently.

"We'll see."

Alex squeezed her again and moved his fingers down into her shorts. Merissa went rigid, refusing to give in to the rush of sensations his caressing fingers evoked deep inside her. But it was hard, harder still when he blew gently in her ear.

She shifted slightly, allowing him greater access and he delved into her folds, searching and finding that tiny nub and moving his fingers unhurriedly against it. She threw her head back and moaned deep in her throat. Her hips lifted off the bed, pushing up greedily for more of his wickedly sweet caresses.

"No other man Merissa," he growled in her ear.

A small sound escaped.

"No other man. Say it," he ordered, moving his fingers faster and faster.

She closed her eyes and bit her lip as his other hand cupped her breast, sweeping his palm across the erect nipple time and time again.

"Say it. Say it!"

He was playing her body to his very own tune. She couldn't think pass the rhythm of her breathing, the thump of her erratic heartbeat, the sweep of his hand at her breast. It was incredible. She hated him.

"You Alex," she breathed. "Only you," she burst out as her body froze, her world tilted, before tumbling from the height of unbelievable pleasure.

Cupping her sweetness, he slid a finger across her wetness with triumph.

"No other man Merissa, ever," he warned, kissing that place just below her ear and rearranging her languid body to his satisfaction.

"Bastard," she whispered.

"I know. Did you see Thomas today?" He asked, changing the subject abruptly as usual.

"Of course." It had taken her a several moments to fight her way out of the erotic fog. "Did you?" she asked, knowing he was a regular visitor.

She started reminiscing and for over three hours Merissa talked, cried and talked some more, exhausting herself. Alex listened, knowing she needed to let all the pain out. Eventually she fell asleep and he just looked at her. A single tear cradled in the corner of her eye. He kissed it away tenderly.

He was in love. She was his.

Chapter Eighteen

Something woke him. Alex snapped his eyes open. The room was different. He was about to get up when he saw Merissa lying beside him, her shirt chugged up, giving him a tantalizing view of one deliciously bare breast.

"Don't Jonas, please don't…" she mumbled beside him. "Don't Jonas…Jonas!" Suddenly she started thrashing almost as though fighting somebody off.

"Merissa wake up," Alex said softly, not wanting to frighten her. He reached over and switched on the bedside lamp. Pale green light touched the corners of the room.

"Wake up!" He shook her shoulders.

"No. Jonas, no! No! Please!" she cried out again. Her head began moving from side to side restlessly. Her fingers clutched the cotton sheets until her knuckles were white. Her legs shifted and she clenched them together. She was whimpering.

Scared, Alex shook her again. "Merissa wake up!"

Merissa's eyes sprang open. She looked at Alex with terror haunted eyes. He could see her trying to separate her dreams, trying to grasp reality as she squeezed her eyes shut and opened them again to stare blankly at him for several seconds. She sat up and buried her face in her knees, rocking herself, searching for comfort.

"You were having a nightmare," he told her quietly, stating the obvious. He moved up beside her and gently stroked her back.

"I know," she said eventually. Her voice was low and shaky. "I always have them." She lay back down and looked at the ceiling.

"So do I." Alex told her lying beside her. He'd never told anyone about them before. "Ever since my parents died."

"You do?" She looked at him, searching his eyes in the dimness of the room. Then she looked pass him and over at the clock on the dresser. "What are you still doing here?"

"We fell asleep." He gave her a guilty smile as he put his hands behind his head in a pose that was becoming very familiar to her.

"Don't you think you should leave?" she asked, feeling very uncomfortable and vulnerable.

"No," he said firmly. "I've already stayed this long and I only have another hour or so before I have to get up and go to work. I'll never be able to get back to sleep if I go now," he finished tiredly. "I'll stay on this side of the bed," he assured.

She could have argued, but she really didn't want to be alone. She liked having him beside her. Besides, it wouldn't hurt.

"Alright, you can stay, *but...*" she stressed, "you stay over there."

She moved nearer to the edge of her side of the bed, turned her back and fell asleep. This time peacefully.

※※※

"Morning sleepy head," Alex said standing over her with a lovely smile on his handsome face.

"Go away. I'm sleeping." Merissa buried herself into her blankets and covered her head with the pillow.

"I thought you said you're a morning person?"

"I am," she peeped at him from under the pillow. "But not right now. Goodbye, I'll probably see you later." She turned around again, giving him a view of her back.

Alex couldn't help himself. He took off his shoes and lay on the bed, cradling her warm body into his.

"Mmm," she said sleepily and wiggled unconsciously against him.

Alex shifted so she wouldn't feel his arousal and touched her breast. The nipple sprang to life.

"Alex don't."

"I need to baby," was all he could say.

He began to kiss the nape of her neck tenderly, his warm breath fanning the tiny hairs erotically. His free hand began to explore her body, going over mountains and into valleys. He brought his hand boldly to the very centre of her making, rubbing his palm over her furry mound.

Merissa moaned.

It was the moan that broke his slipping control. Flipping her over almost roughly, he nudged her knees apart and pressed himself against her, rocking his body against hers to the natural rhythm of centuries past. Merissa went berserk. She frantically scratched at his t-shirt wanting to touch him. His back was so smooth and strong, his skin so taut and so sleek the urge to taste him overcame her. She nibbled at his throat, hungry for the feel of him against the warm slide of her tongue. He groaned and lifted his head away from the exquisite torture of her mouth. She pounced on the bare skin now within her reach and bit down hard on his shoulder. Alex was beyond himself. He had to have her. Had to! He pulled away and yanked his shorts down, pulling her roughly up to meet him. His hunger for her was unbearable.

"I need you baby. I need you," he whispered harshly into her ear.

He slid down the bed to use his hot tongue and lips against her core, killing her with unbearable pleasure with his mouth. He released her, whispering sweet promises in her ear as he felt her love bathe his fingers. He glided a finger over her centre, then moved it slowly against her lips. She tasted herself.

Merissa opened her eyes as the cool morning air trickled over her hot flesh. She shivered.

His eyes were glazed as he arranged her beneath him. His pupils lost in the black depths of his desire. His eyes looked so much like another's. His breathing so hot and heavy...like...like *that* man. She panicked, not being able to tell one from the other. Seeing the star studded sky, the ceiling, the brush of the curtains, and the rush of the surf.

She screamed and pushed at him frantically. She kicked out and twisted her body free. She landed with a thump on the floor. Dragging her bed shirt around her, she cowered against the wall.

He went still.

"What the hell?" Alex said in confusion. One minute she was beneath him, holding him close. The next...

Merissa was sobbing and shaking as though he had raped her or something and he quickly pulled up his shorts and went down to the floor beside her. She flinched away from him as he tried to take her hand.

"What is it Meri?" he asked worriedly. Something was going on here and he didn't know what. This was the second time she'd gone crazy like this.

"Leave me alone, you bastard. Leave me alone!" She was trembling violently and with a muffled oath, he picked her up and laid her down on the bed, pulling her into the curve of his arms as he gently rocked her. She tried to fight him off, but he held on until she calmed.

Eventually her sobs subsided and Alex thought her to be asleep. Gently, trying not to wake her, he disentangled himself and sat at the edge of the bed. She was staring at him accusingly.

"I gave you no right to touch my body," she told him coldly.

Alex couldn't believe what he was hearing.

"*What?*"

"I want you and your filthy hands out of this room and this house, before I wake Toby and tell him what you did."

"What did I do Merissa?" he asked chillingly, his eyes narrowing as he caught on to what she was implying. He was livid.

"You were going to rape me," she snarled at him.

"I was not!" He was shocked she could even think such a thing, much less vocalize it. He stood over her, his eyes blazing, his jaw jutting out in menacing rage.

"I told you not to touch me. I told you!" Merissa screamed at him, scrambling away from him.

"Listen lady," he ground out slowly between clenched teeth. "If you didn't want it as much as I did, you only had to say no."

"Get out. Just get the hell out," she growled fiercely.

"I'm going." His face was twisted in disgust as he looked around for his shirt. "You're some mixed up woman, Merissa," he sneered. "You're only lucky it was me you were playing games with. Anybody else…" He smiled brutally as he pulled on his t-shirt. "Anyone else," he said again, "would have taken you and there would have been nothing you could have done about it."

She paled. "Get out. I don't ever want to see you again."

"Believe me," he shot back. "The feeling is mutual." His eyes raked over her breasts. "I don't think you would have been any good, anyhow." He picked up his shoes and left. The door clicked softly behind him.

Merissa hugged the pillows to her and buried her head into the softness, trying to muffle her sobs.

"I hate you Alex York. Hate you, hate you, hate you!" She punched the pillows and rubbed her mouth with the back of her hand.

Thomas left the hospital several days later and Merissa, Thomas and Joseph toured the island, visiting old friends and even taking a three-week holiday in Europe. She left them to explore India, then she flew home to help prepare for the fashion show which was scheduled for later that summer.

She saw nothing of Alex and was grateful. Toby and Cymone seemed to be getting along much better and the work they were all doing together was fantastic.

Chapter Nineteen

"I will not wear that dress!" Angelique said, glaring down at the two ladies, who were now quite used to such outbursts from the stunningly beautiful eighteen year old Jamaican model.

"What's the problem now?" asked Cymone, rubbing her forehead tiredly, a headache was threatening.

They'd been having rehearsals and fittings continuously for the past five days and the show was tomorrow. Everyone was on edge.

"I won't wear that wedding dress," the model pouted, tossing her wavy hair over a skinny shoulder.

"Why not?" Cymone questioned, stifling a yawn.

"Because it's bad luck, that's why. My Grandma told me so." Angelique sat beside Merissa and stretched her long legs in front of her.

"Angelique, I didn't think you were the type to believe in old wives tales? But if you don't want to honour us and wear the most important dress of the whole show, well…" Merissa shrugged.

"What does it look like?" Angelique wanted to know with a flicker of interest.

"It's the best creation Toby has ever made," Merissa answered simply.

"I'll think about it," Angelique muttered.

"Do we really need her?" Cymone asked for the sixth time in the past hour.

"Unfortunately yes. She's the hottest thing around at the moment. She'll draw the crowd," Merissa pointed out, then spotting the twenty children going onto the stage yelled, "ok kids! Take it from the top!"

Merissa and Cymone watched the children and models rehearse two more times before declaring everything perfect.

The bus came for the children to take them back to the Children's Home and all the models left, leaving the three of them alone in the National Arena.

"Well girls, I think we have it," Toby stated, as he jumped off the stage and sat beside them.

"I think so too," Cymone said.

"We might have a problem with Angelique and the wedding dress though," Merissa said, consulting with her clip board.

"That's ok. I have a solution if she refuses," Toby said.

"What?" Merissa enquired.

"You don't need to bother your pretty little head with that detail, I've got it covered." Toby gave her a confident grin.

༺❦༻

Alex stood at the very back of the arena. He'd gone home late, only to find a gilded envelope addressed to him under his door inviting him to the show. He'd 'if'd' and 'butted' for half an hour before changing into his formal clothes.

He didn't sit in the chair reserved for him as it was too near to the stage and Merissa might see him. He couldn't bear to have her scowl at him, it was better like this.

All the models had left the stage and Alex looked at his programme. The wedding theme was next. He sighed.

"May as well watch the end," he muttered aloud to himself.

Pink smoke filtered onto the stage and the lights went down. Two little girls came out wearing long white dresses in taffeta and lace holding baskets of large shiny silver stars. The wedding march was played by a saxophonist at the corner of the stage. Slowly a shadow of a figure stood in the centre of the stage, not moving. The figure was joined by the bride and together they began to move forward, slowly. Ever so slowly in tune to the soft music, the lights went up gradually and Alex held his breath.

"Oh God," he whispered to himself, a thrill or chill, he didn't know which, running through him.

Merissa stared out into the crowd with a gentle smile on her face and white orchids in her hands.

Alex had never seen her so beautiful. All eyes were drawn to her. She was beautiful, truly beautiful. The pale ivory of the gown, the thousands of beads and sequins, the miles of lace and tulle, it was an enchanting dress. Alex felt his gut tighten.

"Merissa," he whispered breathlessly to himself. All of his love poured into her name.

Alex felt a lump at his throat as he watched her walk around the stage and out towards him, getting nearer, ever so near. These past weeks had been hell. Watching her come and go from Toby's house all hours of the day, she haunted his dreams and entered his thoughts at the most unexpected times. He missed her but her accusations that night in the bedroom rubbed him raw.

Rape, she had called it. Even now he was perplexed. She was ready and willing that morning, he was sure of it. Yet he was haunted by dark tides of guilt. Maybe, he had lost control and hurt her, maybe he was a little rough. But it was only because she was so incredibly hot in bed that he assumed she was experienced. No woman had ever responded to him the way she did. Hell he had never responded to a woman like that in his life. They were meant to be together.

He had hardly seen Toby over the past weeks due to the show, and what could he say anyway. "Hey pal, I almost slept with your best friend, but now she's crying rape." The thought alone enraged him again. It was so unbelievable.

The lights came up and photographers were clicking away crazily at her, scrambling closer to get the better shot. After a while, she turned to leave the stage, only the MC called her back out again for one last walk. He then called out Toby and Cymone, who came on stage. Merissa waited for them to reach her, then all three walked down the runway holding hands and smiling triumphantly.

Thomas and Joseph were the first to stand and start clapping and were quickly followed by others. The audience went mad.

The arena eventually emptied and Alex toyed with the idea of going back stage. Without even realizing it, he moved to the side and was picking his way through the crowd to get to her. He had to see her. Touch her. Explain. Beg.

Reporters and celebrities crowded back stage. Alex managed to glimpse her before being pushed behind the door. She had changed and was wearing a bright red evening dress that left her shoulders bare. He moved towards her, shouldering his way through the crowd, only he got pushed back again. Giving up, he looked back one last time before slipping out, but not before Thomas saw him go.

Chapter Twenty

Cymone and Merissa were sitting at a small round table on the lawns of Boon Hall.

"We needed this," Merissa told her friend as she looked around the tranquil gardens, listening to the subtle rush of the passing river near by.

Boon Hall was found a short distance from Stony Hill Square. It was a delightful garden, full of flowers and trees, with a play area for children and an outdoor restaurant. It was a popular place on a Sunday, when most Kingstonians came out to enjoy the buffet brunch whilst watching their children play and the birds entertain.

"I can actually feel my body winding down. It's been such a hectic month or so. Whose idea was it to put on a fashion show anyway?" Cymone asked with a cheeky grin.

"Yours." Merissa laughed at her.

"It's good to hear you laugh like that Merissa. It's been a long time," Cymone told her sadly.

"Yes, well…" Merissa's defences immediately shot up.

"Still no hope for you and Alex?" Cymone pressed.

"Nope."

"Are you sure? He's such a nice fellow," she continued relentlessly.

"Yes well, for someone else maybe."

"Oh stop it!" Cymone scolded in a heavy Trinidadian accent. "The two of you fit together, like two halves of a coconut. You were so happy."

"I really don't want to hear this Cymone. Besides what about you and Toby? Things seem to be smoothing out with you two. I haven't broken up an argument in weeks."

Cymone smiled secretly.

"Mmm, we are getting along better. But nothing will come out of it. I don't want to be involved with another white guy ever again!" she admitted abruptly, only to instantly regret the admission.

Merissa looked at her sharply. "You're not prejudiced are you Cymone? Because if…"

"Don't be stupid!" Cymone shot back. "Sorry that was uncalled for," she apologised.

"Yes it was. What aren't you telling me Cym?"

Cymone looked down at her fork and twirled it between her thumb and finger for several seconds before placing it carefully down with intense concentration on the soft pink table cloth.

"Cymone?" Merissa prompted.

"Alright, I'll tell you." She leaned back and sipped at her rum punch before continuing.

"Remember that evening…sometime back…when you caught me crying over a picture?"

"Yes."

"The little boy…is my son."

Shock made Merissa's mouth drop open. "Your son?"

Cymone nodded then smiled. "His name is Nathan. He's three."

"That's nice. But why have you kept him a secret?"

"It's a long story Meri."

"We've got all day," Merissa pointed out briskly.

Cymone took a deep breath.

"The very first time I fell in love was with this white guy. I stupidly thought he loved me back. We went out secretly for about six months, then I got pregnant. He took off the same day I told him."

"Oh Cym."

"It's ok really. It was for the best. My family didn't approve of him anyway. They – my family – sent me off to my aunt who lived miles away in the countryside. I had my son and they took him," she stated simply.

Merissa gasped, "What do you mean 'they took him'?"

Cymone nodded sadly as her dark eyes went even darker with sad memories. "My mother came one day and took him away with her. She didn't even let me say goodbye." Tears trickled slowly down her cheeks. "To cut a long story short, I found him eventually after months of searching and explained to the family who has him that I want him back.

I told them what my mother did. My mother had told a bunch of lies and they were disgusted and appalled. They are such good people. They promised to look after him until I was able to come for him."

"But why didn't your family take him?" Merissa asked. Cymone had never talked about her family before.

"They were ashamed," Cymone told her simply. "I wasn't married. I had sex and dropped out of college to have a baby. They were horrified." She smiled sadly at the memory. "They told the neighbours I'd gone to England or some such place to study."

"They're ashamed of you and your child?"

Cymone shrugged, "My house in Trinidad looks like the pages of Architectural Digest. Us kids couldn't bring friends over in case they might dirty the white carpet. It was hell growing up in a house like that."

"Oh Cym. What have you been doing for money?"

"My aunt died and left all her money to me. That's what I used to trace my son. I send his guardians money from it every month, pay my rent, school fees…"

"Why didn't you tell me? I'm your friend, I would have helped," Merissa argued, dashing aside her tears.

Cymone smiled and reached across the table to take her hand.

"It's not only my parents who are proud, Meri."

Merissa accepted this, though she would rather not. They were silent for a moment.

"Is that why you react so emotionally when Toby is around?" Merissa asked.

Cymone flushed.

"You really like him, don't you?" Merissa pressed. Now clearly understanding Cymone's reactions for the very first time.

"Yes I do," Cymone admitted reluctantly.

"He loves you, you know."

"I know."

"So what do you intend to do about it?"

"Nothing."

"You can't live like this Cymone. Toby is so in love with you it's not funny. If a man ever loved me the way he loves you, I'd snap him up!"

"Alex does," Cymone said quickly.

"He doesn't count," Merissa shot back hotly.

"Why not?"

"We're not talking about me here," she informed her friend dryly.

"I can't think about Toby right now. I don't want to be involved. I just want to finish school and get my son."

The waiter came then, his pen poised ready to take their order. Cymone was grateful for the intrusion.

Chapter Twenty-One

Alex was sitting moodily staring out of his office window, seeing nothing, hearing nothing. He'd been so stupid, letting a woman like that walk out of his life without a fight. He'd never be able to be with another woman and not wish that it was Merissa he was holding beneath him.

"Damn it!" he muttered gruffly, he missed her.

He reached for his briefcase, he was going over to Toby's. Enough was enough.

"Sir? There's a call on your private line," Mary, his secretary, said via the intercom.

Alex toyed with the idea of just letting the phone ring but decided against it.

"Yes," he barked down the line.

"That's no way to answer the telephone," Thomas said, switching his phone to his other ear.

"Mr. Walters? Nice to hear from you sir," Alex said, surprised.

"Thought I was dead did you?" Thomas asked sarcastically.

"The thought hadn't even crossed my mind," Alex chuckled.

"So how's it going down there in the city?" Thomas asked.

"Pretty much as you left it sir. How was your holiday?" Alex asked politely.

"Should have stayed home. Merissa was sulking about the place. I'm having some friends over for dinner tonight. Be here at seven." He hung up.

Alex sat bewildered for a moment, wondering what had just happened.

❦❦❦

At seven o'clock sharp, Alex rang the door bell to Thomas' house. A uniformed maid let him in and showed him into the living room. Thomas' few consisted of about fifty people, some of which Alex already knew. The majority he didn't.

"Alex, grab a drink and come over here! I want you to meet someone," Thomas shouted above heads.

Alex found the bar and ordered a Coconut Rum and Coke, then moved through the crowd towards Thomas.

"Evening sir. You're looking well," Alex said to Thomas, as they shook hands.

"Of course I am. I'm out of that damn place aren't I? Alex York, I'd like you to meet Sam Parker. Sam is the big fish of Collins' and Parker Real Estate."

Alex shook hands with the bald man and listened politely as he rattled on about several beach front properties up for sale in Hellshire Heights, all the while, keeping an eye open for Merissa. After about two hours of polite chit chat and heavy politics, Alex grew bored. It was obvious Merissa wasn't at the party. Disappointed, he went out onto the balcony.

The view was even more breathtaking at night. The community of Portmore sprawled out below in a mass of orange lights that seemed to merge into one great big fireball. A plane was descending slowly as it moved towards the airport. The house was tastefully decorated in what he would presume to be original Kapo paintings and other Jamaican works of art. He was no expert, but he could tell the exquisite cabinets and tables which dotted the living room, looked decidedly French in flavour and extremely expensive.

Merissa suddenly appeared on the landing and was smiling and talking to the guests. Alex felt his stomach tighten with nervousness and he released his breath in a whoosh, not realizing he'd been holding it in the first place.

It was obvious she knew the majority of people in the room, giving and receiving hugs and kisses as she mingled. She looked beautiful, all dressed in a long electric blue strapless dress. The whole thing clung to her. Hostile rage flowed slowly through his veins and knitting his brows together, he wondered where the hell she'd been and who'd she'd been with!

Alex watched her every move as he sipped his drink in the shadows. She eventually drifted into the kitchen and he followed behind her, oblivious to Thomas and Joseph watching him and smiling to themselves. He closed the door softly behind him and leaned against it.

"Hello Merissa."

She turned, surprised to see him standing there. She took an involuntary step backwards.

"Hello Mr. York," she said coolly, regaining her composure. "How have you been?" she asked politely, turning back to pile food on her plate.

"Can we talk?" he asked abruptly.

"I have nothing to say to you."

"We need to talk Merissa. We can't leave things the way they've been."

She sighed deeply. She didn't want to talk to him. She didn't want him to see the yearning in her eyes. She missed him, knowing she'd overreacted that morning; but she just couldn't bring herself to talk to him. Her life was simpler and easier without the complication of a man in it – especially a man like Alex York. He was too good looking, too confident, too arrogant, and too easy to love.

But damn she missed him!

She finished putting food into her plate and turned to look at him. Really look at him. He looked good. Better than how she remembered.

"We really have nothing to discuss," she repeated tightly.

"Please."

He needed to talk and be with her so bad he felt as though his whole life depended on it.

"Meri, I've had a very bad week, nothing has gone right and this weekend will be the anniversary of my family's death. I don't want to be alone. Please." He begged. Hell, he'd crawl on the floor if he had to!

They looked at each other silently for long, hushed seconds.

"Alright, follow me," she relented and led the way up the back stairwell.

She stopped and opened an ornate mahogany door and went in. A huge carved painted bed dominated the room with its soft canopied cotton in the palest of peach. Bleached wooden floors shone. The walls were hand painted with designs of flowers and vines which had been rubbed down to add a touch of mystery and fantasy. The room extended into what he saw was a bathroom and dressing room. Both of which were decorated in the same ethereal mood.

She walked through, putting her tray on a table, which housed a collection of Victorian glass boxes. Then she went to another door, opening it to reveal a dainty balcony that overlooked the gardens. The subtle smell of freshly mowed grass and the potent perfume of a frangipani plant tickled the evening air.

He could hear the muffled voices of the party going on below them.

"We can talk out here," she told him, going for her tray but he beat her to it.

"You have a nice room," Alex complimented.

"Thank you," she told him proudly. "Toby did the paintings, I did the rest."

"You did?" Now was his chance. "Will you help me with my house?"

"No."

"Why not?"

"You know why not Alex," she told him coldly.

"No, I don't!" he yelled at her.

"Don't you dare get upset with me. I don't want to decorate your house and I don't need to explain a damn thing to you!"

"You have a hell of a lot to explain to me," he burst out.

"Why do I get the impression you aren't talking about your house here?"

"Because we aren't!" He took a shuddering breath and tried to calm himself down. "Look Merissa," he breathed slowly. "The last time we were together we almost made love and then all of a sudden you turned around and started accusing me of…of…" He couldn't bring himself to say it.

"Rape? Assault?" she provided icily.

"Yes. I don't understand," he admitted, a frown creasing his strong forehead. "I never forced you. I admit I became a bit rough…"

"A bit?"

"But I didn't do anything that would warrant such an accusation."

"Okay. I admit I went over the top. I've never been in that kind of situation before…"

Alex latched on to the 'never'.

"Never?" She was still a virgin?

Merissa struggled with her explanation. There was no way she was going to tell him about her past.

"It had been a long time ago," she lied.

"So you're not a virgin?" Somehow he was disappointed.

"No, I'm not."

"And you've had boyfriends?"

"No! Yes! Look I'm not a virgin ok. Leave it at that!" she shouted at him.

"Which is it Merissa?"

"I said I'm not a virgin. It's just been a long time that's all."

"How long?" he persisted. He may as well get the whole story to agonise over.

"What the hell is this? It's not any of your damn business!"

"It is, when you accuse me of raping you," he countered hotly.

"You didn't rape me."

"But you said I did. How am I supposed to feel when the girl I lo-" He caught himself. "When the girl I'm making love to, suddenly panics and starts behaving as though I violated her!"

Merissa made a frustrated movement with her arms disturbing the tray. It tipped onto the tiled floor, the plate breaking in two.

"Let's just forget it. Why don't we?" she said in a reasonable tone as she bent to clean the mess. Alex helped her.

"It's not that simple."

"Look I'm sorry I said what I said. I lost control and my nerve. It should never have happened in the first place."

"I disagree. It was the most incredible love making I've ever experienced. And I want to feel that again," he admitted boldly.

"No!" Merissa's hands stilled at their task.

"It's true. I like you. I like you a lot. You like me." He reached out and stood holding her hands and pulling her to her feet. "Look," he said looking down at their hands, "even now your reacting to me. Your body is quivering under my touch."

"It's nerves."

"It's not." He trailed a finger down her neck and along the top of her dress. "Your body wants mine Merissa. You can't lie about a reaction like that."

He was looking pointedly at her aroused nipples pushing against the material of her dress.

Merissa wrenched out of his hands and crossed her arms over her traitorous body.

"That's just a reaction to the cold."

"It's a warm night," he countered.

"Why are you doing this?" she asked desperately.

"I want you."

"You can't have me."

"Oh I'll have you Merissa. But believe me. You'll be coming to me first. I won't touch you unless you want me to."

"I'll never want you to."

He only smiled confidently and said, "Let's go and get you some more food."

༻✦༺✦༻

"I had a lovely day Meri," Alex said in the darkness of the car as they went down the hill the following evening.

They had talked throughout the night on her tiny balcony, snuggled under the blanket she had pulled from her bed, keeping the chilly night air out. It was only when they heard a single bird, singing a Jamaican morning song, that they finally slept in each others' arms, closer than they had ever been.

"Glad you enjoyed it," Merissa answered. "Where are we going anyway?" she asked, when she finally recovered.

"To my house. I need to take a quick shower and change my clothes. You can plan the rest of the evening."

"Ok."

They reached his house.

"Doesn't look as though Toby and Cymone are home," Alex observed. "Make yourself at home, whilst I shower. . .care to join me?" he asked with a twinkle in his eye.

She shook her head.

She walked around for some time, making mental notes of the changes she would make, and was making her way upstairs when she bumped into a half naked, very wet Alex, during her tour. Merissa snatched a second to examine his body with a thoroughness that was uncharacteristic. Tiny streams of water glided down his hair-roughened chest. Merissa took another moment to follow the progress of a droplet of water as it disappeared into the folds of the minuscule white towel, tied precariously at his waist.

"Looking for me?" he asked, delighting in the hot looks she was shyly giving him.

"Actually," she breathed. "No. I was just moseying around."

"Well have you moseyed in here?" he asked, pulling her with him into a room.

"No. Whose room is this?" she asked, looking around. It was a big room, with only a bed and a plain wooden chair in it.

"I sleep in here, sometimes."

"Oh. And where else do you sleep?" she asked.

"Here and there."

"Is that right?" One elegant eyebrow rose.

"Yeah, I don't like to sleep alone," he said, his voice grim.

"So who do you sleep with?" She had to ask, even though his answer would probably kill her.

"Amber," he replied simply.

"Amber?" Merissa repeated, feeling a wave of something like jealousy sear through her. "Who's Amber?" She couldn't help asking.

He chuckled.

"Would you like to meet her?" Alex offered with polite kindness.

"Actually no."

"Well I think you should." He pulled her out of the room, down the stairs, through the kitchen and out the back door.

"Amber!" he shouted into the darkness.

A Golden Cocker Spaniel leapt into his arms yapping happily.

"Oh, she's gorgeous! Can I hold her?" Merissa was already reaching out to take the tiny dog.

"Not yet. Let her get used to you first."

He put the dog down and went into the kitchen, leaving the two ladies behind.

"Hi Amber," Merissa said bending down to pet the dog.

Amber allowed herself to be patted for a moment then ran into the kitchen yapping for her dinner.

"Have you decided what you want to do yet?" Alex asked Merissa as she entered the kitchen.

"Get some ice cream, come back here and watch a DVD?"

"Sounds good to me," he said, locking the back door and securing the grill.

❦❦❦

An hour later they arrived back at his house. Alex finished his ice cream, helped himself to hers, then promptly fell asleep. Merissa watched the film to the end, loving every minute of it, then gently removed Amber from the bottom of the couch.

"Alex? Wake up, it's finished." She shook him gently.

Alex woke up, his eyes were slightly red.

"Sleepy head," she teased. "The movie is finished," she told him again.

"Oh, ok," he murmured, getting up.

"Alex?"

"Mmm." He was stretching his arms above his head. Merissa watched the play of his muscles with wondrous fascination. Her throat went dry.

"Where do I sleep?"

"With me." He was looking straight at her, his dark eyes making her aware of her body. She could feel the heat spread down between her thighs. Her nipples pinched and she crossed her arms. He raised a knowing eyebrow. "But I guess the room next door will have to do, I suppose," he added with a regrettable smile.

"That's right. Good night."

She gave him a peck on the cheek. Alex watched her go, his eyes full of regret.

Chapter Twenty-Two

"Jonas…no!…No. Please stop…stop!" Merissa screamed and sat upright, completely shaken.

Alex burst into the room.

"Meri! I'm here. Its ok baby, it's ok. Don't cry…I'm here." He repeated this over and over again as he made her more comfortable against him, letting her cry into his shoulder. She was holding him tight.

"I was dreaming."

"I know babe. Stay here while I get you a glass of water, ok?"

"Ok." She answered, trying to smile but failing miserably.

He came back with a glass of ice water and she drank it thirstily.

"Do you want to talk about it?" he asked her gently.

"No!" She instantly stiffened and went to move away from him, but he held her in place.

"Ok. Would you like me to stay?"

"No."

"Alright." He got up stiffly, hurt by her rejection. "See you in the morning," he said gruffly as he quietly left the room.

Merissa lay in the darkness looking at the ceiling. She didn't want to fall asleep, so she got up and tiptoed into the TV room lifting Amber onto her lap as she sat on the sofa, stroking the dog's silky coat.

Thomas had said she would have to tell the person she might be falling in love with. She was sure she loved Alex with a certainty that grew with every second in his presence. For her to go any further in their relationship, she would have to tell him.

Thomas was right. Getting up quickly – before she could change her mind – she went into his bedroom without knocking on the door.

"Alex?" she whispered as her eyes adjusted to the darkness.

"Yeah."

"Can I talk to you?" She went and stood over his bed looking down at his shadowy figure under the covers.

"Now?"

"Yes…please."

"Ok, come here." He shifted across the bed making room for her. Only she surprised him and snuggled up to his side under the cotton sheet, resting her head on his shoulder, and placing her hand on his chest. He didn't dare speak in case she realised what she was doing.

It took a few moments for her to muscle up the courage to begin.

"When I was younger I used to live in a place called Paradise Pass," she began, talking to him in a stilted emotionless voice. It was only when she reached that terrible night that her emotions broke loose.

"It was Jonas," she explained. "I helped him. The worse thing I could ever have done was help that bastard!"

Alex soothed her.

"I tried to get away Alex, I really did. But he was stronger than I was and he pushed me down…Alex…I swear I tried to get away!"

"Shh baby, it's ok, I know you did." Alex knew what she meant, what she was trying to tell him. He held her tighter and rocked her gently, giving her time to compose herself.

"He raped me, Alex," she said quietly.

"Oh baby."

"Don't talk," she put a finger to his lips. She had to go on. "It went on forever and then I passed out – thankfully. And the next thing I know, I was on a yacht, Thomas' and Joseph's. They had found me on a rock out at sea…you see, Jonas not only raped me, but he tried to kill me as well."

"Dear God!" Alex didn't know what to say. He had tears in his own eyes. He couldn't even imagine anyone wanting to hurt her, this beautiful woman, much less kill her!

They held each other for a long time.

"It doesn't change the way I feel about you, Merissa," he told her softly, breaking the silence much later.

"You don't think I deserved it?" A small voice asked him.

"Of course not!" He sat up and turned her to face him. "Baby I love you," he whispered to her, looking into her eyes and wiping her tears away with the pads of his thumbs.

"Oh Alex, I want to make love to you. I really do. But whenever I close my eyes, I see him over me, hurting me…and I just can't…It's better if we don't go any deeper than we already have."

"No! Meri, listen to me! Listen to me," he pleaded urgently. "This doesn't change the way I feel about you. In fact I understand you better. What about your mother?" he asked abruptly, changing the subject, now wasn't the time to tell her what he was feeling.

"She died some years ago."

"Were you close?"

"At times I thought I didn't exist in her life anymore, but I knew she loved me. I'd only seen her once after that night and that was to assure her I wanted to go with Thomas and Josey. We changed my name and I've lived with Tommy ever since."

"Have you ever been back to Paradise?" Alex asked.

"No, I can't face it. I can't even go to Negril. I cannot go back there Alex," she stated adamantly. "My father left almost ten acres of prime beach and farm property and now those bastards have it. We were almost poor, but my father had big plans for all that land. We were going to build a little guest house, only he died before even a brick was laid!"

There was another long silence.

"Why did you tell me this Merissa?" He needed to hear her reasons. She needed to realize just how much he meant to her. "Am I the only other person who knows beside Thomas and Joseph?"

"Yes," she said after a slight hesitation.

"Then why did you tell me?" he encouraged gently.

"Because...I don't know why Alex...it just felt right."

He smiled, hearing what he wanted to hear, if not the exact words.

They talked all night, about their fears, ambitions, and families until the early hours of the morning. Only when the first rays of sun had begun to warm up the world, did they drift off into a contented, secure, sleep.

The following afternoon, they left the house and went for a drive in the countryside. They drove parallel to Wag Water River until Alex pulled off the main road and parked at Castleton Gardens. It was really a beautiful place. Not too far from Kingston, but far enough to leave the hot city frenzy behind.

The flowery garden was a haven for birds. The tiny bee hummingbird danced from flower to flower with its iridescent cousin the mango hummingbird, whilst their red-billed streamer tailed cousin looked on with haughty disdain.

Alex and Merissa strolled hand in hand through the park. After a refreshing lunch of water coconuts and long mangoes, they crossed the street, where they paddled in the river.

"Mmm. Alex this is nice," Merissa said sometime later gazing around from where she sat on the grass, chewing on a piece of sugar cane.

She felt happy and relaxed and it showed.

"Merissa?" Alex asked seriously taking her free hand.

"Yes?"

"I meant what I said last night." He looked into her beautiful dark eyes, trying to convey his message to her.

Merissa swallowed. "You said a lot of things last night."

"I do love you," he said, holding her stare.

"But how could you? We've only known each other a short time."

"I know, because you're all I think about...when I didn't see you all those weeks, I was going out of my mind. We'd only known each other a couple of days. I didn't expect you to get under my skin the way you did and it frightened me. I've never been in love before and I didn't know how to deal with it. Then every time I picked up the phone to call you, I thought you might reject me. It's been torture not seeing you. Not being with you," he admitted passionately.

"What you told me last night doesn't affect the way I feel about you at all. In fact I love you more," he went on.

He held his breath and waited for a response, it took some time to come, but what she said was well worth the wait.

"I...I love you too, Alex...but I..." He put his finger to her lips, not wanting to hear her doubts just yet, he had to do all the talking.

"I know what you're going to say. I'll help you Meri. You'll have no reason not to trust me, I love you." He put his hands on either side of her face and pulled her to him, stopping only when their breath mingled. "I love you," he told her again. "I promise you'll be safe. I will not let any harm come to you ever again. I can't be without you."

Merissa's heart shone. A tiny smile changed into a dazzling grin as she flung herself into his arms, holding him tight. He gave her a soft kiss, sealing his promise.

"Where do we go from here?" she asked some time later, lying on the thick grass.

Alex flicked her nose and kissed her gently, picking up half of a fallen coconut frond beside him and pulling off three of the greener leaves, beginning to plait them expertly.

"What are you doing?" Merissa asked curiously, watching him with a puzzled frown.

"Nothing really," he replied vaguely.

A few minutes later, he looked proudly at the finished product. He pulled Merissa up to him, kissed her tenderly and wrapped the plaited leaf around the ring finger of her left hand, knotting it securely and cutting off the end with the pocket knife sticky with sugar cane juice.

"Will you marry me?" To hell with taking things slowly he thought. He wanted her to be his now! "Will you be mine Merissa?" he said again, more urgently, holding his breath, waiting.

"But what about the things I told you?" she edged.

"I love you. We'll deal with it together. Please say yes," he urged, a wave of apprehension washing over him, knotting his stomach with each passing second.

She took a deep breath and moved away from him. Alex took it as a bad sign. His shoulders slumped.

"Do you love me?" he asked gently.

"Yes."

"Marry me Merissa. I promise I'll look after you and we will be good together."

She smiled through her tears.

"Yes." And then more confidently. "Yes I will marry you Alex."

Chapter Twenty-Three

"Mi seh, mi can't tek it no more," Jonas complained to his younger brother.

"Tek what?" asked Tally, as he sat beside his favourite brother beneath the ackee tree at the back of the yard. Jonas' chest was bare, his massive stomach resting heavily on his knees. Tally grimaced.

The sky was overcast and there had been a severe weather alert for the area, that's why Jonas was lazing around at home.

"Mi head a hurt mi," Jonas whined holding his head in his hands.

"Mi notice seh you nuh get no sleep a night time. Wha mek?" Tally asked. He slept beside Jonas at night and knew he was always having nightmares, waking up covered in sweat.

"Mi miss di likle coolie gal," Jonas lied easily. He'd been using that excuse for years. "Mi jus can't imagine a sweet likle ting like she dead inna di sea. A shame it is, a bloodclaat shame." He shook his head as though in grief but peeped at his brother to see if he was buying it.

Tally looked out at the stretch of blue water in the distance. He never thought about his stepsister, had in fact forgotten all about her. Her body had never been found.

"A wha we a nyam fi dinna?" he asked Jonas as he rubbed his stomach.

"Yuh mussi tink mi a yuh puppa," Jonas growled. "Yuh no av two baby madda down so? And three up so?"

Tally looked in the direction of Cousins Cove and stood up. It was true. He did have girlfriends all around. All of them had given him a kid; seven children so far and two on the way. He could choose who to eat dinner with.

"Si yuh later. Mi a go get mi fill," he chuckled, rubbing his stomach and then cupping his private parts.

Jonas picked up a dry stick and pushed it into the dirt. He had to get out of here. Everywhere he looked he saw the bloodclaat coolie gal. In his dreams, at the beach, at Jack's and even when he went fishing.

She was haunting him. He could hear her screams and see her body as it floated away every time he closed his eyes.

He couldn't eat, couldn't sleep.

He had to get away.

He would go to Kingston.

Chapter Twenty-Four

Merissa watched the sun dip slowly towards the invisible line separating the sky from the sea, signalling its end to another warm, sultry tropical day. She smiled contently. The day had been just marvellous, absolutely delightful as Thomas would say. She chuckled and lifted her left hand, admiring the emerald and diamond ring on her finger.

"Mrs York," she whispered to herself. "Mrs. Merissa York." She smiled brightly and sighed with contentment.

The wedding had taken place just two weeks after Alex had proposed. Thomas – it seemed – had everything planned before hand because the speed in which the arrangements had been made was startling although they had disagreed on the number of invitations to be sent out. Thomas finally relented and cut his own list down to fifteen out of his original ninety-eight.

In all, the wedding had been an intimate fifty with only a few of her friends. Cymone as her only attendant, Toby as Alex's best man. Alex, himself, had invited a handful of people; most of them from his workplace and a couple of old friends. One was female, whom he'd introduced as Vanessa Powers.

Something about Vanessa niggled at Merissa. She was very attractive, a dark chocolate complexion, sultry eyes and long waist length micro braids. She was a lawyer and had worn an attention grabbing, tightly fitted, lime green dress. She was pleasant enough when Alex was around but the way she had looked at her across the expanse of the garden was thoroughly disturbing. The look was hot and accusing, full of raging hostility, and then suddenly bland and innocent when their eyes met. Instinctively, Merissa knew they would never be friends. Vanessa wanted Alex.

Merissa was now at a small secluded beach which was a part of Joseph's property. Scraggy mangrove trees trailed into the sea for quite a distance. Booby birds and pelicans were regular visitors to the natural, dark, eerie tangle.

Merissa never swam close to the mangroves. Although crocodiles had never been seen at this location, they were prevalent in the marshlands and many rivers in the south central parishes. The cottage was found near Treasure Beach, on a small slope of fruit-filled land and just steps from the beach.

The cottage was one of her favourite places in the world. Painted in a sassy shade of pink, with its white louvered windows and shutters and low shingled roofs, Merissa felt at peace there. White latticed work trimmed the edges of everything and cascades of clinging vines surrounded the front door. Small white flowers, delicate against the walls, added to the picture of fairytale quaintness.

Trees of lime, orange and grapefruit were staggering under the weight of their bearing fruit. Everything was in full bloom. The tangy sweetness of a nearby pineapple grove mixed the air with an exquisite blend of flora and citrus.

They had been married up at the house in a beautiful garden ceremony this morning. She turned to look at the cottage and saw her husband holding a silver tray and an ice bucket. He was slowly picking his way down the rough pathway which led to the beach.

Merissa took a moment to admire him. He was very nearly naked she noticed, feeling heat spread throughout her body. He was wearing white swimming trunks that had 'Groom' written in silver script on his left hip. Merissa had the matching bikini. Alex was wearing his proudly, all lean muscle, flat rippling stomach, narrow hips and powerful thighs. He looked good and he was hers. The thought made her nervous. Tonight they were supposed to make love.

"Happy Mrs. York?" Alex asked.

"Mmm. Very."

She smiled and lifted her mouth to receive his kiss then shifted over to give him space beside her, settling against his naked chest.

"It was a perfect day wasn't it," he said, stroking her bare arms with his thumbs.

"Absolutely. We couldn't ask for a better day. Especially seeing you standing there waiting for me. You had this small nervous smile on your face."

"I wasn't nervous!"

"Yes you were!" she teased.

"Ok, maybe a little," he conceded graciously. "I'd been so anxious waiting for this day I couldn't believe it had finally arrived." He sighed. "And there you were walking down to me in *that* dress." He chuckled in awe and hugged her tight. "Can I tell you a secret?" he whispered.

"Mmm."

"I'd been hoping you'd wear that dress. Ever since I first saw you in it, all those months ago," he confessed. "And today coming to me, it blew my mind! Talk about dreams coming true."

"You liked it, huh?"

"Woman. I loved it." He kissed her hard on the shoulder.

They were quiet then.

"Alex?" Merissa asked after a time when the evening stars began to peep out.

"Yes my love?"

"Can I be honest with you?" she asked, licking her dry nervous lips. She was glad that he couldn't see the embarrassed flush on her face. She'd been wondering how she could broach this subject with him ever since the engagement. Taking a deep breath, she plunged ahead. "I'm ne…nervous about to…tonight," she revealed anxiously.

"Tonight?"

"Tonight in b…bed I…I mean," she stuttered.

She could feel him chuckling.

"It's not funny," she said sternly, annoyed at his response.

"I know sweetheart. Sorry," he apologised, easing her up and shifting her around so she was facing him. "I'm nervous too. But Merissa, I'll make love to you only when you feel the time is right. I promise I will never hurt you," he assured. "Whether it's tonight or two years from now."

"Do you mean that?" she gasped. He nodded and kissed her upturned nose.

"Yes I do. I won't rush you."

"How about you just hold me tonight?" she asked, clearly relieved.

He smiled. "Consider it done." He kissed her gently, cupping her face in his hands.

"Really?"

"Really. Now lie down again," he commanded. "I'm getting cold."

For the next two days they leisurely explored the area, swam and fished. Not that they caught anything. They were too busy with each other. The only thing Alex hadn't done was enter her body with his. He'd kissed her in places she never thought to be kissed. Touched her in places she never knew could respond that way. He was using his skill and patience to drive her mindless.

She was no longer afraid of his body. In fact, she had taken great delight in touching him and seeing the way his body responded in rapid jerking movements against her hands. She delighted in seeing the look of sheer ecstasy as she kissed his throat and scraped her nails over his nipples and daring to kiss him along his hard rigid strength, drinking his love.

They decided to explore the island for the rest of their honeymoon and so they left the cottage early on the fourth day and drove westward along the A2. The scenic contrasts were startling. Lush forest green mountains gave way to parched Savanna hillsides and cactus plants. At times Merissa was able to catch a swift glimpse of shimmering sea as they drove along narrow winding roads.

They ate a heavy breakfast in Santa Cruz; fried breadfruit and lapped herring, drank fish tea and enjoyed tall glasses of guava juice. Happy, full and content, they drove through the century old, two-mile long, shaded tunnel of Holland Bamboo, delighting in the tall frilly bamboos standing guard over the road.

Alex surprised Merissa by continuing to drive on, passing their turnoff and continuing until he reached Middle Quarters, a tiny village known for its peppered shrimp.

As Alex pulled over onto the side of the road, they were immediately descended on, by what Merissa thought to be, all of the town's women folk. They were pushing brightly coloured plastic bowls through the car windows demanding they buy their shrimp from them. Ironically they all cost the same price, Merissa noted in amusement.

A little further down the road, they could see two bus drivers arguing loudly. Large women in aprons and straw hats were picking up their baskets and reloading the buses as they periodically joined in the fight. Merissa was watching in relaxed curiosity when, suddenly, a sliver of apprehension skated down her spine. The hairs at the back of her neck stood on end, her breathing laboured. She shivered. She felt as though someone was watching her and wanted to leave.

Alex bought several bags of shrimp, a bottle of Red Stripe beer and a large bottle of Blue Mountain spring water before turning the car around and up the winding track to a cane farm.

Merissa was relieved to get away from the spooky shrimp village.

Chapter Twenty-Five

Jonas found himself on a cramped country bus out of Paradise Pass and into the excitement of the real world. He'd only been to Kingston once before years ago. At the moment the bus was stuck in a chaotic traffic jam in Savanna-la-Mar, so he stood up and pushed his head out of the window trying to breathe in some clean air. The woman beside him stank of sweat and was snoring loudly with her mouth open. A continuous trickle of saliva dripped down her chin and onto her huge bosom. Nasty, he thought as he spat a thick wad of mucous out of the window. Twenty minutes later they were underway.

The bus was packed with country people on their way to sell their produce in the big towns along the way – Black River, Santa Cruz, Mandeville, May Pen, Spanish Town and finally Kingston. Sticks of sugar cane poked into his back. Produce laden wicker baskets scraped his arms and legs.

The driver, a young man who didn't look a day older than twelve, drove as though his house was on fire. They swerved precariously as they turned corners and skidded around tight bends, all the while the loud horn bellowing. Jonas wished he had spent the few extra dollars to travel in a minibus instead of this loud death trap.

As they approached the shrimp capital of Middle Quarters, the bus narrowly missed another country bus coming in the opposite direction. Both buses swerved violently, sending baskets tumbling.

As the buses reloaded, Jonas bought a coconut water and ate shrimp, whilst watching cars full of tourists and locals pass by. Maybe he could bum a ride into Kingston, he thought. Sitting on dusty steps in front of a shop, he watched a rich looking man buy goods from a vendor directly across from him. He looked at the nice executive looking car and the woman inside it, though he could only see her hair and the yellow flowery dress she wore. Maybe he could ask them for a lift, he thought.

Just as he was about to get up and ask, a market woman rushed pass him, knocking him over. By the time he got up the young couple had gone.

At the cane farm they were greeted by a young smiling toothless guide by the name of 'no teet' who believed himself to be the next Shabba Ranks. Everything he said was in a deep rhyming, controlled, DJ voice.

They transferred to a mud splattered tractor, pulling a wooden carriage, shaded by a blue and white striped canopy. They drove along a bumpy, muddy, winding track pass cane fields, cows and horses, through a small stream, around massive guango trees until they finally came to the open splendour of YS Falls.

Arranging a time to be picked up, 'no teet' left them with a cheery grin. Finally they were left alone to enjoy themselves.

"We've got the place to ourselves Mrs. York," Alex pointed out unnecessarily.

"We sure do," Merissa responded while removing her sandals.

Alex lay down beside her sipping his beer. "Mmm, this is good." He looked at the brown bottle with satisfaction. "Want some?" he offered.

She shook her head. "Thanks, but beer is much too bitter for me. Where's my water?"

He reached into a black plastic bag and gave her the bottle, watching the smooth column of her throat as she drank thirstily.

"I've never been here before," she said when she'd finished. "It's so beautifully kept. I'm glad we came."

"So am I. Come here Mrs. York," he ordered softly in a voice Merissa was beginning to know.

She bent over him, knowing he was expecting a kiss and she obliged.

"I love you," he whispered against her lips.

"I love you too. Let's take a swim."

They got up and Merissa pulled her yellow floral dress over her head to reveal a skimpy violet bikini.

Shyly, she waited for Alex to remove his shorts revealing his 'groom' trunks underneath.

"No thong today Mr. York?" she asked tongue in cheek.

He'd modelled one for her the night before – bought for him by Toby as a laugh. "I'll only wear it for you my darling. You don't want me to show off my fabulous physique to just any and anyone do you?" he teased.

"Definitely not. Race you to the water!"

The water was refreshingly cool and they frolicked around in it for hours. Each of the three tiered waterfalls hid a limestone cave, and all had nicely sized pools to swim in. Forests of ferns and mosses banked either side of the river. Tall trees shaded the pools and brightly coloured Red Gingers danced in the cascading mists of the sparkling water.

They were completely enclosed.

Merissa crooked her finger and called her husband over. She lay on her back as he bent over her and stroked his cool skin with her finger tips, tasting the freshness of the water as she trailed her tongue along the curve of his shoulders, nipping at his neck.

Her breasts grew heavy and she delighted in the feel of his chest brushing her nipples. His tongue plunged into the depths of her mouth. She whimpered and pulled him down, holding him tighter. The mossy grass was a perfect cushion against her back.

"Touch me," Merissa urged roughly.

She felt his hot tongue swirl in the curves of her ear, before moving down to her throat where it stopped to play in the delicate nook at the base of her neck, suckling softly on her skin, before moving unhurriedly to the valley between her breasts.

"You like that?" Alex asked hoarsely, as his hands skimmed her smooth thighs and he bit down gently on the inviting curve of her breasts.

"You know I do," she breathed hotly, gripping his shoulders as she tried to control the waves of desire shooting through her body with every stab of his tongue.

"You'll like this even more," he promised, as holding her eyes with his, he skimmed her bikini top aside and lightly trailed his fingers across one deliciously welcoming nipple.

She gasped and dug her nails deeper into his shoulders.

He paid tribute to its twin, licking and sucking the hard nub deep into his hot mouth, until it stood proud, tall and dark against the paleness of her skin.

Her back arched against his mouth as he moved on and she withered in pleasurable pain when his tongue dipped into the small dent of her belly button swirling around before travelling on. Her bikini bottoms were swept off speedily and he kept her tremulous body still by pressing her hips down firmly into the soft dewy grass, as his tongue explored her feminine folds, knowing what she liked.

She had nowhere to go. She wasn't sure she wanted to go anywhere. Tiny sounds escaped from her kiss-swollen lips. She bit down on them hard but something was missing. She felt empty, strangely hollow. She wanted him inside her, filling the cavity that had been untouched by love.

"It's time Alex," she whispered urgently and he looked up, his brown eyes dark with desire.

"Are you sure?" he asked moving up to her and kissing her mouth. She could taste the musky scent of herself on his lips.

"Yes I'm sure."

Gently he kissed her again as he removed his shorts, careful not to press his arousal against her. He didn't want to frighten her.

Going to her breasts, he bit each pert tip tenderly, then more urgently. Suckling hungrily, he could feel her body tremble against him. Her soft cries urging him on, driving him wild. He didn't want to rush things and frighten her and tried to slow down but she wouldn't let him. She held onto him tightly and opened her legs. It was the most natural thing to do. The throbbing in her secret place became unbearable, she needed, no demanded, he do something about her terrible ache. Now!

In one move Alex was over her.

"Look at me Merissa," he whispered and waited until she opened her eyes and focused on him. "I love you," he whispered and entered her slowly. Alex died and went to heaven.

"Am I hurting you?" he asked as he tried to control the natural urge to sink into her body and pound her into the soft grass.

She shook her head. She had a look of wondrous tenderness on her face and she lifted her hips to tentatively meet his.

"I love you Alex. I love you," she breathed as he began to move.

"Look at me," he whispered again when she closed her eyes. "Stay with me."

Her body began to tremble; she was losing control fast, spiralling upwards. Every nerve ending, every pressure point, every cell, moved in time to his thrusting and Alex, not able to stand it any longer, gathered her close and rocked against her, helping her climb into the unknown abyss of erotic sensations. Willing her, demanding, that she let go.

With a scream she fell, tumbling, rolling, collapsing. So shattering was its intensity she bit his shoulder drawing blood and felt his immediate release with pure pleasure and womanly satisfaction.

He groaned deeply in his throat calling her name over and over again until his shudders stopped and he collapsed on top of her, his breathing hard and deep.

"You ok?" he asked.

Her face was flushed, her mouth swollen with his kisses, her eyes filled with love. She'd never looked more beautiful.

"To tell you the truth Mr. York I've never felt better." She giggled and stretched languorously.

He laughed and dragged her into the water, where he again, paid homage to her body.

Chapter Twenty-Six

The heat of the city hit Jonas' face head on as he stepped off the bus in Half-Way-Tree and stood looking anxiously around. The first thing he noticed was that Kingston hadn't changed; or rather Half-Way-Tree hadn't changed much. Granted, a pretty waterfall was over in one corner, a big screen in another and the whole bus terminal looked a lot less complicated. Men and women in brown uniforms patrolled the area.

Maybe I should have stayed on the bus and gone downtown, he thought, glancing over his shoulder only to see it pull out into the throng of traffic. He picked up the black plastic scandal bag which held his few possessions and crossed the busy street walking towards Hagley Park Road. That was one street where he would definitely be able to find work. The road is so bloodclaat long, he thought, quickening his pace and narrowly missing an open man hole along the way.

Jonas couldn't believe it. He'd got a job as a delivery man and security guard for a small flower shop, which had just fired a man for smoking weed in the back of the building. The job came with a room at the back, so he could live on the premises and an old motor bike to make deliveries. He had it made.

Jonas settled in. He tried to sleep but the loud dancehall music at the auto mechanic shop next door kept him awake. The scent of flowers insulted his nostrils. He didn't want to smell roses; he wanted to smell the salty air of the sea, the smell of raw fish, and the smell of his rum. Now that, he chuckled, he could fix.

Bending over the side of the bed, he rummaged through the contents of his bag and pulled out his rum bottle. Twisting the cap off, he breathed the potent fumes, smiling as he took a long satisfying swallow. He closed his eyes and snapped them open again in familiar panic.

That bloodclaat coolie gal! She appeared frequently, night or day, sometimes covered with blood, other times faceless and screaming. It was the screaming he couldn't take. Loud blood curdling sounds that vibrated into his ear drums making him cover his ears in pain.

He knew his brothers thought he was getting mad. So did the people at Jack's, but he couldn't help it. She would scream at him and he'd have to cover his ears and ask people to make her go away. She was turning him into a mad man, playing with his mind.

Tomorrow was a new day. Tomorrow he had to be up early to water and polish the plants. Imagine him, tending flowers! His brothers would laugh and call him a pretty bwoy! Jonas grinned as he imagined what they must be thinking, him perishing away in Kingston. What a joke!

Chapter Twenty-Seven

Merissa stepped off the ladder and looked up to evaluate her paint job. Neat, she thought, pleased with herself. The living room was almost complete. She just needed Alex to come home and touch up the edges and corners that she couldn't reach. Making sure to step on the newspapers which were scattered over the new marble tiles, she went outside to wash out the paint roller and pan. Amber came over yapping and spinning around with excitement.

She set her tools aside to dry and played with the little dog for a while and then sat on the grass. Amber was in her lap, her pink tongue hanging out.

What a day, Merissa thought tiredly. Between trying to make the house into a home and finishing her final semester at school, she was exhausted. She looked over the low hedge separating Alex's house from Toby's. Cymone and Toby are out again she mused thoughtfully. Things were working out well for them. She was so glad.

Merissa got up, dusted off her paint splattered shorts and headed inside, but as she reached the back door a sudden wave of icy apprehension skittered up her spine and spread throughout her body. Goose bumps popped up along her arms and she shivered whilst looking around apprehensively. Everything looked normal, yet the tiny hairs at the back of her neck stood on end.

She hurriedly picked up the dog and rushed inside quickly securing the door behind her.

She could hear the faint buzz of a motorcycle engine nearby and she peeped out of the front window. All she could see was the bulky, uniformed figure of a flower delivery man at Toby's gate.

She watched him cautiously. His hat was pulled low on his head, she couldn't see his face. He leaned over Toby's gate, placed a bouquet of pink roses on the driveway, and tooted his horn twice before riding off. Nothing strange in that, she thought, except that someone was supposed to sign for the flowers.

Beads of perspiration dotted her upper lip and Merissa wiped at it impatiently as she watched the man ride down the street. A fine flume of smoke trailed behind him.

She couldn't understand why she'd had the sudden panic attack. It had never happened before. Immediately she thought of Alex and called his office. He had already left! What if something has happened to Alex?

She was just about to go and look for him when he pulled up in the driveway. Merissa flew outside.

"Oh Alex, I thought something had happened to you!" she cried as soon as he'd opened the car door and stepped out into the sunshine. She held on to him tightly.

"Hey, what's all this?" he asked confused as he leaned back to look into her stricken face. "What's wrong honey?" She was shaking like a leaf as he led her into the house.

"Why didn't you phone and tell me that you were leaving work?" Merissa demanded, unreasonably.

"Phone?" he asked bewildered as they walked into the newly refurbished kitchen. The smell of wood, paint and varnish hung heavily in the air.

"Yes call," she repeated crossly. "I thought something might have happened to you." She sat at the glass table and buried her face in her hands.

"Honey, what's wrong?" She was acting very strange.

"I'm sorry," she said eventually. "It's just that I thought…" She shrugged, laughing at her own stupidity. "Come here," she ordered, gently holding out her arms to him.

He pulled her up, sat in her chair and tugged her onto his lap. He noticed how pale her face was and she had faint blue shadows under her eyes. She looked exhausted.

"Why don't we take a few days off from all of this painting and relax for a bit?" he suggested gently.

"We only have the TV room left to do," she pointed out, "and that won't take two hours to finish."

"We can finish that on the weekend. I think you've been working too hard."

"I've been working at my usual pace," she stated stubbornly, "but I do feel a little under the weather," she admitted ruefully. "Maybe I'm coming down with the flu or something."

Alex only had to hear her admission to take charge. He ordered her to bed and then made some chicken soup.

"I'm fine," Merissa insisted.

She lay down sinking into the downy pillows and tried to relax but she couldn't shake the uneasy feeling that something was about to happen, something dreadful. She couldn't explain it, but she knew. She rang Joseph to check if he and Thomas were ok and was just putting the phone down as Alex entered the room.

"Who were you just talking to?" Alex asked casually.

"Joseph," she replied. "Thomas has just called him. He's in Moscow now." She knitted her brow.

Alex was so protective and sometimes it really worried her. Then again a little protectiveness was nice. Wasn't it?

Alex changed into a comfortable pair of shorts and lay beside her.

"I think you should go and see a doctor," he suggested. "You really don't look so great." He traced a finger along her brow.

"I'll go soon," she replied, not sounding very committed. "How come you left work so early?"

"I wanted to come home."

He looked around their bedroom, liking the decor of pistachio green and cobalt blue and silver. It had been years since he'd even called this place home. He shifted and hugged her into the nook of his shoulder. "To tell you the truth I missed you and had to see you." He tweaked her nose and kissed her forehead.

"Mr. York, you can't keep leaving work like this. It gives a bad impression," she admonished playfully, fighting a yawn.

"I'm newly married and have a very demanding wife to satisfy," he teased, nuzzling the valley between her breasts. "Are you up to being satisfied?" he asked, already moving a finger over her flat stomach, stopping to play in her belly button before casually exploring the soft curls between her legs.

"You bet," she whispered.

༄༄༄

The following morning, dragging a reluctant Merissa out of the house, Alex sat waiting impatiently in the sterile looking waiting room at the medical centre Merissa always used. He had grown tired of watching the fish swim aimlessly up and down the huge aquarium opposite his chair. He was now flipping nervously through a decade old magazine.

She'd been inside the office for over half an hour and he thought again that something must be terribly wrong. Even this morning she had looked tired and pale. Deep circles were under her eyes. He was worried, no he corrected, he was worried sick!

Minutes later, his wife emerged. She gave him a small nervous smile before being taken into a lab. Why the hell did they need her in the lab? If anything happens to her...

A short time later, his wife walked up to him with a small pale pink plaster on the inside of her elbow. She gave him a quick reassuring kiss on the cheek before disappearing again.

"Alex," she called out moments later.

"Alex?" she said again, when he didn't hear the first time.

"Yes." He cleared his nerve-clogged throat and tried to smile.

"The doctor wants to see you."

What did the doctor want to see him for, he wondered. Something's wrong with his Merissa, if she was dying...

"Good morning Mr. York. Please have a seat," the young doctor told him cheerfully. Alex sat and looked worriedly at Merissa who was looking nervously down at her hands. Alex took one of them.

"I'm Dr. White," he introduced, "I've been your wife's doctor for years and years."

Alex only stared, his body tense.

The doctor cleared his throat.

Alex sat silently, stunned with what the doctor told him next.

Baby. Daddy. Two words he'd never used in his vocabulary were now going to be a part of his life. It was all so unbelievable.

The doctor gave him a list of written instructions, to ensure Merissa followed her own list down to the last dot on the paper. Then on a more serious note he told Alex that her blood pressure was abnormally high. She and the baby may be at great risk with that and the blood test had detected anaemia. She needed strict medical supervision.

Alex wanted to question him some more about the risks, but Merissa stood up abruptly, saying it was time to go. Alex was puzzled for a moment. Something was going on here and he looked back at the doctor for confirmation. The doctor wouldn't meet his eye. Merissa didn't want him to know about something. He looked at her suspiciously.

Out in the parking lot, Merissa peeped at her husband. He was awfully quiet and she was wondering how he was taking the news. She was still in shock. They'd never discussed having a family, especially one so soon. Yet they hadn't been using any precautions against it either.

Alex didn't drive them home but went to Devon House instead; a 18th century Georgian Mansion located at the intersection of Hope road and Waterloo Road. It was a tourist attraction with its lush grounds, hops, restaurants and famous ice cream.

"Are you tired?" Alex asked, as he went around helping her out of the car and holding her hand tenderly, as he walked over to a grassy verge concealed by flowers.

She smiled, "No, I'm fine."

"Are you sure?" he asked anxiously.

"Sweetheart, I'm fine, honest," she pressed. "Now are you going to get me some ice cream or not?" she asked, trying to lighten the mood.

"Not. You're having a callaloo loaf." He looked at her, ready to knock any objections she might have down flat.

She wrinkled her nose but made no comment.

He went over a quaint bridge spanning a small pond chocked with lily pads and disappeared inside one of the many restaurants.

Merissa sat on the grass and looked around, her hands unconsciously straying to her stomach. I'm pregnant, she thought, looking down at her stomach. She didn't feel pregnant; then again she didn't know how she was supposed to feel. Smiling, she rubbed her hand over her flat tummy. In a couple of months she'd be huge and walking like a duck. She laughed.

Alex came back with her callaloo loaf and what looked like a chicken patty for himself. He gave her hers and sat beside her.

"You really did buy this thing! I hate callaloo loafs!"

"You heard what the doctor said, you need iron," he said with a finality that ended her objections.

Merissa gave up, knowing she couldn't argue the point. It was for the baby's sake after all. She took a small bite.

"Good girl. I'm going to be a daddy." He said the word 'daddy' as though he couldn't quite believe it.

"How do you feel about it?" she asked him anxiously.

"I don't know…I've never even thought of being a father before," he admitted honestly. "I like kids, don't get me wrong. It's just that I don't know what to do with them." He shrugged.

"I don't know what to do either," she admitted softly.

They were both silent for a while, eating, lost in their own thoughts.

"How do you feel about it?" Alex's cherry brown eyes bore into her darker ones.

"I'm not sure. I'm just getting used to the idea of motherhood but what can we do? You do want it, don't you?" she asked suddenly.

She was terrified of what his answer might be, and more so when he seemed to take a long time to answer. He didn't want it! The thought brought a huge wave of gushing disappointment. Even though it wasn't planned and it was a high risk pregnancy, she wanted her baby!

"I don't want anything to happen to you," he admitted cautiously, still aware she wasn't telling him the whole story.

"That isn't what I asked," she pointed out, her voice ten degrees cooler.

"I want what you want. I want you to be ok. I *don't* want anything to happen to you and if that means terminating the pregnancy until later, so be it!" he growled.

Merissa couldn't believe her ears.

"You don't want to have this baby!" she whispered harshly. "You want me to have an abortion?" She couldn't believe her ears.

She stood up with tears in her eyes. He was immediately beside her, trying to console her but she wouldn't let him near her.

"Don't touch me! Just don't touch me!" Merissa backed away from him, her eyes round with despair.

"Merissa!" Alex held her roughly by the shoulders. "Honey, it's not that I don't want it. I just don't want to lose you. Can't you understand that?" He looked at her, his pain reflecting hers.

"No, I don't understand it but what I do understand is that we made this child, you and me. It was irresponsible of us not to consider that we may be creating another life in the process but we have. You and I made love, shared our love and this is the result." She touched her stomach possessively. "It's with *my* love that I'll keep this child, whether you want to or not!" Her chin went up and she looked at him hurt and angry.

"Merissa? Hear me out," he begged.

"No. You've already made yourself clear." She stalked off towards the car.

Alex stood watching her for a moment, fighting with himself to go over and make her listen, or to wait until later when the two of them had had time to think things through.

He decided to wait.

For the rest of the day Merissa stayed in her sewing room and sketched designs, trying not to think about what Alex had said. He had gone straight out as soon as she had gotten out of the car and let herself into the house. He hadn't spared her a glance. She couldn't believe this, refused to believe it.

Throwing down her pencils, she took a quick nap on the couch. An hour later he still wasn't back so she made herself a sandwich and went out. She needed some fresh air and a drive out alone would do her good.

Alex came home to find the house in complete darkness. His eyebrows drew to an angry line. Toby had once told him that she always drove around when she was upset.

He called Joseph but there was no answer. Swearing loudly, he locked up and went up the hill. Minutes later he pulled up in front of the house. Her car wasn't outside and Joseph wasn't in. Where the hell was she? Running his hands through his hair and down his neck in angry frustration, he drove speedily down the hill and went home. She wasn't there and he didn't have the first clue where to look for her. Toby and Cymone weren't home either.

He waited for her sitting in the darkness of the living room trying not to think about all the things that could happen to her. Oh God! It was his fault! Why couldn't he have been more sensitive to her needs? She had needed him today. And what did he give her? Nothing! Nothing but rejection!

He looked at the clock. It was almost midnight. Where the hell was she?

Amber's barking outside drew his attention and he let her in and fed her whilst he waited. He thought about what he would do to Merissa when she came back. He had never struck a woman before but right now the urge was great, very, very great.

Merissa listened to the waves crashing against the pebbly black sand. Her eyes felt swollen and gritty. She was exhausted. She'd driven out to Buff Bay and parked her car at the bottom of one of the many streets that led directly to the beach. She stretched out her aching limbs and walked quickly to her car thankful that the moon was out.

She was tired, hungry and wanted to go home, not to Alex, but home up the hill. She knew she couldn't do that. She had to go back to her own house and see if Alex had come to terms with the pregnancy. She would have this baby; she didn't care if it killed her in the end. She would have this baby. She wanted it and she loved it and she would try with all her might to keep it healthy, even if it meant her own life. Why didn't Alex understand that? She wanted to give him a child.

Alex woke with a jerk and he gazed around the room, wondering what he was doing downstairs, then he remembered. Looking at the clock, he heard her keys in the door. Scolding red-hot rage gushed heatedly through his veins. In the darkness he went to her. She made a small sound of fright as she turned on the light and saw Alex standing behind the door, his eyes blazing with fiery rage.

They looked at each other, long and hard, both not daring to speak; neither one trusting themselves.

Merissa made to move pass him but he grabbed her arm, stopping her. She looked tired and ill, the circles under her eyes looking darker and deeper than this morning. Her eyes were red and puffy and Alex felt his anger drain away. He pulled her into his arms and held her tight, thanking God she was home safe, even if it was after four in the morning.

"Are you alright?" he asked, gently stroking her hair.

She nodded and hugged him, fresh waves of tears trickling down her cheeks. They stayed holding each other in the hallway for long silent minutes. Then Merissa pulled away and stared up at him. He couldn't look her in the eye.

"You haven't changed the way you feel," she stated quietly and not waiting for an answer, went up the stairs.

"Merissa..." he appealed, moving to the foot of the stairs, his foot on the bottom rung.

She stopped half way up and turned around, her lovely face a frozen mask.

"You can sleep in the spare bedroom," she said coldly. "If I do, it might make me and *my* baby sick." She stressed each word pointedly.

Alex couldn't believe his ears, he must sleep in the...not on your life! He rushed up the stairs too late. Merissa had locked the door.

Chapter Twenty-Eight

The next morning Merissa struggled to get out of bed. When she finally made her way downstairs, feeling quite ill, Alex had already made breakfast and was sitting waiting for her at the table. She looks dreadful he thought to himself, knowing better than to let her know that.

"Morning," he said. She just looked at him and for a dark moment he thought she wasn't going to answer.

"Morning," she replied tightly, sitting at the table and reaching for the orange juice at the same time.

Alex watched in dismay as she tried to pour orange juice into a glass but her hands were shaking so much, juice was sloshing everywhere but in the glass.

"Here, let me help you with that," he said standing up and going around to her side of the table to help.

"I can manage," she snapped, jerking the carton away from his hand only to end up dropping it onto the floor.

He sighed with annoyance and got some paper towels.

"What time is your class today?"

She looked at him suspiciously. "Eleven until four."

"It's a long day. I'll take you."

"I'll be fine."

"I said I'll take you!" he yelled, glaring at her, his brown eyes daring her to argue.

"Fine. You can do whatever you want." She paled, clapped her hands over her mouth and rushed into the bathroom, throwing up uncontrollably again.

Alex was beside her holding her hair out of her face. She didn't even have enough strength to hold herself up. He was scared. Damn scared! She was not having this baby.

When she finished, he wiped her face with a damp cloth, picked her up and carried her upstairs. She looked so pale. So fragile. He set her down in the bed and covered her up.

"I need to get ready to go to class," she mumbled hoarsely.

"Lie down. Take a nap and I'll wake you when it's almost time to go." He left the room when she closed her eyes.

Downstairs, Alex dialled Dr. White's number.

"Morning, Mr. York, what can I do for you?" the doctor said cheerfully when the call was passed through to his office.

"What weren't you telling me yesterday?" Alex asked abruptly.

The doctor cleared his throat, "Mr. York, I have an obligation to my patient. I cannot divulge that kind of information without her consent."

"You told her the baby might kill her didn't you?"

Silence.

"Mr. York..."

"Didn't you?"

"I made certain recommendations yes...for medical reasons."

"What reasons?" demanded Alex promptly.

"I'm sorry Alex; I can't say but come into my office on her next visit. I can only tell you she needs rest, lots and lots of rest. I…we are going to give this pregnancy a chance."

Alex let out a breath he didn't realise he was holding.

"I do not want to lose my wife," he said through gritted teeth as he gripped the phone tightly.

"I understand Alex, but Merissa has made a decision." He sighed. "As a doctor I have to support my patient, no matter the decision rightly or wrongly made."

"She's not keeping it," Alex whispered more to himself, then without hesitation added. "Thank you for your time doctor."

Alex hung up and moved to the window, staring at nothing, his eyebrows drawn into a deep angry frown. She is not having this baby! Later after her classes they would talk. I won't lose my temper. I'll be calm and talk reasonably, he told himself. He didn't want anything to happen to his wife. She was more important to him than having children.

Later that day, Alex tucked Merissa into bed after picking her up from her classes. She looked deathly pale and barely ate the soup and crackers he'd made for her.

"I'm sorry. I can't eat anymore." She put the tray beside her on the bed.

"Honey, we need you to eat some more. We have to get your strength back up…for the baby's sake," he added reluctantly.

She looked at him with eyes clouding with simmering rage. "Don't you dare talk to me about what the baby needs! How do you know what it needs? If it was up to you, you'd have carted me off to the abortion clinic yesterday!" The tray dropped to the floor as she moved her legs in agitation. Neither of them looked at it.

I won't shout, I won't get mad, Alex reminded himself. He counted to ten and breathed in deeply.

"I don't know what's going on, the doctor wouldn't tell me…"

"You spoke with Doctor White?" Merissa asked instantly.

"He didn't tell me anything. Wouldn't tell me anything." Alex raked an unsteady hand through his hair. "But I do know you're going against his wishes!"

"You had no right to talk to him!" she attacked.

"Merissa," he started again carefully. "Your life is at risk. We can have children some other time," he added reasonably. "But this one is putting you in danger and I won't lose you. I love you too much to have anything happen to you." His eyes became glassy with tears.

As he spoke, he'd come over to the bed and was kneeling down beside her, holding her hands.

"Don't do this, please," he begged gravely.

"I have to," she whispered, her own eyes misting.

"Why?"

"Because I need to have this baby," she whispered. "I want to give you a child more than anything in this world."

"Even if it costs you your life?"

She sighed before looking at him pleadingly.

"Yes."

He shook himself. He couldn't believe what he was hearing.

"No! I won't let you!"

He moved violently away from her. His face twisted with pain.

"I don't want you to have it," he stated adamantly, when he got control of himself again.

"I've already made up my mind," she told him tenaciously, her chin rising in stubborn defiance.

"That's it, is it? It's only your decision to make?" He swore violently and she grimaced. "I'm your husband damn it! I do have a say in what goes on around here and I forbid it!" he roared.

"I'm having this baby, with or without your help."

Alex felt a deadly chill sear through him. "So that's it?" he whispered gruffly.

She looked away as she couldn't bear to see the hurt and pain in his eyes. She refused to be swayed.

"You've made your choice," he went on filling the tense silence. "If you have that child, Merissa, you will be alone. I won't be around to watch you die! Make your choice Merissa, now," he challenged. "Me or the baby."

Several minutes ticked by, the clock the only sound in the room.

Tears ran down her cheeks, stopping at her trembling chin before dripping onto the cotton sheet.

"Don't do this Alex," she pleaded.

"*You* don't do this to us! Merissa please," he beseeched. He was beside her again, burying his head into her soft neck. She held onto him for dear life knowing, deep down, this would probably be the last time she would ever hold him again.

"I…" She broke down and he moved away so he could hold her face, wiping her tears with his thumbs.

"Me or the baby Merissa," he whispered again.

"Alex," she looked at him, afraid for the first time. "I love you, but I…I have to have this baby," she finished quietly.

Her answer knocked the very breath out of him. He couldn't believe it. His whole life was lying in that bed and she'd just told him that she would rather have this child – which would probably kill her – than be with him!

He was crushed. Enormous waves of despair engulfed him, suffocating, killing him. He had to get away from her! He couldn't stand the sight of her. Without looking back, he left the room, hearing her sobs as he closed the door.

For the rest of the week Alex took her to her classes and looked after her without saying a word about the baby. Merissa felt guilty but knew she was making the right decision and tried to act as though the conversation a few days ago had never taken place.

At her next doctor's appointment Alex was adamant that he would be involved and though Merissa was furious, he still went in to see Dr. White with her.

Dr. White went through the usual routine, taking Merissa's blood pressure again and shaking his head when he consulted her file.

"It's gone up," he told them both with a frown, checking her pulse.

"Complete bed rest for the next few weeks. I don't want you to lift a finger. You're in danger of losing the foetus. I'll have to put you on a low-salt diet which you must stick to. *Must* Merissa," he stressed. "And come in for blood pressure and weight checks every other day."

"You're in great danger," he told her, his eyes begging her to reconsider. "The foetus may die if we can't control your pressure and more seriously you may start having seizures or even a stroke." The doctor held nothing back.

Alex made an animal-like sound and looked at her with pleading eyes.

"I'll take my chances," she said to the two men. Her back stiff, her chin high.

Alex's shoulders sagged and the doctor shook his head in bewilderment.

"I strongly recommend that you terminate the pregnancy Merissa. We don't know what's going on in your body…"

"I'll take my chances," she said again, more determined. If anything her back went even straighter.

The doctor sighed in defeat.

"Ok. Go to the lab," he ordered.

❦❦❦

Alex was infuriated. Merissa, he thought, how he loved that woman. He loved her so much and now she was destroying herself. It was so ironic that she wanted to have this baby for him, yet she was willing to lose everything they had ever shared because of it. Every day she looked weaker and weaker, even though she tried to hide it from him.

He couldn't understand it. How she could risk her life over an unborn child, when they could have other children? Why didn't she even consider the doctor's recommendation? It wasn't for religious reasons. He just couldn't understand it.

Things had changed. He didn't even want to see her anymore. Couldn't bear to see her looking the way she did. It was sickening that she chose the baby over him; willing to die for it than spend the rest of her life with him like she had vowed, just three short months ago.

He slept permanently in the spare bedroom now. He didn't want to make love to her. He couldn't stand the thought of seeing her listless body. Why he'd never protected himself he didn't even try to guess. He blamed himself for the trillionth time. She wouldn't be pregnant now and everything would be just the way it was if only he had protected them both from this!

"Oh Jesus!" He thumped his desk causing the computer to wobble and he was just about to get up when the door opened suddenly.

"My, don't you look happy today?" Vanessa Powers said, striding into his office, her long false braids swinging wildly.

"I'm not in the mood Vanny," Alex told her darkly. He just wanted to be left alone.

"Poor darling. Problems already?"

She smiled sweetly at him before moving around to slide onto his lap. She planted a kiss on his stiff lips, leaning forward so that her jacket would gape, giving him a glimpse of her bare unfettered breasts.

He wasn't looking.

How she had ever let this man get away she didn't know. But, if he was having marital problems maybe…

"Vanessa, get up," he ground out, lifting her off his leg and standing up himself. "What do you want?"

He looked at her hard, trying not to breathe in her sweet, overpowering perfume.

"I came to take you to lunch," she told him, moving next to him and trying to take his hand.

"I don't want lunch," he told her, removing her hand from where it was sliding up and down his silk tie.

"I insist. You look as though you haven't had a good meal in days."

She moved around him and picked up his jacket. "Come on," she encouraged, tugging on his shirt sleeve.

Alex looked at her knowing full well that when she was set in one direction, she wouldn't move in another. Oh what the hell, he thought, he needed to think about something else.

"I'll be back later Mary," he told his secretary.

Mary nodded, hating what was happening. She didn't like Miss Powers at all, she could see right through the woman. She was a bitch.

Vanessa took him to an expensive restaurant close by. It was always full of old company founders and members of their families. Alex never ate here, he felt too uncomfortable.

Vanessa smiled at various old men as she passed, relishing the attention, in her navy blue Chanel suit. She didn't care that it was too tight and too short for the office – even if she was almost partner in a law firm. They were looking on in distaste rather than admiration. The majority of the men told their 'been there, done that' jokes as she passed.

"I hate this place," Alex told her when they were seated in the centre of the room – Vanessa's choice – oblivious to the disapproving stares.

"Sweety, don't be a prude. This is where people who want to reach places eat," she pointed out, whilst reading her menu and ordering a simple chef salad.

Salad – Alex thought with disgust. His wife would have ordered the steak with all the trimmings, he mused sadly. He missed her company more than ever.

"So what's on your mind? Merissa giving you problems already?" Vanessa asked, a small smug smile on her face. Alex failed to notice.

"She's pregnant," Alex told her simply, only Toby and Cymone knew about it. Not even Thomas who was still in Moscow.

"Oh my, so soon!" Vanessa exclaimed dropping the cigarette that was in hand.

Alex gazed at her.

"You don't look like a happy father to be," she pointed out. "What's wrong darling, don't you want to have children?"

Alex stared at her as though he didn't understand her language. Then leaned forward, placed both hands on the table, breathed in deeply and told her everything. When he'd finished, Vanessa knew that if there was any time to get him back, this was it.

"I'm so sorry," she told him sweetly, taking his big hands and rubbing her thumbs over them gently. "You've tried talking to her?" she suggested innocently.

"I've tried everything." He pulled his hands away abruptly and raked them through his hair, his eyes full of pain and misery.

"How could she do this? It's not as though you can't have other children. She is *young* enough," Vanessa spat, hating the other girl's youth. *She* was almost thirty-five and she hated it!

"I know."

"What she's doing is selfish," she fumed. "If she loved you the way she says she does, she wouldn't hesitate to get rid of it," she pointed out maliciously, watching the flicker of emotions passing across his face. Alex was so easy to read. "It's obvious she doesn't care that she's hurting you." Vanessa let this sink in before continuing spitefully. "Maybe you should have waited before going off and marrying her Alex. The two of you never really got to know each other properly. I don't suppose you had even talked about having a family?"

"No we didn't," he admitted reluctantly.

"If she was a responsible woman, she would have taken precautions against it, at least until later down the road. Anyone else would have. Maybe all she really wanted was a child, and didn't want the stigma of being an unwed mother. It's looked down upon in her circle you know."

Alex looked up from his plate and stared at her, contemplating what she had just said.

No, Merissa wasn't like that. Was she?

Vanessa smiled as she saw the seed of doubt plant itself in his mind. Now all she had to do was be there for him. Be his friend and he would be hers. Just like when his parents had died. Only back then, she had been foolish enough to let him sleep with her too fast. Not this time. This time, she would plan carefully. Alex was her one chance to marry a wealthy young executive.

Merissa lay down on the sofa. Alex had just pulled open the door and was in the kitchen warming up the dinner she had left for him in the microwave. This had been a new routine for them. Only a few short weeks ago the two of them would make dinner together, eat, clear the table and make love in the kitchen. Now she was always alone. He came home well after nine o'clock and she was usually sleeping by then. She missed him terribly but if he didn't understand…

"Hi," Alex said standing in the doorway of the TV room holding his tray. He was surprised to see her up.

She smiled at him and moved her legs so that he could sit beside her. He looked deliciously sexy in his light grey suit, his deep yellow tie hanging loose about his neck. She felt her nipples tighten.

"Hi."

"How come you're still up?" he asked as he sat in the chair opposite.

He doesn't even want to touch me anymore, she thought sadly as she stretched her legs out again.

"I don't know. I was watching a film."

"Oh yeah, which one?" he asked politely.

Which one?

"I don't remember the name of it," she replied vaguely, "but it was good. How was your day?" she asked him, wanting desperately for him to hold her. She needed him.

"Long. I had lunch with Vanessa," he said casually.

Merissa instantly bristled. She had never liked that woman. She couldn't keep the coldness out of her voice when she said, "That was nice. Where did you go?"

She was angry, very angry.

Alex glanced at her with a frown, sensing her changing mood. "The Pelican Room."

"I thought you hated that place?" she said, her eyes flashing.

"I do. Only Vanny took me out to lunch," he shrugged, his eyes narrowing at her tone. "I couldn't very well tell her where I wanted to go, could I?"

Merissa saw orange then red. How dare he go out with that trollop when I'm here alone waiting for him to come home?

"Did you have a nice time?" she asked through gritted teeth, not wanting – but needing – to know every single detail about his lunch date.

"Not really. We talked about you," he said nonchalantly.

Merissa's anger blazed and she leapt off the chair and was in front of him in a second; her flaming red nightshirt enhancing the angry flush on her cheeks.

"Oh really? How dare you discuss me with that woman! She isn't even a friend of mine. What gives you the right to talk to her about our personal problems?"

Alex stopped chewing and stared at her wide eyed. "Vanessa is a friend of mine…"

"But she isn't mine! How could you?"

"I needed someone to talk to! You go to bed as soon as I come home. You don't want to discuss it! So what do you expect?" he yelled back angrily.

"I don't expect you to go running off to that woman! Of all people! And if you came home at a reasonable time I wouldn't be in bed!" she back shot.

She felt hot and flushed and before she could do anything about it, she fainted.

Alex sat beside her on the couch wiping her face with a cold cloth. He was a fool. Why did he let her get so mad at him? Her blood pressure must be sky high by now. He was just about to call Dr. White when her eyes fluttered open.

"You fainted," he told her.

"Sorry," she told him, trying to get up.

"Stay still for a bit." He pushed her down gently. "Have you been sick today?" he went on, holding her hands with his.

"Only a little bit. It seems to be passing," she lied. She was sick a whole lot and it seemed to be getting worse.

"That's good." He touched her hair, and then trailed his finger over her face as though touching her for the first time. "I'm sorry," he said.

"Sorry for what?" she asked breathlessly, hoping he would say the words she had been longing to hear ever since she'd decided to have the baby.

"For upsetting you," he told her, seeing the way she seemed to droop and realizing what she must have been thinking. "I still haven't changed my mind," he went on ruthlessly. "You're foolish, Merissa, very foolish."

She pushed his hands away and sat up, her eyes as dark as his. Then, without saying a word, she left the room to go to bed.

Chapter Twenty-Nine

The following weeks were extremely tense for Alex and Merissa. Alex stayed away as much as possible, leaving Aggie to take care of Merissa. He came home long after Merissa was asleep and left the house before she woke each morning.

Thomas was back, but didn't seem to sense anything wrong and to the outside world they seemed like the typical just married couple – almost.

Thank God I have Vanessa, Alex thought. He wouldn't be able to get through all of this if she hadn't been his rock once again. She had kept him preoccupied, distracting him from all of the problems at home. It was just like old times when he'd had the death of his family to deal with. Vanessa was a God send.

He hadn't seen Merissa in days and for a moment, felt a pang of guilt. What kind of husband was he? She needed him right now, but then again, she had pushed him away. She had made her choice. So what was he needed for? He thought dejectedly.

Glancing at the clock on the wall, he realised it was after two in the afternoon. He hadn't eaten lunch yet, so he stood up and stretched before picking up his keys. He wanted to go home.

The house was very quiet when he arrived. Usually Aggie kept the veranda door open during the day, whilst keeping the grill locked, but the door was locked. He found it odd. He went into the house and listened intently for any sound, maybe Merissa was sleeping and Aggie had gone shopping. Then a sound in the back garden caught his attention.

Merissa was laughing. He'd forgotten how that sound used to send tiny thrills up and down his spine, like it did now. His body tightened in response. He listened for awhile, relishing the sound, before going outside. Merissa was lying on the grass wearing white skimpy shorts and a blue bra top. Her hair was loose and bouncing all around her in a curly mass. She was playing with Amber.

Alex felt all the tension of the past few days melt away, like an ice cube left out on the pavement. Walking over to them quietly, he slung his jacket over his shoulder and waited for her to notice him.

She didn't.

He moved closer until he cast a shadow over her. She scrambled to her feet, ready to run, before realising it was him.

"Hi, I didn't mean to frighten you," he told her, taking in her shapely legs and softly rounded stomach, and how her shorts were unfastened, all in one scorching glance.

"Hi. What are you doing here?" she asked, breathlessly aware of his stare.

"I came for lunch. Where's Aggie?"

Merissa watched him for a moment, before turning her back and sitting back down on the grass.

"She asked me for some time off so I gave it to her. She's gone to see her brother in New York and will be back the week after next."

Alex dropped his jacket and sat beside her, careful not to get too close. She looked like his old Merissa again – slightly tanned and healthy. His body was responding ferociously.

"I see. When was this?" he asked her casually, whilst tugging off his tie. There was no way he was going back to the office when his wife was looking as delectable as this!

"Last week sometime," she replied vaguely.

Alex looked at her hard, feeling his temper rise. "Last week when?"

"Monday," came the innocent reply. If he'd had any interest in her and his house he would have known sooner.

"Monday! You've been alone since last Monday!" he exploded.

She smiled sweetly. "Sure, it's been quite nice actually not having Aggie clucking around me all the time. She made me promise to tell you that day, but you came home too late and this is the first time I've seen you." She continued to smile as if it didn't bother her in the least.

Alex had the decency to flush.

"I took my final exam, it was a breeze. I've been up the hill a few times. Thomas and I have had lunch together. I've made up some of my orders and given them out and Cymone and Toby have been coming over every evening to keep me company," she listed.

Alex felt guilt, shame, and then blinding rage flow through him. Why hadn't she told him about Aggie? Why hadn't she told him she was feeling better? A lot of questions came to his head but he knew all the answers. He hadn't been around to tell.

Alex stretched out beside her and looked at her profile, before leaning on an elbow to touch her.

"Are you feeling better?" he asked as he touched her cheek with his finger.

"A long time ago."

"Why didn't you tell me, Merissa?" he asked quietly, watching his finger travel down between her breasts and over her tummy, stopping just above the unbuttoned opening of her shorts.

"I didn't want to bother you," she admitted and heard his sharp intake of breath with satisfaction.

"It wouldn't be a bother to hear that my wife was feeling better and…"

"Stop it, Alex. You made yourself quite clear the last time we spoke…which was a long time ago. I've been fine, I feel fine and I've been enjoying the solitude."

She knew that last remark would sting and it did. She looked at him and saw a tiny flicker of anguish in his expressive chocolate gaze.

He was silent for a moment.

"I've been wrong to stay away Meri," he started, "but I couldn't bear to see you the way you were, insisting on…" He didn't want to get into that. "Damn it Meri! You could have at least called and told me about Aggie."

"Oh stop it!" she fumed again and made to get up, only he pulled her back down and flung a well-defined leg over hers.

She bit her lip, trying not to respond to his nearness. He smelled so good. Her nipples pushed against her bra top, heat pooled at her centre. It had been so long.

He looked down into her eyes, seeing them darken even more. He knew she wanted him and his already aroused body surged against hers. He kissed her, kissed her long and hard, drinking the juices she had denied him all these weeks. How he missed her.

Within seconds he was inside her, her warmth wrapping around him, keeping him snug within her. He released her mouth and pushed her bra aside, latching on a plump nipple and he felt her shudder beneath him. Her walls gripped him and with a moan ripped from his very soul, he spilled himself inside her.

Alex flopped onto his side and watched as Merissa pulled on her clothes with an unsteady hand. She was so beautiful, his wife. Maybe now they could get back to how they were, he mused. He pulled her back down to him. They had found each other today and he would never let her go again.

"Alex, I've got to get ready," she explained against the lips that were whispering across hers.

Alex stilled above her, lifting himself onto his elbows.

"To go where?" he demanded looking at her sharply, as jealousy surged through him. This was the first time he had touched her in weeks. He wasn't about to let her go.

"I have a business lunch to go to."

"With whom?" he asked suspiciously.

"Alex please, you haven't expressed the least bit of interest with my life lately. I could have been dead from last Monday and you'd only just be finding out! I'm having lunch with a prospective client." She pushed him away and rushed into the house before she lost her temper. Being alone had really helped her lower her blood pressure and she wasn't about to jeopardize it.

"*You* hold it right there!" Alex barked as he strode into the kitchen just in time to see her put one foot on the stairs. She kept on climbing and had almost reached her bedroom when he grabbed her and propelled her into the room, sitting her down on the bed as though she were a naughty child. "You will not be going anywhere if you don't give me some answers!" He loomed over her in a rage.

Merissa didn't let any of it get to her, but actually moved up to the top of the bed and arranged the pillows behind her with patient ease, before looking at him with a tiny indulgent smile on her face.

He stood glaring at her for several seconds, willing himself to calm down. Her expression didn't help.

"Who are you going out with?" he asked again between clenched teeth.

"James Edison," she replied.

"Who the hell is he?"

Merissa feigned impatience. "I've already told you that he's a prospective client who is thinking of using my line in his stores. Alex, it is only lunch." Then couldn't help adding, even though she had told herself she wouldn't. "You've had enough yourself with Powers, so I don't think you have the right to tell me what to do and who to see. It's only lunch!"

Alex was stunned to know she knew about his lunches with Vanessa.

"You're not going," he told her.

"Oh yes I am." Her chin went up.

"Merissa…"

She cut him off. "I have a chance to send my clothes to Europe. And just because you're feeling more than a little guilty for leaving me on my own all these weeks, just to find out, that hey your little wifey has been surviving without you and doing fine, doesn't mean you can walk in here and dictate to me what to do!"

Each word was like a slap in his face.

"You've already made yourself clear on where you stand in my life and have displayed…for all of Kingston to see…that you're definitely having a good time without me around," she seethed. "So go back to your office, call Powers and have one of your usual 'power' lunches at the Pelican Room, because I won't be making you any!"

She slid off the bed and moved pass him, only to be grabbed and kissed so hard her neck hurt. When he finally let her go, he saw hostility in her eyes.

"Go. But if I don't see you back here in two hours, there will be hell to pay!"

He stormed out of the room.

Alex watched his wife leave and felt jealous rage simmer through him once again. She looked like his old Meri, beautiful and confident in a nicely tailored grey and white linen business suit he hadn't seen before. She didn't even tell him goodbye, as he watched her walk pass him, her head held high and her wild hair pulled back and secured with a white clip at the nape of her neck.

He wanted her again with a fierceness that overwhelmed him.

He walked out with her to the car and opened the door for her. She looked at him for the first time.

"Bye," he said, looking at her cherry red lips and gave in to his urge. He kissed her softly and felt pulses of excitement flutter through his veins when, with a sigh, she kissed him back.

"Bye," she told him, feeling her insides burn for him.

They smiled at each other in understanding, before he closed the door and watched her drive away. He felt elated and wonderful, his wife was back. He started to plan the evening ahead.

Chapter Thirty

Vanessa had just started her car when Merissa drove up and parked in a space opposite. Vanessa watched the younger girl through narrowed eyes. Heated surges of anger grabbed her and twisted her inside out. It wasn't fair! How dare the bitch be up and about looking as lovely and young as ever?

Alex wasn't hers yet, she thought frantically. If Merissa was almost back to normal, she wouldn't have a chance. She had to move things along.

Vanessa began to plan. She reached for her car phone and rang Alex's straight line to his office. No answer. She called the regular line and spoke to his secretary, only to be told that he had gone out to lunch. Maybe he was having lunch with Merissa. She immediately looked around for his car. On impulse she called his house. He answered on the fourth ring. She hung up without speaking. She smiled, a plan already forming. She needed to find a florist.

※ ※ ※

Alex was happily preparing a special dinner for Merissa when he heard a car pull up. He looked at his watch and frowned, she'd only been gone twenty minutes. He walked to the window and groaned before going to the door.

"Hi Vanny, what are you doing here?" he asked as he opened the door for her.

"I came to see Merissa. Is she home?" she asked innocently.

"No." He was still holding the door knob.

"Can I come in?" she asked.

"Sure." He reluctantly moved aside. "She won't be back for another hour or so."

"That's ok, I can wait. Mmm that smells good. Cooking?"

"Yep." He walked into the kitchen.

"Here, I brought these for her." She handed him the vase.

"That was thoughtful of you, but..."

She interrupted him before he could go on.

"Making a special dinner? Let me help, I'll be out of here before she gets back."

She'd already put on the 'hers' to the 'his' apron he was wearing.

Alex looked at her for a moment, and then shrugged, what the heck, he could do with some help, he thought. Together they made a huge dinner of roast pork, baked potatoes and salad. Vanessa was watching the clock closely; she had to time this just right.

"Can I borrow your phone? I need to call the office," she told him a short time later.

"Sure, you know where it is." Alex was making salad dressing.

Vanessa called the restaurant and quietly asked to speak to Mrs. York. She was told Mrs. York had left ten minutes ago.

She went back to the kitchen and pretended to stir the gravy. She then purposely splashed it on herself.

"Oh no, my suit!" She watched the brown stain spread with false horror.

Alex grabbed a hand towel and began to wipe it off roughly.

"It's no use. Can I take a shower?" she suggested and seeing the look of indecision in his eyes, quickly added, "I'll be as fast as I can. I just need to rinse my skirt before it stains." She pleaded with just the right amount of anguish.

"Ok. But please be quick about it," he pressed.

Vanessa rushed upstairs and took a long shower until she heard Merissa's car outside. She then switched off the tap and towelled herself off, rubbing herself hard so that her skin glowed; she bit and sucked her lips hard. They needed to look as though she'd just been kissed. She donned Alex's black rob, leaving it gaping slightly and sprayed herself liberally with Merissa's perfume before going unhurriedly downstairs with bare feet.

⁂

Merissa was enjoying the welcome home kiss from her husband, when she heard someone walk towards the kitchen. Moving apart, both she and Alex turned.

Alex was stunned.

Merissa was furious.

"Hello Merissa, nice to see you up and about," Vanessa said as she approached them. It was all she could do to hold back and not scrape her nails down the other girl's face.

Merissa looked at Alex questioningly before ignoring the woman's earlier remark.

"Vanessa, what are you doing here?" Merissa asked frostily.

"I brought you those." She pointed to the vase of fragrant roses on the kitchen counter.

"That was nice of you." Merissa forced a smile to her stiff lips.

"She was helping me with dinner," Alex rushed into the loud silence, "when the gravy spilled all over her." He tried to explain knowing exactly what his wife must be thinking. "Vanny was just leaving. Weren't you Vanny?" he prompted.

"Of course," she replied, running a hand over her hip suggestively. "Merissa can I borrow some clothes please?" she asked sweetly.

"I don't think so." Merissa allowed her gaze to slide insultingly along the woman's figure. "They won't fit." She turned, shrugging off her husband's hand and went into the living room, fuming with resentment.

"Sorry," Alex apologized to Vanessa, "let me get you a pair of my shorts and a t-shirt."

"I hope I haven't caused you any trouble," she said as he handed her his shirt. "Don't worry about it." She slipped the robe from her shoulders, revealing her nakedness beneath, but he had already turned away.

"Meri, I..." he began when he entered the living room.

Merissa held up her hand, stopping him from talking.

"Well thanks again for a *lovely* afternoon Alex and I'll drop these things off by your office," she told him. "Bye Merissa, nice to see you looking better."

Merissa smiled tightly and waited for the other woman to drive off before she looked at Alex.

"Explain," she said simply.

Alex shifted under her accusing glare. He had never seen her so angry. But hell! It was an innocent situation.

"Meri." He sat beside her and took her hand. "I was fixing you a nice dinner when Vanny came by," he started awkwardly. "She offered to help and reluctantly I let her, that's all."

"How did she end up in your bath robe, looking as if you had just made love then? Explain that to me?" Merissa was losing control fast. Everything she had heard seemed to be true, Alex was having an affair with Vanessa! In their own home! This wasn't real, this wasn't happening. Her head started to pound.

"Merissa, please!" He turned her to face him. "I swear nothing happened. Why would I jeopardize what we have for her? Nothing happened. She's just a good friend of mine who wanted to help out, that's all!"

Merissa stood up. "I don't believe you. I trusted you damn it!" She dashed her tears aside with shaky hands.

Alex stood also and reached for her. She flinched away. "Don't touch me! How could you do this to us? To me?" she wailed.

"I didn't…"

"Spare me your explanations! You brought that woman into this house, knowing how much I hate her? Knowing that I wouldn't want her here, much less cooking my food? Alex how could you? How could you after what we shared this afternoon?"

"Merissa, it's not like that, I didn't invite her here, she just…"

"How did she know that you were here?" she demanded, cutting him off abruptly.

"I don't know."

"Why did you let her stay?" Her eyes were accusing.

"I don't know, Meri…I…"

She held up her hand and began to walk away.

"Where are you going?" he asked her. "I made dinner."

She rounded on him. "Do you really think I would eat the food you and your woman made? Everybody was right. Everyone told me. I just refused to believe…until now."

Merissa didn't wait to hear what he had to say, but rushed up the stairs and closed the door, letting wave after wave of tears wash over her.

Alex stood in the living room in a state of shock. Him and Vanessa? That's what Meri has been hearing? Oh God. Why hadn't he realised things would get back to her, even if it was all innocent.

Why did things always go wrong with them? Why was it that something or someone always seemed to come between them?

He looked up when he heard her door open and was shocked to see her lugging down a suitcase.

"Where are you going?" he asked as he went to take the heavy suitcase from her. She refused to let him take it.

"It's better this way, I can't live like this anymore. Please Alex, let me go."

"No!" He held her arms tightly before crushing her to him. "I won't let you do this." His words were filled with pain. "Don't do this Meri, I beg of you, please don't." He buried his head in her neck, refusing to let her go. "We'll work it out."

"I have to, we have to be apart for a while…"

"No!"

"Alex…"

"No! You're not leaving me," he stated stubbornly. "You're my wife, you belong here with me damn it! Meri please honey, don't do this." His eyes pleaded for her to listen.

"Alex I…"

He let her go and took the suitcase from her abruptly. "You're not going," he stated arrogantly and glared at her, his stance rigid.

Merissa squared her shoulders and looked at him coldly. "I am going with or without my clothes. You've made it plain you no longer care. It took you over a week to even realize Aggie was gone. Maybe we rushed into marriage. You don't know me. What I feel inside," she thumped her breast, "and I definitely don't know who the hell you are!" She flicked a tear away. "I can't live like this under your roof, I feel like a lodger! Alex, I've had enough. The atmosphere isn't good for me or the baby, I'm going away for a few days…"

"Where?"

"I'll call and let you know."

"You'll tell me where now! Damn it!" he exploded, his nostrils flaring with his fury.

"Alex…"

"Where?" he said trying to calm down and forcing himself to breathe regularly.

"Joseph has an empty apartment up Red Hills. I'll be over there for a while. I don't want to worry them," she told him sadly.

"What's the address?"

"If you think I'm going to tell you that you're sadly mistaken. I need some peace. I need to think about us and decide what to do."

"There's nothing to decide," he told her adamantly. "You'll have your few days, then you're coming back home," he told her matter-of-factly. Merissa bristled.

"This isn't my home," she told him sadly, looking around the freshly painted walls, new tiles on the floor and the new paintings on the walls. "I doubt it ever was."

"Meri, please, don't go. Give us another chance. I love you."

His eyes looked sorrowfully into hers and she could feel her anger evaporating. She had to get out of here before she changed her mind.

"I have to," she told him and watched the hope die in his eyes. He let her go, picked up her suitcase and walked out of the door; his shoulders slumped over in defeat.

"Drive carefully and call me when you get there, ok." His voice was thick with emotion. There was nothing more to say.

Merissa walked behind him and wiped the tears from her eyes. He opened her car door for the second time that evening and waited for her to get in. His eyes were begging her to stay.

"I'm sorry," she began to say, only he put his finger to her lips to silence her.

"Don't talk, honey. Please don't talk," he said hoarsely, "I never meant any of this to happen, you must believe me. I could never hurt you. I love you too much to ever want to hurt you." He lifted her chin and kissed her gently, before softly closing the door.

She looked at him through watery eyes. "I'm so sorry," she said and pulled him down to her, giving him a deep kiss. Alex felt as though there was a finality about the way her lips seemed to cling to his, as if she wanted to remember him by it. He moved away and smiled weakly, not daring to speak.

It had started to rain. A steady downpour that mixed with the tears he didn't bother to hide.

She started the car and moved off slowly, not putting on her head lights until she was on the main road. She stopped and waved before moving off again.

He went in and looked around the quiet house then went to the bar in the living room. He looked and found his over proof white rum and swallowed it straight from the bottle. A strong urge gripped him and he relieved it by throwing several glasses. Feeling unfulfilled, he threw the heavy bottle of liquor and watched as the clear liquid trickled down the wall like the tears on his cheeks, and the rain drops on the windows.

Chapter Thirty-One

Merissa spent the next few days trying to relax and not think about Alex. She hadn't shed a single tear since she'd moved out and she was thankful. She missed him terribly, but knew this was the right thing to do. She had already planned to move in permanently at the apartment and had even asked Joseph if she could. Of course they had asked a lot of questions and she noticed more than once the way Thomas glanced at her stomach. It was so hard keeping things from them both. Alex had made her into this – a liar.

A routine check at the doctor told her that her pressure was still high, so she stayed off her feet most of the time.

At least she didn't have Thomas to worry about. He was looking wonderfully well and was in the process of planning another trip for him and Joseph.

She looked at the clock, it was time to go and see Alex at his office. Getting up and glancing in the mirror, she stopped and looked at herself with a very critical eye. She looked good. She hadn't felt this good about herself in a long time. The black long vest fit snugly over her hips and she wore a short fitted skirt that showed off her long legs. Her hair was pulled back and held with a scarlet red clip and bright red low heeled shoes completed the look. Eat your heart out Alex; you gave up this for that tramp!

"Afternoon Mary," Merissa said to Alex's secretary as she approached. "Is he in?" She indicated the closed door with her head.

"Afternoon Merissa, nice to see you. He sure is and he's making his presence felt. He's been in an awful mood lately."

Just as Merissa was about to answer, Alex's voice boomed through her intercom.

"Mary! Where's that file? Or would you like me to come out there and get it myself?" he drawled sarcastically.

Mary looked at the little device on her desk as though she wanted to shoot it. It had become her worst enemy.

"I'll take it in Mary," Merissa told her.

"Thank you." Mary smiled with relief and gratefully handed a set of files to her.

"What took you so damn long?" Alex roared as soon as the door opened.

"Sorry sir, I didn't know which one you wanted, sir," Merissa replied, as she walked over and sat opposite him, slamming the files on the desk between them.

He looked a mess, crumpled, unshaven and his tie was askew.

Alex thought his eyes were deceiving him then blinked several times. "What are you doing here?" he asked abruptly, taking her in from head to toe. "You look well," he added with marked reluctance.

"Thank you. You look as though you haven't slept in days."

Alex gave her a dry look. "I haven't. When are you coming home?" he asked, getting straight to the point.

"If you want me to be as blunt as you, I'm not."

Alex stared at her hard. "What the hell do you mean you're not?"

He stood and leaned over the desk, his knuckles pressing into the glass top painfully. Alex ignored the pain as he glared at her, fire in his eyes.

"Calm down," she stated. "I've decided to live by myself for a while, that's all." She stood also, but moved behind her chair as though shielding herself from the verbal attack that was sure to come.

"You can't live by yourself. What if something happens to you? What if…"

"Save it Alex. I've made up my mind. I'll be over at the apartment for the next three weeks. Then Joseph and Thomas will be going away for several weeks and I'll be looking after the house."

There was silence as he digested this.

Merissa made to leave.

"Is this it then?" He looked at her sadly not believing she was walking out on him.

She smiled when he walked around his desk and took her hands.

"I think so." I won't cry she willed herself. I won't cry.

"Don't do this to us Meri," he said quietly, as he pulled her tenderly into his arms.

Merissa could feel the day old beard on his jaw as he rubbed his cheek to hers lovingly.

"I have to." She pulled away and opened her bag. "This is the address and telephone number." She reached up and kissed his cheek and then touched her hand to it as she looked up at him. "I have to," she repeated and walked out.

❦❦❦

Flowers had been sent to her from Alex every day since then and he called every night and they spoke for hours upon hours in the weeks that followed. It was amazing, now that they were separated, they seemed to be closer. They openly discussed the baby and she told him her plans about her line of designs. But she still refused to let him come and see her. She wasn't ready yet and was just enjoying the new found friendship they had formed.

Alex occasionally lunched with Vanessa and other persons, some of them female businesswomen; but he always made sure to tell Merissa about it before she got wind of it through other channels. The society papers seemed to get bits and pieces of them from time to time. Where they got the information neither one of them knew nor cared. Merissa was used to it, being Thomas Walters' daughter always brought news, none of it was damaging – yet.

Alex hated reading about himself in the papers and they always seemed to make him look like the villain with heavy speculation about his relationship with Vanessa. He just hoped Merissa wouldn't judge him by any of it.

Several weeks later, Alex was standing outside Merissa's door like a nervous teenager.

"Hi," she said as she let him into her apartment.

"Hi. I hate to say it, but this place suits you," he admitted jokingly, as he walked into the living room, handing her the bunch of long stem yellow and red roses he'd been holding – yellow for friendship, red for love.

Alex looked around the apartment. It had one bedroom and a tiny kitchen. But it was warm and welcoming, decorated in blue, orange and cream.

"Thank you. I'll be running out of vases soon," she said as she arranged them in her last crystal vase. "Please sit down Alex, you're making me nervous," she admitted.

They ate and talked for most of the night, all the time yearning for each other. When it was time for Alex to leave, he was reluctant and told her so.

"You can't stay, Alex," she told him again as they put the dishes away.

"I miss you Meri, I can't sleep knowing that you're all the way over here, alone…"

"That's not the reason and you know it," she teased.

"It's part," Alex smiled down at her, God she was beautiful. Her stomach was blossoming and was nicely rounded; he wanted to touch the changes in her. "When will you start to really show?"

"In a few weeks."

"Do you feel it move or anything?"

She laughed. "Not yet."

"Do you still get sick?"

"No."

"Do you still feel tired all the time?"

"No...well sometimes."

"How's your blood pressure?"

"What's with the sudden interest?" she asked as she hung the dish cloth on a hook and went into the living room.

Alex followed.

"I'm concerned, that's all. I do have a right to be you know," he pointed out defensively.

"It's a bit late for concern, don't you think?"

Alex squashed the heated reply before it built up inside him.

"You're putting on weight," he pointed out instead, trying to lighten the mood.

"Good weight or bad weight?"

"Good weight, definitely good weight." He smiled at her, longing to touch her.

"You can."

"Can what?"

"Touch me. You can touch me."

Alex grinned and picked up her hand. "Let me stay Merissa," he asked again. To hell with pride, he'd roll around in the mud and beg like a dog just for her to say yes.

"No."

"Why the hell not!" he yelled, immediately regretting his outburst. Her smile faded and she pulled her hand away.

"Don't raise your voice at me Alex York. I don't want you to stay, let's just leave it at that."

"Come back home Meri."

"You know I can't do that."

"Please, I'll make everything up to you. I'll be there for you, please say you'll come home, honey."

"No, I can't Alex. I'm happy here. This is the first time I've been happy in weeks," she admitted. "It's better this way."

Alex looked at her, his pain intense.

"I think you'd better go now," she told him. It was obvious he was wrestling with his conscience.

Just then the phone rang.

"Hello?"

Alex got up and looked out the window, giving her some privacy.

"Oh hello James."

Alex stiffened.

"Yes…tomorrow?…Ok I'll meet you there…bye take care…yes bye." She hung up.

Alex went rigid with rage; he blindly rounded on her without thinking. "You don't want me to stay over because you have this James person coming over, don't you? Don't you!" He grabbed her arms and shook her.

"I don't have to explain anything to you, Alex." Her statement did nothing to alleviate his anger.

"Like hell you don't!" he exploded. "Who the hell is this James anyway? Has he been over here? Well has he? Has he!"

"Alex let go of me. You're hurting me!"

"I bet that baby you're carrying isn't even mine!" he spat out viciously.

Merissa paled.

"Get out."

"Don't worry I'm going." He grabbed his keys, glared at her once more in disgust and left, leaving the door open behind him.

Chapter Thirty-Two

Merissa left the building very satisfied. She got the contract and had to start preparing her new line straight away. Nothing or no one could put her in a bad mood today, she thought, as she left the restaurant and went into the parking lot. Not even her husband.

She stopped at the doctor's office on her way to the apartment and was told her blood pressure had gone down just a little. It was good news, but she still had to be careful.

As she let herself into the apartment, she felt a twinge of pain followed by another in her back. She thought nothing of it and made herself a sandwich before buckling down to work on new sketches.

The constant ringing of the door bell broke her concentration and she got up quickly.

"Who is it?" she asked through the door as she looked through the peep hole rubbing her back.

"Flower delivery ma'am," a deep voice called through the door.

"Send it back."

"Yuh haffi sign for it first ma'am, might lose mi job," the flower man said.

"Oh alright." Merissa sighed and opened the door to a fat man dressed in a navy blue uniform.

Taking the clip board from him she signed her name quickly then glanced at the card. It was from James.

"I've changed my mind, I'll take them."

"Yes ma'am."

The man handed her the large bouquet of tiger lilies with a smile. The smile froze on his face.

Blood shot beady eyes, clashed with horrified brown ones in swift recognition. All the colour drained out of Merissa's face as she looked at the man. No, it can't be! It can't be! She was close to fainting and only just managed to slam the door in his face. Her body shook in terror. A cold sweat broke out all over her body. She reached for the phone as an intense pain ripped through her body and a hot thick sticky gush washed down her legs. Blackness engulfed her and then nothing.

Cymone kept ringing the door bell. Merissa was supposed to be home. They had arranged to meet fifteen minutes ago and her car was outside.

"Toby, she's not answering!" she called down to him.

"Maybe she's sleeping!" he yelled back reasonably. "I'll call her." He used his mobile. The line was busy again. It had been like that for the past half an hour. "It's still busy."

"Toby, something's wrong. I just know it!" Fear made Cymone's voice seem unusually shrill.

"I'm coming up."

Seconds later Toby joined Cymone outside the door. He pounded it loudly.

"Merissa! It's me, Toby, open up!"

He pressed his ear to the door, there wasn't any movement inside. He got nervous.

"Cym, does she have a balcony?"

"I'm not sure. You go round the back and see. I'll keep knocking."

Toby left her then, but came back a short time later with a khaki uniformed maintenance man.

"This one," he told the man. Cymone moved aside to give the man way.

"Mr. Joseph place. Me did tink me did see Miss Merissa ere, not so long ago, ma sa," the man told them as he tried several keys.

"How long ago?" Cymone asked.

"Let me see. Mi did see a flowers man."

"Oh." Cymone looked at Toby. Both of them wondering who had sent Merissa flowers.

"Ere we go."

The door swung open and Cymone ran inside, only to stop and scream.

"Oh God, Toby!"

"Jesus."

Merissa lay in a pool of blood, lifeless and blue, her hands still clutching the phone.

"Who's her doctor?" Toby asked, recovering quickly.

"The same as mine, I'll call him."

Cymone stepped across her friend, almost in tears. "Toby don't move her!"

"I have to make sure she's alive." He moved her hair aside. "Thank God."

"We have to get her straight to the hospital now!"

"Alright, I'll take her down, you call Alex. Now Cym!" Toby ordered when Cymone didn't respond.

Cymone flew into action and made the necessary calls. Then got into the back seat to hold her friend's head, all the while praying she'd be alright.

Toby drove as though he was at Dover Raceway and got them to the hospital in less than ten minutes. Five minutes later, Alex rushed in, his face pale.

"Where is she?" He was panicked and couldn't think straight. "Where is she Toby?" He was close to tears.

"They've taken her into surgery Alex."

Alex stood stunned for the second time in half an hour and openly began to cry. Cymone held him.

"She'll be alright, she's strong." Cymone was crying too. The three of them held each other as they waited.

Three hours later, Dr. White came out and looked at the three persons holding hands in the corridor.

"Alex?"

Alex looked at him and slowly separated himself from his friends. The doctor indicated a room and went inside. "Sit."

Alex remained standing. "How's my wife?"

"Merissa will be fine." He watched as relief made the younger man's features soften. "I couldn't save the baby. I'm sorry."

Alex nodded. "Can I see her?"

"Only for a short time. She's lost a lot of blood and was haemorrhaging heavily when she came in. It's lucky she was found. Things may have been different. She's up in the private wing. Stay five minutes."

"Yes doctor. And thank you." They shook hands. Then Alex went over to Cymone and Toby. "She'll be fine. Thanks for finding her, you both saved her life." He hugged them both and then went to Merissa's room alone.

He held her hand as he looked at her. She was so pale and tubes were up her nose and in her mouth. He had almost lost his wife. His whole life lay in that bed. He'd never let her out of his sight again he vowed to himself. He'd never leave her side.

"I'm sorry sir but you have to go. You can come back later around six, normal visiting hours. You'll need to bring some toiletries for her anyway," a nurse kindly informed him before leaving the room.

Alex kissed Merissa's hand and reluctantly left the room.

An hour later, he was back after getting the necessary things and making several phone calls. Cymone and Toby had gone to find Thomas and Joseph, who had flown in from the Cayman Islands.

Guilt consumed him; none of this would have happened if he had stood up and told her point blank she wasn't leaving. All he had given her these past few months was pain. He hadn't even been her friend and those last words he had spoken to her at her apartment the other night made him hang his head in shame. He put his head down on the side of the bed, his Meri could have died today if she hadn't been found. He could have lost her for good.

Thoughts like those consumed him, making his guilt even thicker. He squeezed her hand.

"You bastard! You…" Thomas came storming into the room and grabbed the front of Alex's shirt, pressing him into the wall with amazing strength. "You did this to her! You almost killed my princess!"

"Thomas please!" Joseph cut in and pulled a furious Thomas from the younger man. Joseph just glared at Alex, his eyes and stance telling the younger man that he'd better keep his mouth shut.

Thomas went over to Merissa and held her hand as he stroked her hair.

"Princess, why didn't you come to me? Why didn't you tell me?" Thomas let his grief out and cried openly as he held her.

Joseph stood by and watched quietly from the side, his own sorrow making the lines on his face deepen.

Thomas rounded on Alex again.

"You did this to her, I don't ever want to see you again. Get out!" he said calmly, his eyes changing to the colour of an ice-cold, unforgiving river.

Alex didn't breathe but didn't move either. He matched Thomas' stare.

"Get out!" Thomas yelled again.

"No."

Just then Merissa moaned and Alex jumped quickly to her side, picking up her hand.

"Merissa?" he said softly, hoping she was coming back to him.

She moaned again.

"My God," Joseph whispered. "Look."

All eyes followed Joseph's eyes to the bed. A dark sticky red stain of blood was seeping through the covers.

"Get the doctor!" Alex ordered savagely. "Merissa don't die, I beg of you, please don't die."

He held her for anxious seconds before he was pushed out of the room by a buxom, no-nonsense nurse. Alex watched as medical equipment was rushed into her room and nurses and doctors walked quickly back and forth. Minutes later, Dr. White came out and told him they were preparing her for surgery. She was haemorrhaging again.

Chapter Thirty-Three

Merissa woke to find her tongue feeling thick and dry in her mouth. She was so thirsty. She turned her head to look if she had put a glass of water on the side table. It wasn't there, neither was her table.

Lifting her head in confusion, she looked around the pale green pristine room. The smell of antiseptic tickled her nostrils. She was in a hospital?

Alex heard a sound and leapt off his bed and was beside her in a second. He was happy to see her eyes open, even if they looked at him with uncertainty.

"You're in the hospital," he answered her silent question. "Don't move, I'll be right back," he told her before turning to leave, only he turned back and kissed her tenderly on the cheek. "Welcome back." He smiled down at her then left to call a nurse.

He came back a short time later with two nurses and a doctor he had found walking down the corridor on his way home.

"Everything is fine, Mr. York." The elderly doctor told him yet again as Alex walked him out to his car. "My, you're a persistent husband!" The doctor chuckled.

"Are you sure?" Alex asked the doctor again worriedly.

The old wrinkled doctor should have been insulted to have his professional integrity doubted but he was amused.

"Yes I'm sure. Now don't you think you should go back inside and give your wife some love and support?"

Alex grinned for the first time in days.

"Thanks." He turned to go inside. It was after three in the morning.

"Hi Meri," he told her as he took her hand. She was crying.

He pulled up a chair and sat as close to her as he could.

"I lost my baby didn't I?" She looked at him, her eyes huge in her paper-white face.

Alex swallowed. "Yes," he said simply.

She turned to look the other way.

"Toby and Cymone found you at the apartment."

She looked at him again. "How long have I been here?" she asked.

"Since early yesterday afternoon."

"What time is it now?"

"Almost four in the morning."

She fell silent.

"You had to have surgery twice."

"Why?"

"To stop the bleeding. You started to haemorrhage again after they brought you in. You went into shock."

Merissa stared at him, not believing her ears, then became sad, as her eyes drifted over her breasts. They still felt a little tender as though they didn't know that the baby had left her. Tears overflowed once more.

"Merissa, I love you. We've been going through some rough times lately but no matter what I've said to you in the past, I want you to put it there. I'm sorry for all the pain I've caused you and I want us to start over." Alex looked at her, only to smile softly and brush a lock of hair away from her face tenderly. She was sleeping.

Merissa sat up slowly in her bed and looked around, her eyes resting gently on the sleeping form of her husband across from her; she smiled. Even though she felt detached from him right now, it was comforting having him here.

Her baby, she had lost her baby. She moved her hand to her stomach. She felt as though a part of her had been yanked out of her very soul. Her eyes misted over. She wondered if it was a boy or a girl. Why me Lord? She screamed silently to herself. What had she ever done to deserve something like this?

She sat up even straighter and arranged the pillows behind her back. It was still very early and she could just make out the early morning rays of sunshine as they tried to reach her through the hospital curtains.

Alex opened his eyes and saw her sitting up. She was crying quietly and he didn't want to disturb her. She needed to grieve. She had loved that child more than she loved him. It still hurt him to think about it, especially now when she had miscarried, but deep inside he was glad that it happened this way. She wasn't going to die, or have convulsions or anything; she was going to lead a normal life. Losing the baby had saved her life.

After a time, she looked over at him and smiled a tiny smile when she saw him watching her. She watched as he got out of bed with blue striped pyjamas on.

"That's a first," she pointed out.

He looked down at himself and grinned. "I didn't even know I owned a pair. Cymone brought them over last night. Good morning, how are you feeling?" He stood by her bed for a split second before brushing his lips against her forehead.

"As though my whole life has been taken from me," she admitted honestly. "I feel empty as though a part of me is missing." Her eyes misted again.

"We almost lost you yesterday," he told her. "You gave me a bad scare."

She smiled thinly. "This doesn't change the way I feel about you. I'm not going back to the house," she told him adamantly, wanting to settle the matter right here, right now.

"We'll talk about it, but not right now. Look Meri, the other day, I'm sorry for what I said. I don't know what came over me. I guess I'm just a jealous old fool, who didn't think."

"You said it and I heard."

"Honey I'm sorry. I just felt rejected and then to hear you make plans with another man... I just blew my top." He looked miserably at her.

She was silent.

"Where's the bathroom?" she asked eventually in the stretching silence. Alex sighed in defeat.

"Good morning Yorks," Dr. White greeted them as he came into the room much later. "Alex? Leave us for a few minutes, whilst I run a check on Merissa here please. I'll call you as soon as we're through."

Alex reluctantly left the room and waited in the passageway.

"Merissa you did know there was a high chance this might happen didn't you?"

She nodded, whilst brushing the tears aside.

"We couldn't save the foetus. It had already detached itself from the uterus when you were brought in. I had to do what we call a suction abortion to pull the remains out."

Her face went white as she thought of her baby being sucked through a vacuum, then discarded like rubbish.

"I'm really sorry Merissa, but it may be extremely difficult to have other children in the future." Merissa gasped as pain like no other ripped through her. "I'm keeping you here until the end of the week; we have to find out why your blood pressure was so high. Ok?"

She nodded. He listened to her heart beat, and then checked her pulse.

"That husband of yours is a good man. He cares about you Merissa. I know the two of you had been on different sides with the pregnancy thing, but you must see things from his point of view. You're his wife, the woman he loves and you chose to risk your life to have this baby. As your doctor, all I can say is that it was a brave thing to do, even if you did go against my advice, but as your friend, you were very foolish."

Merissa looked at him, her eyes hardening.

"I wanted this baby," she told him.

"Yes. But Merissa, it was medically impossible that you would carry it to term."

"I don't care. I needed the almost."

"Why?"

She looked at him again, "Why?"

"Yes, why? Why did you have to put yourself at risk like that?"

"Well I...I needed to have this baby."

"That's not the only reason and you know it. When you're ready to talk about it just let me know. But whilst you're here I want you to think about what you did, what you put your husband through. He must really love you, because many a man would have left you by now."

The doctor left her then, telling her that he'd be back later.

Merissa looked at the closed door. Nobody understands! She thumbed her pillow and moved down under the covers.

※ ※ ※

Thomas approached Alex when he spotted the younger man leaning against the wall opposite Merissa's room. He apologised for his manner the day before and with a beseeching look the two men held each other, before moving into the waiting room to talk privately. Alex told him everything, holding nothing back.

※ ※ ※

The next few days passed by slowly. Merissa was getting bored and was itching to dig into her work. Alex never left her for more than an hour. They hadn't talked about their living arrangements once she was released either. She still had no intention of going back to his house. She needed time to be alone and she also had to think about that flower man.

What if it was Jonas? She remembered the little eyes and she could have sworn he recognized her. Dear God? What if it was him? What should she do? Tell Thomas and Joseph? No, she couldn't. They had enough on their minds, besides they'd be leaving in a few days to continue their tour of the smaller islands. If she told them, they wouldn't go. Maybe she should tell Alex? That was a possibility but she really didn't want to tell anybody. It might not have been him.

She'd make a few phone calls herself and call the flower shop, the number must be on the card.

Chapter Thirty-Four

Later at the hospital, Thomas sat alone with Merissa, watching her sleep.

"Hi Tommy," she said as she opened her eyes expecting to see Alex but pleasantly surprised to see Thomas instead.

"Hi. I was watching you sleep," he told her unnecessarily.

She smiled at him.

"I'm sorry," she told him simply, knowing she had hurt him. He took her hand.

"Why didn't you tell me Princess?" He looked at her sadly, the blue of his eyes darkening with sorrow.

"I couldn't. It was my problem and I didn't want to upset you."

"You've upset me more by not telling me," he pointed out. "I thought you and I had a special relationship? I never thought the day would come when you would be afraid to come to me."

"Tommy, it's not like that." She bit her lip. "I've only just been married. I couldn't come to you with my problems. My husband should have been there for me and I didn't want you to think things had already gone wrong, especially this soon."

"Meri, you're my daughter. Everyone has problems. The very first year of marriage is usually the toughest. Both you and Alex have handled it all wrong, but that is your own business. You're both adults and belong together. Work it out," he told her abruptly. The words he swore never to say tumbled out. "Meri, if I was married to you and you chose to have this baby…I would have killed you myself!"

She gasped.

"What were you thinking?" he went on. "You're young, you could have had other children. What were you thinking of Princess?" he repeated.

She turned her head away, ashamed.

"I just wanted to have my baby."

"I understand that but…"

"How can you?" She sat up and glared at him. "How can you understand? For once in my life, I had the chance to give a child – my child – everything you had given me. I wanted this baby so that I could love it and be loved by it. I wanted to be a mother! You can't possibly understand that!"

"I understand your instincts, but I refuse to understand why you made the choices you did – against your doctor's orders!" he bellowed.

"I had to!"

"Why damn it! Why did you want to put yourself at risk and almost lose your life?"

She was silent.

Thomas shook his head. He didn't understand it. Couldn't understand it.

"Alex has gone to get you some dinner. The doctor said you could eat out tonight," he told her, changing the subject suddenly.

"Thanks," she mumbled, refusing to look at him.

"Merissa please, we've always been able to talk."

"I don't want to discuss it anymore, Tommy. I lost my baby. The one thing I could call my own..."

"So that's it!" He leapt on her explanation. "You wanted something that *I* had nothing to do with!" he bit out tightly.

She looked at him stunned.

"Of course not!" she exclaimed. "The thought hadn't even entered my mind!"

"Then why? You're my daughter, how do you think I would feel if you died? I guess you didn't think that far ahead did you?" He didn't wait for her to answer. "How do you think Alex would feel if you'd died?"

"The same way I feel about you keeping your illness to yourself!" she snapped back. "I'm sorry Tommy, forget I said that." She shook herself, hardening. "Alex wouldn't care Tommy."

"Merissa how can you say such a thing?" Thomas gasped in disbelief.

"Tommy, you don't know everything."

"Then tell me," he urged. "What aren't you telling me?"

"Alex and I are on different levels right now. When I leave here, I'll be living at the apartment, for good," she revealed.

"Why?" Thomas asked bewildered.

"Because Alex is having an affair."

There was a long silence.

"I can't believe that," Thomas dismissed with a flamboyant wave of his hand.

"Why not damn it! I'm always in the wrong it seems but go and ask him. Ask him!"

"It's not my place. If he was having an affair Merissa, believe me I'd be told about it."

"By whom?"

"By the whole of Kingston and beyond, that's by whom. Nothing passes me, don't you know that, especially something like that. You're my daughter and everybody knows it. I'd be told about it before it even began."

"He's having an affair Thomas. I confronted him about it and he didn't deny it."

Thomas was silent.

"Did you give him a chance to explain himself? I know your temper Princess. Sometimes you just don't listen when you're all fired up."

"I heard right Tommy, and I almost gave him another chance until she was in the house in his dressing gown!" she seethed.

"Who?"

"It doesn't matter." She turned her face away and looked out the window.

"Yes it does."

"Vanessa Powers," she told him simply. Not expecting him to know who she was.

"The lawyer?" he asked incredulously, his eyes wide with shock.

"One and the same," she replied tersely.

"The woman is nothing more than a common whore!"

"My sentiments exactly."

"I'll kill him! I'll bloody well kill him!"

Merissa smiled. At least someone was on her side.

❦❦❦

Alex had no sooner put the tray down on Merissa's table before Thomas dragged him by the arm and into the empty waiting room.

"You had better have a damned good explanation!"

Alex looked at him tiredly. He wondered why Thomas hadn't pulled him up about it before.

"She told you," he said simply.

"Yes she did. Explain!" Thomas roared.

"Thomas." Alex turned and looked the older man in the eye. "There is nothing to explain." He shrugged his shoulders.

"Then you're saying that Merissa is lying?" His blue eyes were blazing with fury.

"I'm saying," Alex said patiently, "that Merissa has put two and two together and come up with seven."

"So you're not having an affair?"

"No-I-am-not and I'd appreciate it if you could tell your daughter that!" Alex snapped.

"I'm sorry Alex. I did find it rather hard to believe," he recanted. "Then what is it all about, if you don't mind my asking."

Alex sat down and faced him. "Merissa has it in her head that I've been having an affair since we found out about the baby and I told her I didn't want her to have it. Thomas, we haven't lived as man and wife in weeks and I'll be the first to tell you that I have been seeing more of my friend Vanessa Powers. Meri hates her guts for some reason, but I needed to talk to someone." He shrugged again.

"How well do you know Miss Powers?" Thomas asked him. Surely Alex must know what type of woman she was.

"Very well. We've been friends since high school. She was also there for me when my family died. She'd been a good shoulder."

Thomas shook his head. "Sorry Alex, but I'm just looking out for my misguided daughter."

Alex smiled sadly.

"Put things right boy, or else," Thomas warned, before leaving him alone in the room.

Chapter Thirty-Five

The apartment was filled with flowers when she opened the door a few days later, a blend of flowery fragrances met her and she breathed in deeply.

"This is nice, whose idea was it?" she asked him as he walked in behind her, closing the door.

"Only me, myself and I," he told her with a small smile and gentle eyes.

Merissa felt a strong urge to go and give him a long hard kiss but she turned her back instead. He had hurt her too much for her to even start forgiving him now.

She opened several cards, each said something different, something loving.

"Oh Alex this is a lovely surprise." She smiled then looked around the small apartment.

The place was clean and neat. Cymone had brought someone in to clean whilst she was away. Then, her eyes rested on an unfamiliar piece of furniture.

"What's that?" she asked, going over to the black leather love seat and sitting in it.

"I bought it," he told her uncomfortably, putting his hands in his back pockets and looking at her with quiet diffidence.

"Why?"

Here it comes, he thought and pulled himself up to his full height. "It's a fold up bed."

Merissa looked at him, then at the bed, then back at him again, wide eyed, waiting for an explanation.

"You won't come home – where you belong – so I thought it best if I stayed over here…on this bed of course…until you're feeling a lot better." He waited for the explosion. He didn't get one.

The next few days passed by nicely until the night before his supposed departure.

"Will you be leaving tomorrow?" she asked him, knowing that if she didn't make him leave, he'd probably stay for forever.

He looked at her hard. "If that's what you really want," he told her gruffly.

She was silent. She liked having him around; it was almost like their first weeks of marriage. He waited for her to answer. They stood, staring at each other with the bed between them.

"It's what I want."

He sagged in front of her and sat abruptly on the bed holding his head in his hands.

"Why can't we go back to how we were before? Why do you hate me so much? Why don't you want to come home?" he asked in a sad frustrated rush.

She moved around and knelt in front of him.

"Because, I need to be alone right now," she answered passionately. "I need to find myself. I got the Italian contract and I'll be working hard on that. I can't have the distractions of you and your mistress…"

"She is not my mistress!" he roared, twisting round to glare at her.

"Whatever," she dismissed with a wave of her hand. Then continued. "I have enough to worry about."

"Are you seeing someone else?" he asked her quietly.

"No."

The silence pulsed.

"Neither am I," he told her. She shrugged. "Why don't you believe me, damn it?" He stood up and moved away.

"Because, I can't trust you. You know it's hard for me to trust and you've made me doubt you more than once. I can't be around you Alex. I need time."

"How much time?" he asked gruffly. His eyes glazed. He loved her, really loved her, how could she doubt that?

"I don't know," she told him honestly.

"That's not good enough," he grated out.

She licked her lips. "A few months? A year?" She shrugged.

"Did you just say a year?" he burst out incredulously.

"Yes."

He stood staring at her for long timeless seconds. Then something in his eyes changed and Merissa didn't know what it was.

"You don't love me anymore do you?" he asked her sullenly, pain making his throat tighten.

"Yes I love you." She touched his arm. "I'll always love you. But I can't be around you just yet Alex. Please try and understand," she pleaded.

He smiled sadly down at her and then lifted her chin to kiss her. The fire that he had made in her insides all those months ago, blazed into renewed life. It was almost as if kerosene had been poured on them. She wanted to kiss him again and again, and it showed. Only he looked at her tempting mouth but moved away instead.

"I won't wait around forever," he warned as he let himself out.

For days Jonas had parked under a Poinciana tree watching the apartment from the road. She hadn't been there in days and he'd made inquiries, the girl was in hospital. He had to see her again just to make sure.

She was dead, he had seen to it. It couldn't have been her…could it? Her eyes looked just like the coolie gal's; he could still see them now, the fright in them, just like that night. It had to be her and if it was…what was he going to do about it?

He continued to watch for several days and saw when her boyfriend – or whoever the man was – left with a suitcase. He hadn't seen him since. Good. He needed to plan.

※ ※ ※

Vanessa drove up Alex's driveway and climbed out of her vehicle with a huge bunch of flowers in one hand and a box of chocolates in the other. Alex had just finished watering the garden around the back and was walking around to the front with the green hose trailing behind him. He grumbled something intangible, and then put a tight smile on his face.

"Hi. Is Merissa home?" Vanessa asked innocently. She knew full well that the little bitch was staying at another place, but Alex hadn't told her that.

"She's not here Vanessa and you shouldn't be either," he told her tightly.

"Why not?"

"Because if you'd like me to be blunt, Merissa doesn't like you and that little stunt you pulled the last time you were here didn't help the situation. Now if you don't mind, I have some grass to water." He walked pass her.

"Well can you at least give her these for me? I'm sorry about the baby," she told him, wanting to make love to him right there on the grass.

"Put them inside. I'll pass the message on," he said dismissively.

She put them on the kitchen table, then walked out. "How about dinner tonight," she suggested lightly.

"Not tonight," he answered, not turning around.

"Tomorrow then…or maybe we can have lunch sometime. It's been a while since we had lunch," she continued.

Alex turned to stare at her. Why doesn't she leave? What if Merissa was to come and see her here? He needed to get rid of her and fast. "Ok, lunch one day next week," he told her and turned back to water the grass.

Vanessa got into her car and drove off smiling. Now it was time for plan B.

Chapter Thirty-Six

"Cymone? What do you think of this? Will it work?" Merissa asked her friend across the table. They were at Toby's house and Cymone was helping her plan her next line.

"Put the green against that saffron." She tilted her head. "No, put it with the burnt orange instead."

Merissa looked at the two colours and agreed.

"We make a great team, Miss Miller," Merissa grinned at her friend.

"Yes we do," Cymone agreed. "Now, how about a break?" She stretched her arms high above her back and arched her back deeply before shaking out her shoulders.

"Alright, but I just need to finish this pattern first. Go ahead, I'll be right behind you."

Cymone waited for Merissa for over twenty minutes, before she emerged and poured herself a cup of coffee.

"You're working too hard," Cymone pointed out. Only last night she had told Toby the same thing.

"No, I'm not, and besides, I have to finish this."

"But he did give us three months, not three weeks. Meri, you've got to slow down. You've not been well, remember?"

"I'm fine Cym. What time is it?"

"Twenty-five after five. Why?"

"I need to pick up something next door before Alex gets home." She stood up and pushed back the chair.

Cymone shook her head sadly. What had happened to her friends?

"I'll be right back!" Merissa called from the driveway and hurried over to his house, with her key.

The place was a complete mess and she remembered that she had given Aggie time off. Dirty dishes were piled high in the sink. Meat had spoiled in the fridge, and wrinkling her nose, she wrapped it in newspaper and threw it away.

She went upstairs but avoided looking into their bedroom. She went straight to her sewing room instead, got the sketches she needed and a few other things – just in case – and was just about to leave when she saw flowers on the dining room table.

She looked at them suspiciously, then picked up the card.

Love Vanny.

Scolding hot rage churned up her insides, her eyes blazed.

"You bastard! You hateful, hateful, bastard!"

She picked up the flowers and tore the petals off and threw then on the floor. She locked up quickly. She just needed to get away from him. The lying deceitful louse! She stormed up his driveway and he almost ran her over as he turned into it. He swerved out of her way and parked the car quickly, just in time to see her round the corner and go over to Toby's house.

"Merissa wait!" he yelled. He hadn't seen her in weeks.

"What for? You and I have nothing further to say to each other. It's over Alex. Over!"

He jumped the fence and grabbed her. "What's wrong now?" he asked. He was tired, hungry and all he wanted was for his wife to come back home to him. Not this.

Her eyes flashed angry tears. "There's no hope for us Alex. I give up." Her shoulders slumped.

A chill went through him. "What's wrong Meri?" He looked at what she was carrying and knew she'd been in the house. But what had upset her?

"I was going to clean up this evening," he told her quietly.

"Don't you try to be funny with me Alex York! Tell me something? Do you and Miss Powers use the same florist?" She spat the words at him.

He looked at her with stunned confusion. What was she saying to him? Florist? "I don't understand?"

"I understand perfectly. I'll be over to remove the rest of my things in the morning. I'd appreciate if you weren't there and another thing, you can have this back." He watched in horror as she took off her wedding ring.

His confusion was quickly replaced by anger. She was not leaving him without a fight! But first he had to know what had upset her so much to want to do something like this to them.

"Like hell I will!" He shouted back at her and with a suddenness that took her by surprise, flung her over his shoulder and strode over to his house.

"Put me down, you arrogant bastard. Put me down!"

He did. Once he had the door closed behind them and he was leaning against it.

"What is this all about?" he asked her calmly, too calmly.

"Those!" She pointed to the floor.

"Flowers?" He looked at her in confusion.

"Yes flowers!"

"You're getting upset over flowers. Flowers that were sent to you?"

"Sent to me? Don't make me out to be a fool Alex because I'm not. Read the damn card!"

"Calm down," he told her quietly. He'd forgotten about the flowers Vanessa had sent to her. "Vanessa sent them for you, only she didn't know you weren't here, so she left them with me. What are you getting so upset about?"

"Read the card damn it!" she yelled at him marching pass him to retrieve the card on the floor and then stood in front of him, fuming as he read it.

"Love Vanny. So?"

"Don't you play smart with me! Why is Powers sending me flowers? I hate her guts and she hates mine…"

"She does not," Alex cut in, "they are for you and some chocolates in the fridge."

Merissa was silent. Was he telling the truth? She watched him closely, he looked as though he was. She changed tactics.

"What was she doing here?"

Alex made an impatient gesture, he'd had enough and he sighed deeply and took off his tie before replying. "She came with those the day you kicked me out…"

"I didn't kick you out, I asked you to leave," she corrected.

"Whatever…it amounts to the same thing. I was watering the garden and she came. I asked her to put them in the house. I'd forgotten about them until now." He looked at her dejectedly.

"I guess I shouldn't be coming in here without your permission," Merissa mumbled.

"Damn it Meri! This is your house! You can come and go any time you feel! You're my wife, this is your house!"

She watched him open the fridge and take out a beer.

"Aren't you having any dinner?" she asked before she could stop herself.

He didn't look at her. "No."

"Why not?" she persisted.

"Why do you care?"

That stung.

"I'd best be leaving," she mumbled, looking everywhere but at him. She had no right to care about him anymore.

"No!"

With a swiftness that left her breathless, Alex caught her against him and kissed her deeply. His mouth was hard and demanding, forcing her to open to him. For a moment she resisted, but his hands, his beautiful hands, curved her body into his, pressing her into the hardness of his arousal.

She moaned low in her throat and kissed him back, matching his hunger, greedy for his kisses. Her shorts pooled at her ankles, she kicked them off, wrapped her legs around him and without releasing her mouth, Alex plunged into her. It was fast, it was hard, it was explosive, and it had never been like this. With a scream, Merissa came and could only hold on tight as Alex, with a few more powerful thrusts, followed her.

For timeless minutes they stayed fused together until Alex shifted to look at her. His eyes were dark and vulnerable. Merissa had never seen him like this. He released her and then turning around, adjusted his trousers. When he turned back around Merissa was dressed.

Her mouth was swollen with his kisses, her hair in a dark tangle around her face. She looked lost. Neither of them was willing to question the madness that had just overtaken them. She bit her lip and simply shook her head as a single tear slipped down her cheek as she turned to leave.

Alex didn't know how long he stood in the doorway. He looked down at the round piece of metal that was now imprinted in his palm. She'd given him back his ring. She was leaving him slowly but surely and he didn't know what to do about it.

Chapter Thirty-Seven

Vanessa looked over the hotel balcony and watched the tiny cars below. Things weren't going the way they were supposed to and she was very upset about it.

"I'm going to kill the stupid bitch!" she exclaimed loudly.

She wanted to hurt her and take everything she had – money, name, beauty and now her man. Alex was hers!

She flung the cigarette she was inhaling over the balcony and watched it fall. That's exactly how you'll be Merissa Walters! You're going to fall. And I'm going to be the one to push you.

Vanessa stalked inside the hotel room and poured herself a generous glass of vodka in seething frustration.

The expected knock came and she glared at the door wishing she could ignore it and pouring herself another drink, swallowed it down quickly before reluctantly going to answer it.

"What took you so long?" Roger Coombs asked as soon as the door opened, pushing his way aggressively inside.

She didn't answer but looked at the man with open distaste instead. He was wearing his brown suit again. It seemed he had only the one suit. His shoes were caked with red mud, and he left a trail of dirty footprints on the carpet.

"Pour me a drink," he ordered. "A double," he went on to demand.

Vanessa did what she was told and waited impatiently over on the couch. She just wanted the evening to end. Give him whatever he wanted, then be out of here.

They had been meeting like this, two nights a week for the past few weeks. He hadn't signed with her company yet and she was beginning to wonder if he ever would.

"You look bored, my dear. Liven yourself up!" he roared as he came beside her and pushed his hand roughly up her skirt.

You are not my man, Alex is, she fumed silently, whilst forcing a moan from her lips.

She smiled at him sweetly then took his hand, pulling him up with her.

"Let's go into the bedroom," she cooed falsely.

I want to get this over with as fast as possible. Ten minutes max, she calculated silently.

"Move!" He thundered above her moments later. "Move!"

She arched her back and moved her hips.

"Yes…yes," he panted. "Just like that."

Just as she thought he might be coming, she held onto him tightly and dug her long nails into his flabby bottom.

"You bitch!" he yelped in pain and slapped her hard across the face. He was shocked by what he had done and opened his mouth to apologise. Then a sly glint came into his eyes. He slapped her again.

She looked up at him stunned and he smiled chillingly, before hitting her again and again. All the while exciting himself as he sexually assaulted her. Finally he released her and lay beside her breathing deeply.

"Keep up like that and the contract will be yours," he chuckled, before going into the bathroom to take a shower and change back into his suit.

"Breathe a word about this to anyone and you'll be history," he warned from the doorway. "Be here with the contracts next Sunday about eleven. I'll be at my in-laws all day, I can't make it any earlier," he said.

"One day they will all pay." Vanessa vowed to herself. "One day. Hunter, Merissa, Coombs, all of them," she promised. "One day, starting tomorrow," she promised as she curled into a foetal ball, bruised and battered, feeling nothing.

Chapter Thirty-Eight

Merissa drove up the hill, very slowly and very carefully, hoping that the Pyrex dishes she had on her back seat, weren't spilling over onto her upholstery. She'd made Thomas his favourite Italian dish, Lasagna, hoping it would cheer him up.

"Thomas!" she yelled, as she walked into the kitchen and placed the food on the counter.

"Tommy! I'm here!" she called out again, walking with bare feet up the stairs and into his bedroom. She'd almost closed the door again when she saw the flume of smoke from his cigar burning in an ashtray on his private balcony.

"Tommy darling you must be going deaf, or are you just ignoring me?" she asked him jokingly, as she walked around in front of him and collapsed on the lounger beside his. "Tommy wake up. I brought you your favourite," she said and reached over to shake his hand.

His arm fell off the armrest and dangled down lifelessly to the floor.

Merissa stared, afraid; afraid to look into his face as unexpected dread raced darkly through her veins, strangling her.

"Tommy?" she whispered, her voice quivering with apprehension.

The world stood still and watched as she slowly moved and knelt in front of him. Her whole body trembled as she took his hand. It was still warm as she held it to her face. Silent tears fell as she held his hands tightly and put her head in his lap.

"Bye Thomas," she whispered a long time afterwards. She kissed him gently, then smiled through her tears. "Bye Tommy. I love you." She pushed back the stubborn lock of silver hair that always fell into his eyes one last time.

Tears blinded her as she held onto him. She wanted to leave him and get Joseph, yet she couldn't bring herself to leave. She reached for the lit cigar that was smouldering slowly. She lifted it to her nose and inhaled the rich aroma deeply, before putting out the fire.

"Bye Tommy. I love you."

She looked at him one last time before leaving the room.

Joseph had just entered the house and was watching her walk down the stairs towards him, the smile on his face slowly dying as he looked at her closely.

Oh God no! Not now. He wasn't ready! He knew, even before she told him. He knew.

"He's left us Josey," she said softly, before rushing into his open arms.

They held each other for long moments.

"Merissa we've got to make plans and you have to call Alex," Joseph told her sometime later when he'd said his own farewell to his life long friend.

Merissa nodded and reached for the phone.

"Alex it's me," she said when he answered on the third ring. "It's Thomas…" she broke down, unable to go on.

"Merissa are you up the hill honey?" he asked urgently, knowing what had happened.

She nodded.

"Are you at the house, honey?" he asked her again gently.

"Yes," she finally said.

"I'll be right there." He hung up.

Merissa put down the phone feeling an inward calm float around and inside her. She took a deep breath, the air smelt of Cuban cigars and Old Spice.

"Goodbye Tommy," she whispered.

The funeral was held the following Thursday, in the afternoon. The weather was perfect – sunny, with a cool breeze. Finally, the thousands of flowers were removed and the elaborate silver and blue coffin lowered into the ground. Merissa, Joseph and Alex all walked up to the edge hand in hand and each threw a single white rose onto the lid.

Merissa watched the men shovel the dirt onto the coffin with detached horror. It was then that she realised the finality of the gravel. They were covering her father, her friend; she would never see him again. She began to shake violently and reached out blindly. Everyone's face became a blur. Alex stepped behind her just in time to catch her as she fainted.

Several days later she was jogging up the driveway, sweating and panting; she could see Alex in the distance. He was sitting on his car waiting for her. He had barely left her side since the phone call.

It had been good having him around. She would not have managed on her own, having to cope with all the funeral details and her own grief, as well as Joseph's. She didn't want to be apart from him ever again. Thomas would have wanted her to give her marriage another chance. Alex smiled as he watched her make her way tiredly towards him.

"Hey," she said, standing in front of him, trying to catch her breath.

"Hey yourself," he grinned. The past couple of days had been good between them. "Feeling better?"

"Yes, much better," she replied truthfully.

"I brought dinner," he told her. He was careful with what he said to her. Things were going so well between them right now, he didn't want to say the wrong thing.

"Oh yeah what?"

"Chinese."

"Mmm. Sweet and sour pork?" she asked, her eyes sparkling in delight.

"Yep, and a whole bunch of other stuff. Whoever it was that said food was the way to a man's heart forgot to mention yours," he teased. Then immediately wished he hadn't as her beautiful face became still and serious.

"Ha, ha, ha. How about I invite myself over to your house Sunday night. Make you dinner, then breakfast the following morning?" she suggested breathlessly.

Alex looked at her silently, not daring to believe what she had just said.

"Well do you want me to or not?" she prompted anxiously, biting her lip.

"What are you saying?" he asked cautiously.

"I'm asking if you'll take me back."

Alex's heart surged against his rib cage. "Are you saying what I think you're saying?" he asked quietly, hope sparkling in his cocoa brown eyes.

"Yes," she replied simply.

He grinned and pulled her gently between his legs.

"Can I tell you what I want for dinner?" he teased as he held her tighter, ignoring the dampness of her t-shirt. It just felt so good to hold her again.

"You my darling have no choice, me for your appetizer." She kissed his eyes. "Me for your main course." She kissed his nose. "And a very sweet and delicious me for dessert." She kissed him long and deep.

"I've missed you," she whispered against his mouth when she finally released him.

"I've missed you more," he replied, before taking her mouth with his and sliding off the car to stand. "Where's Joseph?" he asked when they came up for air.

"Mrs. Dobbson's."

Alex's eyes blazed and he swung her easily into his arms and marched into the house.

Saturday was the first time she went off the hill in days, she had a lot of things to do. But first she went to the apartment to pick up a few things and the daily newspapers that had been crammed into her letter box. Afterwards she went and picked up Amber, knowing the little dog must be lonely. It was almost six in the evening, before the two of them headed back up the hill.

That same evening, Jonas followed the white jeep. He'd almost blown his cover when she'd driven into the apartment complex this morning just as he was driving out. It was definitely her. The newspapers had been a great help. Even though he didn't read well, he had managed to get the information he was looking for. Merissa Walters, now York, adopted daughter of one of Jamaica's wealthiest men, who was now dead.

Jonas' body had shaken with hungry anticipation. She was rich, very rich. He wasn't going to kill her again after all. Oh yes. Blackmail was a beautiful weapon! Miriam Evans! Very beautiful. He smiled in satisfaction.

When she had turned off the main road and into a posh looking estate, he pulled over and switched off his engine before getting off and peeping through the bushes. She'd stopped in front of an impressive three storey house. This must have been where the rich man lived, he thought gleefully. He waited until dark, before riding closer to the house. He heard a car turn in just as he was about to go and peep in the windows. Quickly he turned his bike around.

"You lost boss?" The man driving the fancy car asked.

"Yes sa. Me did tink dis was a road. Sorry," Jonas said quickly, holding his head down.

"No. This is someone's driveway – mine – so take yourself off," Alex said to the man who smelled as bad as he looked.

"Yes sa. Tank yuh sa." Jonas bobbed and rode off smiling.

Alex entered the house and was pleasantly surprised to find Amber sniffing around with excitement.

"I'm home," he called out. One thing he hated with big houses, you never knew where everyone was.

"Honey I'm in the kitchen," Merissa called out.

"Hi," he said, coming up behind her and kissing the nape of her neck, delighting in the smell of that very first perfume he had bought her almost a year ago.

"Hi yourself. Do me a favour and look beside my handbag and bring me the black scandal bag please."

"Ok."

Alex left the room to search for her bag. It was where she usually left it only it was hidden by a whole load of last week's newspapers.

Alex glanced at the headlines then froze.

Pictures of him and Merissa were on the cover – their wedding picture. Only they had been separated with a jagged scissor cut. The headline read:

JAMAICA'S MOST LOVABLE COUPLE, BREAKING APART. ALEX ENJOYS EXTRA CURRICULAR ACTIVITIES WITH OLD FLAME WHILST MERI MOURNS LOSS OF BABY AND FATHER.

Alex saw red. Anger made him crumple up the paper tightly in his fists as he read on.

Who had given them this kind of information? Had Merissa seen it? He looked towards the kitchen, hearing her singing happily.

"Alex, can't you find it honey?" she asked.

"Yeah, I'm coming," He looked around worriedly. She couldn't have seen it yet!

He hid the paper behind the chair then went back into the kitchen. His mind was ticking. Who would do something like this to them?

Chapter Thirty-Nine

"See you later at home, sweetheart," Alex told Merissa as she walked out to his car with him. It was the following morning. She would be coming home to him today.

She grinned, wrapping her arms around his neck and standing on tiptoe to kiss him.

"What time will you be back?" she asked, knowing he had a seminar to go to.

"About six," he replied, kissing her nose. "I can't wait to drag you upstairs and make love to you, in *our* bed," he stressed with a grin. Then he stilled as though remembering something important. He held her head and stared into her eyes.

"Merissa my love, we need to have a serious talk tonight," he added seriously. "Something you need to see."

She nodded.

"I'll be there. Promise."

Merissa frowned as she walked back into the house. What did he need her to see? She needed to tidy the house. Everything should be alright now, she thought. They had started rebuilding their marriage. It was amazing how things had almost turned out between them.

Thomas would have been proud of her.

With upstairs clean, she walked downstairs with Amber quick on her heels, and then went into the kitchen to wash up the breakfast dishes. Amber wandered into the living room. Half an hour later Merissa walked out of the kitchen, ready to clean the living room only to stop dead in her tracks.

"Amber!" she yelled, looking for the dog. "Amber!"

She couldn't believe it. Amber had found her newspapers and had chewed parts of it up all over the Persian rug. Amber, she noticed, was nowhere to be seen. Sighing, she bent down and picked up the torn papers.

She was just about to throw them into the rubbish bin when a piece of a picture caught her eye. Standing up straight, she moved to the table and put the torn pieces together. It was a wedding picture of her and Alex. She put more pieces together to read the article. Waves and waves of scorching hot rage swept through her body.

She sat in stunned silence. Why was he doing this to her? Why did he marry her? She read on and found the answers – her money, her name and all the frills that went along with it. His affair with Vanessa was public knowledge; it showed a picture of the two of them together enjoying a candle lit dinner.

"Oh God!...Oh God...No!"

Dashing the tears aside she went into fast action. It was over. He could have Vanessa but he was never going to touch her again! Damn him! Damn him for doing this to me! She fumed.

"I loved you! I really loved you!" she cried aloud, as she drove down the hill at break neck speed.

Vanessa drove up Alex's driveway, then stopped midway. His car wasn't there. She gripped her steering wheel in frustration. She'd been trying to find him for the past few days but he hadn't been in. Later she had heard he'd been sleeping at Merissa's house. Green jealousy had swamped her since then. How was she supposed to work on her plan if he wasn't around? She had even toyed with the idea of going up to their house on the hill but had changed her mind. She didn't want a confrontation, yet.

Turning her car, she was about to leave again, when Merissa pulled up looking all distressed. The two women looked at each other hard, both sitting in their respective vehicles.

It was Merissa who moved out of the way first, then got out of her car and slammed the door. Her eyes still holding Vanessa's.

Vanessa followed and calmly walked over to the younger girl. They stood almost nose to nose in the middle of the driveway. Vanessa gleefully noticed the newspaper article in Merissa's hand. Well, well, well, things might just work out my way after all she thought smugly.

"I'm sorry you had to find out that way Merissa," she told the girl with false sincerity, flicking her long braids over her shoulder.

Merissa looked at her willing herself to stay calm. She was not going to give this woman the satisfaction of seeing her crumble. Nor, was she about to bring herself down to her level, by scratching her eyes out, even if that was what she really wanted to do.

"Where's Alex?" she asked calmly.

"He went out." Vanessa leaned even closer to her. "I'm really sorry. We didn't mean for you to find out like this." She shrugged apologetically. "He was going to tell you about us tonight," Vanessa finished, not realising she had struck gold.

Merissa paled, remembering Alex had wanted to talk to her this very evening. As much as Merissa tried to control herself, her hand connected with the other girl's cheek, leaving her stinging finger marks behind. Vanessa was shocked, she really hadn't expected the little bitch to hit her, but before she could hit her back, Merissa had walked off and was opening the front door and had gone inside, slamming it behind her.

Vanessa put her own hand to her cheek, feeling several welts on it. She smiled. Alex was hers.

Alex walked out of the conference ten minutes early and bought Merissa a large chocolate sundae before heading home. Home, he thought. His wife would be waiting for him and he couldn't wait to take her upstairs, or even on the kitchen table and make love to her in their own house. It had been months since he'd slept in their bedroom.

With growing excitement he pulled into the driveway. Her car wasn't there. Thinking nothing of it, he glanced like he normally does, over at Toby's house. They were still in Trinidad. Quickly he switched on Toby's house lights for him, before going home.

Alex stepped into his house, noticing it looked a little odd. He left the door open as he looked around. Things were missing. Merissa's collection of crystal had been taken off the shelves and so had her favourite picture frames. Something wasn't right. Had they been robbed?

Walking around quickly, it dawned on him that it was only her things that had been taken. A strong surge of apprehension chilled him. Panicked, he rushed through the kitchen intending to go upstairs, when several papers on the table caught his eye. It was the newspaper article and picking it up, he realised she had found it before he could talk to her. She must have assumed the worst. He sat down suddenly on the chair, defeated.

How could he forget about that damn article? By the looks of it Amber had found it behind the chair. Merissa had taped it up. A smaller piece of paper slipped out of the side and he picked it up. It simply read:

There are too many pieces to pick up.
It's over.

Merissa.

Alex began to shake, before leaping up the stairs and going into her wardrobe. Nothing. Everything was gone. Nothing was left. But damn it to hell! He was not letting her go! Vanessa pulled up, just as he had closed his front door.

"Hi Alex," she called out cheerily through her car window, not noticing the look of bitter hatred on his face as he walked menacingly towards her.

She got out and stood with her car door open between them.

"What have you done?" he snarled, grabbing her arm and dragging her away from the vehicle.

"I don't know what you mean," she told him, frightened. He was looking at her in a strange way.

"I think you do. You little bitch. The article!" he growled in uncontrolled fury.

Vanessa decided to play innocent.

"What article?" she asked, trying to free her arms. He gripped her harder then shoved the article in her face. "Oh, is this what's getting you upset?"

He gripped her harder still.

"I read it the other day. I tried to get a hold of you but you weren't around. I thought…" She didn't get a chance to finish.

"You gave them this story, didn't you?" he ground out through clenched teeth.

"No." He gripped her arms even harder and shook her. She made a small frightened sound. "Yes. I gave it to them…" she admitted quickly.

He let her go in disbelief and stepped back, stunned.

"But I did it for you, for us. Alex we were meant to be together…"

"Woman, have you gone mad!" he swore violently. "Merissa is my wife. I love her!"

"You only think you do, darling." She held onto his arm, as he made to move away. "I love you, always have. Don't you see? We can be together now." She looked at him smiling and played with the buttons of his cotton shirt, before reaching up to kiss him.

He shoved her away and she stumbled.

"I've never hit a woman before," he warned darkly, "but if you don't leave this house…this very second…I will. You have never meant anything more to me than a friend, I never loved you and I never will. Merissa is my whole life. Not you! Get out!" She made no move to leave. "I said get out!" he yelled angrily at her, then walked slowly towards her.

Vanessa couldn't move. "I love you!" she shouted at him. "I've always loved you. She can't love you as much as I can!" She began to cry. "We were meant to be…"

"You'd better leave Vanessa," he said with amazing calm, his anger tightly reined into a stiff coil. "I won't be responsible for my actions otherwise. I don't *ever* want to see your lying face again!"

She looked at him hard then squared her shoulders and lifted her chin in glinting defiance.

"You'll live to regret this Alex," she told him icily, "You and the rest of them will live to regret treating me like this, using me!" She got into her car and roared up to him. Alex had to jump out of the way before she ran him over. The girl was crazy!

Chapter Forty

Vanessa waited expectantly for Roger Coombs. He was late as usual, but tonight she didn't mind. Alex was on her mind. After her anger had settled and she had several straight Vodkas, she felt much better. She didn't realize what a fool he was. How could he say that he loves that witch? Obviously he really didn't realize how deeply he loved her and how much she loved him, but one day he would.

"Hi Cym, it's me."

"Oh, hi Meri. Where are you?" asked Cymone through the faint static on the phone.

"Miami," came the simple reply.

"Still?"

"Yes. How did it go in Trinidad?"

"Wonderful. We have Nathan with us now. He and Toby are outside playing football." She smiled as she glanced out the window, and saw her two men playing happily together.

"That's great Cym. So everything is ok with you two then?"

"Almost."

"What do you mean by almost?"

"Well, you're our best friend and you're not here. When are you coming home Merissa? Alex told us you've been away for almost a month. It's Christmas in two weeks."

"I know. What else did he tell you?"

"Nothing much really. Meri, the boy is frantic with worry. You need to speak to him."

"And say what exactly? Cym whilst you were away, I almost moved back in. Only this newspaper article came out and gave a very descriptive piece on my life, including the miscarriage that only you guys and Vanessa Powers knew about, and how very close my so-called husband and the tramp is! Cymone I'm not going back to him."

"Oh Merissa, I'm sorry and I feel like such a rogue. Here I am, all happy and content and there you are all sad and miserable."

Merissa smiled sadly. "That's the way it goes sometimes."

"Come back Meri. Nathan needs to meet his godmother."

"Godmother?"

"Yes Godmother and besides, we'll be having his fourth birthday party for him in a week, you've got to be here."

Merissa bit her lip. "Ok. Actually, it was the birthday party part that convinced me. Can I speak to Toby please?"

"Sure, hold on a minute. Merissa I miss you. Oh I almost forgot. James Eddison is back and he wants more of our stuff. You have to come back. Toby and I can't manage it on our own."

Merissa smiled. "I'll be back. Don't tell Alex that I'm coming, will you."

Cymone sighed. "No, I won't. Let me get Toby for you."

Merissa waited on the line for her friend. She really missed them and was dying to meet her godson.

"Hey you, aren't you coming back?" Toby said, as soon as he picked up the phone.

"Yeah, in a couple of days. How's it been?"

"Just great. I'm a dad," he pointed out proudly.

"Well congratulations. Just legalize it all now please."

"I'm working on it," he told her with quick confidence. "Alex has been looking for you. He's been to Miami twice."

Merissa was surprised to hear that and the silence told Toby the same thing.

"Oh."

"Merissa," he sighed, "you have to come back and deal with it. You can't stay in hiding…"

"I am not in hiding!"

"Then what are you doing over there? You're my friend and I've known you a very long time and I've never known you to run away from your problems."

"There's more to this than you know Toby," she told him icily. "Alex has hurt me. Really hurt me. I really don't think I can forgive him this time." Toby could hear the tears in her voice.

"Look, Merissa, Alex told me everything. Not even Cym knows what's been going on. He told me about the article. He's been equally hurt by it all. But he's hurting even more, because you never gave him a chance to explain."

"There's nothing to explain. The paper said it all."

"You can't possibly believe that."

"It's true," she stated stubbornly, "I don't want to see him Toby," she told him, her throat tightening. "All I've had was a few short weeks of happiness with him, then it all went away. I'm not going to compete with Vanessa Powers. She wants him and it seems she'll do anything to get him. I can deal with that. Only Alex doesn't love me enough to put her in her place and to stop flaunting her around. I can't live like that."

Toby was silent.

"He's hurting Merissa," he told her.

"It's his own fault," she told him stubbornly.

"The two of you need to talk."

"Yes, but not yet. I don't want to see him Toby. Don't you understand! Why don't you understand?" she questioned.

"I understand, but I also know you're needed over here. Poor Cym is working her ass off trying to fill our orders. We went into a partnership and your services are needed, so get your ass back over here before the week is out!"

She was silent for a long time, torn between guilt in not helping them and her peace of mind in staying in Miami, away from Alex.

"Alright, I'll be on a flight on Thursday and I'd appreciate it if you could open up the apartment, no, let Joseph know I'll be coming home and staying up by the house."

Toby grinned. "Sure, anything else?"

"Not that I can think of right now."

"What flight will you be on?" he asked, ready to go next door and tell Alex.

"If you think I'm about to tell you that Toby Chase, you're sadly mistaken. I'm not sure, and besides, I'll take a taxi from the airport."

"But that will cost you a small fortune," he argued.

"Maybe so, but I can afford it."

Toby sighed loudly. "Alright, it's your choice, I would have gladly picked you…"

"Sure Toby," she cut in, "and cart Alex along with you. Let us work it out please. Don't interfere." As soon as she said it she regretted it. "I'm sorry Toby, I didn't mean that the way it sounded."

"It's ok. Just make sure you bring my son a present and call us as soon as you reach home. Alright?"

"Ok. See you Thursday."

"Yep. Bye."

"Bye."

Jonas was busy pacing in his tiny room feeling very frustrated. He'd been trying to track the gal down but it was as though she had disappeared off the face of the earth. She wasn't at the apartment or at the house on the hill, and he needed some money now. As soon as he could get some out of her, he'd go back home to Paradise Pass and live a happy life.

He sat down heavily on his narrow bed. I want to have her one more time, he thought, licking his lips. I want to hear her scream and plead with me to stop, just like before. I want to feel her as a woman.

Grinning, he reached for his glass of rum. Yes, it's been a long time since she felt a real man.

It's good to be home Merissa thought, as she made her way back down the hill. Joseph and Mrs. Dobbson hadn't asked any questions – thank God – but she knew she had some explaining to do to Joseph who'd looked at her sadly when she had asked if she could live at the apartment.

She pulled into Toby's driveway and avoided looking over the fence. But her eyes refused to cooperate with her brain and she found herself looking anyway. Alex's car was parked on the grass, glistening in the sunlight. He'd just washed it.

Climbing out quickly, she rang the little bell Cymone had installed and waited for her friends.

"Look Nathan, it's Aunty Merissa!" Cymone told the chubby almost four year old boy she was holding in her arms.

"Hi Nathan," Meri said after kissing his cheek and hugging her friend.

"Say hello to Aunty Meri, Nathan," Cymone encouraged her son.

"Meri, Meri, Meri!" The little boy began to bounce happily in his mother's arms, his mop of light brown curly hair flopping around madly.

"Oh, no, I've just started him on a new word," Cymone groaned good-naturedly.

Nathan wriggled out of her arms to go to the floor where he promptly ran off to find his daddy.

"You're looking well Cym," Meri told her friend, as they walked into the house.

"Thank you. I can't say the same to you though. You've lost weight."

"I have? I didn't realize."

"Sure..."

"Didn't I tell you to call me when you got home?" Toby demanded as he reached to kiss her on the cheek. "You've lost weight," he told her unnecessarily.

"Toby? Is that you?" Merissa gasped, stunned, noting the shiny bald head and the absence of earrings.

"Yes it's me," he replied, embarrassed, avoiding Cymone's scowl.

"He came home without hair the other day. I got the shock of my life!" Cymone said tightly.

"She doesn't like the change even though I did it for her," he admitted.

Obviously this was a bone of contention between the two of them. Merissa simply smiled.

"Meri I hope you're not tired, because we have to start working right now. Hungry?"

"No. Mrs. Dobbson made me something to eat not so long ago."

"Why doesn't she and Joseph get married?" Cymone asked, as she watched Nathan reach up and turn on the TV. "Nathan, you know Mommy doesn't like when you do that. Don't be naughty."

Nathan turned and looked at her but turned it on anyway, then turned and grinned.

"Meri, Meri, Meri!" he shouted happily, before noticing that his Daddy had left the room and ran after him.

"I hope you realize that you have to help me plan his birthday party," Cymone said, watching her son fling himself at Toby in the other room.

"Doesn't anyone ask me anything these days? I'm just ordered around," Merissa teased. "When is it anyway?"

"Next Saturday."

"Ok. Now show me the things James wants to be done."

They worked late, making plans and chatting. Alex's name never came up and she was very grateful. She couldn't deal with that right now. She just wanted to settle back down and go on with her life and try and find that flower man, before he finds her.

Chapter Forty-One

The days flew by and Merissa was thankful that she had the party to plan and orders to fill. She even babysat a couple of times for Cymone and she loved every minute of it. She always became anxious when it was time for Alex to get home from work but thankfully, he hadn't been over and she hadn't seen him.

She pulled up and parked on the road, smiling when she glimpsed the hundreds of helium balloons and the bright, bouncy castle jerking about madly on the grass. Toby had invited about thirty kids to the party from all over the neighbourhood, but at least forty-five were there. Cymone must be pulling her hair out by now.

"Aunty Meri, Meri, Meri." Nathan ran happily into her arms and squeezed her tight.

"Hi young man. Happy Birthday."

Nathan pointed to his child size Jeep. "Mine."

"Well isn't that nice. Where's Mommy?"

"Inside."

"Ok, go and play with your friends whilst I help Mommy ok?"

He grinned, "Ok, Aunty Meri, Meri, Meri." Then ran off.

"Does he always say your name in threes?"

Merissa spun around to find Alex behind her with his hands stuffed in his pockets.

She gasped and took a step back. She wasn't prepared for this. He looked much too good. Her senses rocked as she took in his casual jeans and long sleeved white shirt casually rolled up on his forearms. Like her, he'd lost weight. His face, though still handsome, had a certain hollowness about it.

They looked at each other for long seconds, before a child crying nearby pulled her out of his warm hypnotic gaze and she walked away. She picked up the child and escaped into the house. Alex stood watching her go, his heart still hammering against his rib cage. He'd wanted to take her in his arms and hold her and never let her go. It had been almost a month since he had even seen her, and it looked as though she wasn't about to talk to him either, but she still wanted him. Oh yes he'd noticed the fluttering pulse at her throat and her nipples suddenly noticeable through her shirt.

❦❦❦

Much later, all four adults sat on the grass in exhaustion. The last child had just been picked up and the place looked liveable again.

"It went well Cym," Merissa told her friend tiredly.

"Yes it did. Thanks to you. But Meri? Can you do me one last favour?" Cymone pleaded.

"Sure."

"Put my little man to bed for me. I can't move another muscle."

They all grinned and looked down at the sleeping child in her arms.

"Pass him over." She stood and reached out to take him, holding him lovingly to her chest as she walked into the house and put him down on his bed.

She stayed with him for a while, stroking his head and for the first time in a long time, thought about the baby she had lost. Getting up, she turned to find Alex standing in the doorway watching her.

"Hi."

"Hi."

"The party was a success," he went on.

"Yes it was." She stood still. He was blocking the entrance and if she tried to pass him, she'd only end up touching him and that would be a mistake. Even now, her body was responding to him and he wasn't even near. "I'd best be going now," she told him.

"Stay a while."

"I can't, I have a lot to do tomorrow and I need a good night's sleep."

Alex shrugged but didn't move. She'd been avoiding him all day and this was the first time they'd been alone. He needed her alone for a while, just so he could talk to her and touch her.

"Your hair's grown," he told her, looking at the way it fell pass her shoulders.

"I know. I'll be cutting it shortly."

"Why?"

"Because I can't manage it."

"Oh." He took a step towards her and she backed up.

"I really must be going Alex," she told him, stepping back again and feeling the cool wall against her back.

"I'm not keeping you here Merissa," he told her quietly.

She squared her shoulders and her chin went up. It's true, he wasn't, but why wouldn't her damn legs move! She looked into his eyes and he took another step towards her and brushed her shoulders with the back of his fingers. He didn't speak but just looked at her deeply, speaking to her with his eyes and watching her skin quiver beneath his touch. Just as he bent to kiss her, Nathan made a sound and they both looked at him. Merissa used that distraction to quickly step pass him and leave the room.

Later that night, she lay in bed looking up at the ceiling thinking of Alex. They can never be alone together. Her reaction today was a typical example why. She would have let him kiss her, then she'd be begging him to take her to bed. No, they must never be alone together again.

She sighed and rolled over. It was almost two in the morning and she still couldn't fall asleep. She got out of bed and padded across to her balcony. She opened the door and sat on the swing, deep in thought.

She missed him or rather her body missed him. The way he made love to her, touched her and made her feel cherished. It had been a long time since she had felt that way and her body was responding to the memories.

Just then, the faint buzz of a motor bike in the distance caught her attention and she stood up to gaze out onto the road. She was just in time to see the small red tail light of it go through her gate and move onto the road. She knitted her brow in thought. Why would someone be down here this time of night? Was someone watching her? She gazed around into the darkness. Could the flower man have found her? It had to be Jonas.

She had tried looking for him and had even contemplated hiring a detective, although she really didn't want to do that. The newspapers might get a hold of it and she couldn't afford for that to happen. She had to find him herself. But what would she do when she did?

Moving quickly, she locked the door securely.

Jonas was a very happy man. Miriam had fallen into a habit of leaving the house around nine in the morning and going to her friends' house, where she would work until eight or so and then head home. He noticed the old man had gone away and that she was alone in the big house. She also had a terrible habit of leaving the upstairs balcony door open in the evenings, whilst she took a swim.

Oh yes. Over the Christmas holidays he'd be paying her a long overdue visit.

Chapter Forty-Two

Christmas day, she awoke to an empty house. Joseph and Mrs. Dobbson had gone off to spend the holiday weekend at one of the all-inclusive hotels on the North coast. They had felt awfully guilty about leaving her to spend the holidays alone, but she had told them she'd been invited down to Toby and Cymone for Christmas dinner. Only then did they feel a little better.

She got out of bed and went down the stairs where she had a lonely breakfast, showered and then put on a blue patchwork skirt and a white frilly peasant blouse. She left her hair down in a mass of black curls and added large loop earrings as her only jewellery. She looked and felt like a gypsy – unsettled.

She really wanted to stay at home alone but her beloved godson wanted her there.

Later in Toby's kitchen, Merissa was helping Cymone glaze the ham when the door bell rang.

"Get that for me please," she told her.

Merissa wiped her hands, then moved towards the door, stepping over several toys along the way.

"Hello Merissa. Happy Christmas," Alex said to her as she opened the grill for him. She knew he was coming but she couldn't do anything about it. It wasn't her house, nor was it her place to voice her objections.

"Hi, same to you." She moved away quickly.

"Where's my tiger?" he yelled, as he walked into the T. V. room and flung Nathan up in the air.

The child was laughing and screaming loudly.

"Those two are going to spoil my child," Cymone said with a groan. "Did you see that thing Toby bought him for his birthday?" She didn't wait for an answer. "My poor boy can't even steer it properly yet, much less drive the thing."

Merissa smiled.

Several hours later, after putting a reluctant Nathan to bed, Toby announced that he and Cymone would like to go to the movies and if they didn't mind baby-sitting for a few hours.

Merissa looked at him in shock.

"Sure," Alex said before her objections came out of her mouth.

Cymone and Toby left quickly after that, promising they wouldn't be too late.

Merissa's eyes narrowed. It was so obviously planned!

"You all planned this," she told Alex when the other two had left.

"Actually, I had nothing to do with it."

"I don't believe you."

"You don't believe a lot of things that I say."

"That is so true," she pointed out sarcastically.

He sighed but made no comment.

"We need to talk," he eventually said.

"Yes we do, but not tonight."

"When?"

"When it becomes convenient."

"And when will that be?"

"When I can deal with it."

He was silent.

"I didn't know about it Merissa," he told her softly.

She jumped off her chair. "I don't want to discuss it right now. It's Christmas and I don't want to fight." She went and poured herself a glass of Sorrel.

"I don't want to talk about it tonight, Alex," she told him again on her return.

He nodded in acceptance.

"Here." He held out a small package wrapped in blue and white shiny paper and had a pretty blue bow on the top.

"What is it?" she asked.

"Take it and open it. It's for you."

"Why would you do this?" she asked him, feeling her cheeks flush.

"Because it's Christmas and your last name is still York." He looked at her sadly.

Timidly, she reached out and took the small box from him, careful not to touch him. She put the present on her lap and looked at it wearily.

"I didn't get you anything," she told him with some regret. It was Christmas after all.

He smiled. "My Christmas present is having you here with me right now. This is all I wanted." He looked into her eyes and smiled tenderly.

Merissa felt her insides melt and bit her lip trying to control the tears that threatened. Slowly, she unwrapped it, folding the paper neatly before opening the box.

"Oh Alex, it's beautiful." She touched the gold unicorn.

"Do you like it?" he asked nervously.

"I love it."

"Let me put it on for you." He moved and sat behind her and fastened the chain, whilst she held her hair up out of the way. Alex took his time and brushed his finger purposely against her neck more than once.

"Turn around and let me see it," he told her.

She turned. He touched the chain with his finger, moving it down until he reached the pendant that rested just above the curve of her breasts. Their breaths mingled.

"Thank you Alex," she whispered softly. "It's very beautiful."

Slowly, she moved forward and touched her lips to his in a gentle whisper of a kiss. They had barely touched but the heat gushing between them was overwhelming.

Quickly, she broke the contact and stood up. "I'd better be going now."

"Why?"

"Why?" Merissa asked frowning in confusion before she realized Alex was talking to her and not her inner voice. "Well, because it's getting late and no one is home."

"You'll be alone?"

She debated whether to lie to him.

"Yes."

"Why don't you stay down here tonight?" he suggested reasonably.

"You know I can't do that."

"Stay until Toby and Cymone come home and then I'll drive behind you up the hill. It's late and I don't want you driving up there alone. Ok?"

She thought for a while. She really was scared of being alone, especially since Jonas was back in her life. If only she could find him!

"Ok."

He smiled and then went to look at Toby's collection of DVDs.

"How about a film?"

"Sure."

They settled down, Alex sitting on the cushions again, whilst Merissa lay on the sofa. It wasn't long before she was struggling to stay awake. She woke with a scream.

"Hush Meri. It's ok, it's ok honey," he told her.

"I had that dream," she told him unnecessarily.

"I know."

She let him hold her for a long time, before getting up to wash her face. Toby and Cymone had come back, just as she left the bathroom.

"Thanks Merissa," Cymone told her friend.

"You're welcome."

"I hope you're coming to help us finish the leftovers tomorrow," Toby told her.

"I'm not sure yet. I really must be going."

Alex stood up and picked up his keys.

"Thanks again. Goodnight."

"Night."

She waited for Alex to drive out with his own car, before she got into hers, then drove off in front of him. She wished he could stay with her. She wanted to be loved again, held again. Things had gone so wrong between them.

Chapter Forty-Three

Jonas walked around the house. The girl was very stupid he thought yet again. She'd actually left her balcony door unlocked and all he did was break into the work shed by the pool and get out a ladder and here he was, living like a king.

He'd been here all day and was making himself comfortable, drinking expensive liquor and helping himself to the food in the fridge. The gal had it good.

Walking around, he switched off all the lights and went into her bedroom to lie down on the bed.

It wasn't long before he heard cars outside.

He was surprised to see her unfaithful, no good husband outside with her. Now what? What if he comes in? He peered out worriedly again. They were talking, then he kissed her and watched as she went inside before driving off again.

Jonas sagged in relief.

Swiftly, he went inside her closet, hid behind her clothes and waited for her to enter.

Merissa kicked off her shoes and locked the front door securely. The place smelled weird. She stopped and breathed in deeply. The place smelt different. Shrugging, she checked all the windows before going upstairs and into her bedroom.

She went to her dresser to replace her earrings and touched the pendant Alex had given her. It was truly beautiful, she thought yet again. I only wish…

She decided she had to get her man but before she chased after him, she decided to freshen up. She walked into her bathroom, brushed her teeth and removed her makeup before going into her closet. It was then that the same smell hit her senses. Wrinkling her nose, she looked on the floor for a dead rat or something.

Just as she turned and started to walk out again, she was grabbed by the hair from behind.

"I'm back, Miriam," Jonas told her cheerfully whilst he covered her mouth with his dirty hand, capturing her screams in the palm. He walked her out of the closet and over onto the bed, where he pushed her down and followed behind her.

Forcefully, he turned her around and sat on her legs laughing.

"You can mek as much noise as yuh want, but yuh know an' mi know, that no one nuh deh ere!" He laughed again and Merissa struggled against him in fright. "Mi gwine soon gi yuh sinting fi scream bout," he threatened.

Slowly, he removed his hand, cautioning her to be quiet with his filthy, stained finger. Merissa took a deep breath and let out the loudest scream she could ever make.

"Bitch, yuh nah ere!" He slapped her across the face. She continued to make noise.

He pulled her up roughly and dragged her out of the room.

"Gi me di money."

"We don't keep money in the house," she told him fearfully, as he dragged her down the stairs by the hair.

"Mi seh, fi gi mi di money!" He yanked her back against him and ran his free hand over her breasts. "Yuh fill out nice gal, very nice."

Merissa twisted in his arms and punched him in the face before jumping down the last few steps and running into the kitchen. He chased her but stopped as soon as she turned around with a kitchen knife in her hand.

"Put it dung," he said calmly. His beady eyes narrowed. This is going to be a fun night, he thought. She made no move to put the knife down. "Mi seh fi put the rassclaat knife dung!" he swore loudly at her, but she just looked at him in a crazed way, her chest heaving.

"I'll kill you for what you did to me. I swear I'll kill you."

"An' all dis time mi did tink you did enjoy it." He laughed then made to grab her.

She side stepped and sunk the knife into him.

"Jeezas Christ yuh dead." He looked down at his cut. Luckily it was his arm that she caught. She stood stunned for a moment as blood squirted out. It was a moment too late.

Jonas brought his fist down hard on her jaw. She saw bright white spots before her eyes and she had to shake her head to get rid of them.

"A wah yuh tink dis is? Dat mi a joke bout dis. Gal, yuh come from nowhere, you're nutten but a bloodclaat coolie whore. A whore!" He hit her again and again, backing her up into a corner.

She stayed on her feet. Something told her that if she ever fell to the ground, he'd probably kill her. Rape her first, then kill her. She fended off most of his punches as best she could, all the while thinking how she could escape.

Glimpsing a large piece of yellow yam beside her, she reached for it, stood up and brought it down over his big head. The yam broke in half. They both looked at it.

He laughed.

Using the piece she still held, she pushed it into his eyes. He swore but let her go.

"Bitch!"

Merissa picked up the blood soaked knife again and ran out of the room. She found the spare house key, which was always kept in the living room cabinet and she leapt to the main balcony door knowing she wouldn't make it to the front door. She fumbled with the keys, dropping them twice.

The door finally opened and she tackled the grill. She looked over her shoulder and saw him watching her with one eye.

"You bloodclaat coolie gal," he swore viciously as he walked slowly towards her. Blood was pouring through his fingers as he covered the deep slash on his arm, dripping onto the floor.

She pressed her back to the grill and watched hopelessly as he came closer.

"You come near me and I'll kill you. I'll kill you!" she screamed at him.

He walked slowly towards her. "Yuh can't get weh. Jus show mi di money and mi will leave. Show mi di bloodclaat money!" He was getting impatient.

"We don't keep money in the house!" she told him again, stalling. Her arms were aching from holding the knife out in front of her for so long.

He lunged for her and wrestled the knife out of her hand, holding it to her throat as he dragged her by the hair once more and moved to the living room and stood in front of a framed picture of a yacht.

"Open di safe!" he demanded. He was tired of playing games and wanted to enjoy her body for a while. But not before he got the money he knew was in the safe he'd found earlier.

"I don't know how," she lied.

"Yuh tek mi fi a fool." He yanked her hair and twisted it around his fist painfully. "Mi bin watchin yuh fi a very long time. Mi no when yuh tek yuh bath, eat, sleep an tek a shit. Mi no everyting." He pushed his face into hers and licked her cheek.

His foul breath made her heave.

"I don't know the combination," she told him quietly.

He pulled her hair even harder then pushed his hand up her dress and groped her.

"No, please." She began to cry. "Please don't."

"Yuh like dat?"

"No!" She tried to kick out at him but he moved away, then pressed her to the wall, grinding himself against her bottom.

She was sickened to feel his stiff arousal against her.

If she didn't give him what he wanted, he'd rape her.

"Alright I'll open it, but on one condition."

"Yuh can't come gi mi conditions. Yuh nuh look like yuh inna good situation to come gi mi condition! Now open di rass safe!"

The alarm! She forgot about the alarm. All she needed to do was open it and not press the digital numbers inside to release the alarm. The police will call and she wouldn't answer it and they'd come up!

She just had to survive the wait. She slumped as though defeated. He moved her back a little bit but didn't release her. Slowly she opened it and stood back. He smiled.

"Tek it out," he told her, "an put it in dis." He took a black plastic bag out of his pocket. "How much is it?" he asked greedily, licking his thick lips as she slowly filled the bag.

"A couple hundred thousand." This was the petty cash safe as Thomas was fond of calling it. The main safe was elsewhere in the house.

He grinned widely.

Just then the phone rang. He looked at it, debating whether he should let her answer it. He walked over to the phone, dragging Merissa with him and was about to lift the receiver when it stopped ringing.

"You have just made a very big mistake," Merissa told him. "You see that thing over there?" She pointed to the little box inside the vault. His beady eyes narrowed on the box.

"That little thing is an alarm device," she explained with a bloodied grin. "You see, if I don't put in the combination, the police will call and guess what." She smiled wider through her tears and pain. "They just did."

Jonas looked from the safe to the phone frantically, hoping it wasn't true. He wanted to have his fill of her first before leaving!

"Yuh bloodclaat bitch!"

He brought his fist down hard on her cheek and she fell to the floor. He kicked her viciously in the stomach with his booted foot before leaving the room quickly and opening the front door. Merissa rolled on the ground in agony but with the last of her strength managed to get up and stumbled to Thomas' office. She found his gun still in the drawer in his desk.

She staggered outside just in time to see Jonas running towards his bike. She stood in the middle of the road and aimed. "This is from me you miserable bastard," she whispered and pulled the trigger, time and time again.

Jonas screamed out in pain, stumbled to the ground and then tried to pull himself up. His bike was nearby. He had to get to his bike! Grasping his bleeding leg he scrambled to his bike and took off. He heard the distant blare of sirens coming up the hill. He trembled with fright. He moved swiftly into action and drove up the hill, instead of down. He didn't know Red Hills but all these roads must lead to somewhere.

Merissa sat down in the middle of the road, the gun still posed in the air. She was crying and her finger kept pulling the trigger. "You bastard, I hope I killed you," she whispered to herself over and over again.

The neighbours rushed out of their houses firing questions at her.

The police found her like that, kneeling in the road, wet and bleeding, surrounded by people who hadn't thought to help her get up from off the cold ground.

"Mrs. York?" One of the uniformed men spoke gently to her, whilst taking the gun out of her hand. "What happened?"

"I've just been robbed, but I shot him. He went up through the hills on a motor bike. I shot him."

The officer spoke to several of his comrades and soon three cars and several motor bikes left and went to find Jonas.

"Are you hurt? Do you need to go to the hospital? he asked kindly.

She shook her head.

"We need to take a statement."

She nodded and then collapsed into tears, reaction finally setting in. Minutes later, she was sitting down in the living room, telling the kind officer what happened and insisting that she didn't need to go to the hospital.

"You can't stay here tonight Mrs. York. Do you have anyone you can stay with?" he asked when she had finished.

She nodded and explained.

"Ok, we'll take you down. Do you need anything?"

"No."

Half an hour later, they pulled up in front of Toby's house. The gate was locked, so she started banging on it.

"Who dat?" Toby called out cautiously.

"It's me Merissa. Toby please come quick!"

Several seconds later, a bedraggled Toby and Cymone were at the gate.

"She's been robbed," the officer told them. "The thief hasn't been apprehended yet, so we thought it safer if she stays here."

"Ok officer. Thank you," Cymone replied in shock.

"Thank you Officer Andrews," Merissa told him kindly.

"Your father was a very good friend of mine. Don't worry Mrs. York, we'll catch him." He gave her an encouraging smile.

The policeman left and the three of them walked into the house.

"I'll call Alex," Cymone said. "Toby, make her a cup of tea. She's still shaking."

"Ok. Merissa it's safe here now."

"You don't understand, he's been watching me. He knew everything about me!" She began to cry harder.

As soon as Alex walked into the room she lurched to her feet and into his arms, holding on for dear life.

"Oh Meri," he rubbed her back, as she clung to him, then moved her to the couch. "What happened?" he asked after a while, looking at her battered face.

She told him the whole story, but not that it was Jonas. Toby and Cymone were still in the room.

"He knows where to find me. He knows that you're my friends." She looked wide eyed at Cymone and Toby. "I can't stay here."

"Of course you can," they both replied.

"You can come home with me," Alex told her. Their eyes met.

She nodded.

"I shot him." She tried to smile through her tears.

"Good for you." He smiled back at her, then pulled her to him and held her.

"Come on, let's go." He stood up when she had finished her tea.

"Thanks you guys," she told her two friends.

They just smiled sadly. Why did everything always have to happen to Merissa, they thought silently to themselves and locked the house up, extra carefully.

Chapter Forty-Four

Next door, Merissa sat in the TV room and waited for Alex to come back with a glass of brandy for her.

"This has been a hell of a Christmas," she told him jokingly.

He didn't answer but sat down in the lazy boy instead, his eyes serious.

"It was Jonas," she told him quietly.

He looked at her alarmed.

"Are you sure?"

"I could never forget a man like him. It was him."

"But how did he find you?"

"There's been a lot of publicity on me recently..." She left the sentence open.

"Oh dear God." He pushed his hands through his hair.

"He took the money Alex, but I don't care about that, but he'll be back. If they don't find him or if he's not dead, he'll be back."

"They'll find him. Did you tell the police that you know who he was?"

"No."

"Why the hell not!" he exploded.

"Because then my whole life will be public knowledge. I don't want that. It would hurt me too much. I got this new identity for protection from them all."

"Oh honey. We'll find him before they do and believe me, I'll kill him. Did he hurt you?"

"Only a little. He was going to rape me again Alex, if I hadn't told him about the alarm. He would have raped me again!" She began to cry.

Alex went over, picked her up and carried her upstairs to their bedroom where he cleaned her cuts and grazes with antiseptic.

"I'm going to make a hot bath for you, ok?" He placed her on the bed. Merissa noticed that it was still made up.

"Ok." She tried to smile but failed miserably.

Several minutes later, Alex came back with a large fluffy towel and began to undress her. She closed her eyes. He was very gentle, yet his touch didn't ignite the fires inside her. She heard his sharp intake of breath and opened her eyes. He was looking at her stomach.

"He did this to you?" He looked at the large, dark, boot shaped bruise on her stomach.

She nodded.

"The man dies!"

The warm water did wonders to her and she felt herself relaxing.

"You'll have to put on one of my shirts," he told her through the door.

"Ok." She reluctantly stood up, dried herself off, and then wrapped the towel around her. Alex was waiting for her on the bed, his eyes skimming over her, looking for more injuries.

"Do you need anything else?" he asked kindly after she put on his shirt.

She shook her head then looked outside.

"Everything always happens to me at this time in the morning," she told him sadly, watching the first rays of dawn dilute the darkness of the night.

"Go to bed. Tomorrow is going to be a long day." He turned the sheets down and waited for her to settle herself, before kissing her gently on the forehead and leaving the room.

Jonas drove his little bike out onto the main road. Red Hills definitely had too many roads. Parking under a street light, he looked at the knife cut. It had stopped bleeding but the leg wound would need attention and fast. Luckily the bullet had gone straight through.

Just then a police car passed and he ducked as though examining his bike tire.

What a rass mess, he thought.

He couldn't stay in town, she would tell them who he was and then they would come looking for him. He had to go to Paradise, at least for a short time. No, she will send them there as well. He took a deep breath; he'd be able to hide out at home though. He knew his territory well.

"Yes," he said aloud. "I'll go home."

Turning his bike around, he headed for the North coast. He couldn't risk driving along the South coast. They might have set up road blocks for him.

It wasn't until two weeks after the incident and she had completely healed, that Merissa broached the subject that had been on her mind.

"Alex?"

They were around the back picking oranges.

"Yeah?" he replied as he stretched to pick an orange that was just out of his reach.

Merissa took a moment to admire his athletic body, naked, except for cut off jeans.

"We need to talk."

"I told you that a long time ago."

"I can't stay here much longer."

He stopped what he was doing, and looked at her inquiringly. She was sitting on the grass hugging Amber as though the dog could protect her.

"It's too dangerous to go anywhere else. You'll be alone," he pointed out bluntly.

Everywhere she went, he went with her and they never left the house unnecessarily.

"I know but Alex I want to go and find him."

"Don't be ridiculous."

She wasn't expecting to be put down so bluntly and lifted her chin defiantly.

"I'm dead serious," she replied through tightly clenched teeth. "I have to find him, don't you see he's ruining my life! I can't go anywhere and feel safe anymore. I'm always looking over my shoulder! I need to find him and only I know where to look."

"You want to go back to Negril?" he asked in amazement, putting his bag of oranges down and sitting beside her.

"Yes."

"You're not going. He's too dangerous. Let the police do their job, Meri. They'll find him."

"They won't without my help," she pointed out.

"They will," he went on, "it's only been a couple of days."

"But I can't sleep, work or do anything without thinking that he could be watching me! I hate this. I hate living here with you. I hate having to look over my shoulder. I want to go home!"

"It's not safe."

Her words had hurt him but he tried not to show it. "If you go back up the hill, I'll be coming with you."

"I don't want you with me!"

He got angry, as much as he tried to remain calm, his anger escaped.

"You are still my wife! And if I say that you won't be leaving this house, you won't!" he ended on a furious note.

Merissa looked at him with her mouth open. She was stunned at the passionate violence of his reaction.

"I will not stay here Alex," she said calmly but firmly. Her lips pressed together tightly.

"Why the hell not. Have I touched you?" he asked and answered his own question. "No. I've kept my distance. I love you damn it – though only God knows why – I want you to live here. This is your home!"

"I can't stay here. What if your woman comes here again?"

"What do you mean here again? And what woman?" Alex demanded hotly.

"Forget I said that." She tried to get up but he held on to her. "Alex, I don't feel comfortable here, it's better if I left."

"You must have a better reason than that."

"I do. I don't trust myself. I want you," she admitted softly.

His stormy expression changed to one of pure unadulterated pleasure.

"What's wrong with wanting your husband?" he asked, his cocoa eyes warm and soft as marshmallow.

"Because, you don't love me."

"I do love you Merissa," he stated firmly, "only you don't want to admit that you've been wrong. Me too, I've been blinded, but I do love you and I want us to start over again." He inhaled deeply and captured her hand raising it to his lips.

"We can't," she whispered as she tried to control the spasms of desire shooting down her body.

"Why not?"

"Because…" She licked her lips and looked at him. "Because I don't want to be married anymore."

Her answer knocked the very breath right out of him.

"You don't love me anymore?" he asked hoarsely, his throat constricted with suffocating pain.

"I love you," she admitted adamantly, "Only I just *don't* want to…if that makes any sense."

He half smiled, his eyes dark and sad.

"You never gave us a chance to…" he started.

Just then, Vanessa walked around the house in a very short pair of red shorts and a black sparkly halter top. Her long braids were swinging from side to side in rhythm to the exaggerated sway of her hips.

"Hi. Oh I'm sorry Alex, I didn't know you had a…" she gave Merissa a derisive look. "Guest," she finished sweetly.

Merissa bristled, then stood up. "How can I give you a chance when you haven't given *her* up yet?" She looked at him, hurt beyond belief.

Alex stood up and held onto her wrist tightly knowing that if he released her, she'd leave the house, probably for good.

"Vanessa, I told you never to come over to this house," he said darkly, a flint of steel making his voice hard and emotionless.

Merissa had never seen him look so enraged.

"Oh Alex darling, stop pretending," Vanessa grinned.

"Get out Vanessa," he grated as Merissa tried to tug free.

"But I thought you wanted me to spend time with you. You did say you'd be rid of her." She pouted her lips and fluttered her eyelashes. "He can get awfully lonely you know," she confided. "Especially, when you went away. He needed someone and of course, I was available," she continued with a syrupy smile.

"Merissa don't beli…" Alex started to explain.

Vanessa stepped closer to him, her body screaming intimacy.

Merissa couldn't take it anymore.

"I'm sure he was," Merissa chocked, willing the tears not to fall.

"Get out!" he ordered, as his control slipped and hit the grass. "You and I never had anything and never will! I told you once and I'm telling you again!" he warned. "This is my wife, I don't want you."

"Sweetheart don't do this," Vanessa cried desperately. This wasn't going as planned. Merissa should not have been here! "I've brought the papers. See?"

She dug into her bag and pulled out a set of official looking documents, shoving them at Merissa to see.

"Divorce papers Merissa. It's a good job I'm a lawyer. I drew them up myself," Vanessa explained charmingly.

Merissa felt her world tilt. She held herself rigid. She turned hurt filled eyes at Alex.

"Don't believe her Merissa," he said before releasing her to grab Vanessa by the shoulders and shake her violently. "Get the hell out of my house before I call the police!"

Vanessa smiled up at him, then flung herself into his arms, wrapping herself around him, so that he couldn't move.

"Don't do this Alex!" she begged. "I love you. You can be free now. I have the papers. You can sign them now and then we can get married, just like we planned."

"No!" He tried pulling her off him as he saw Merissa pale then run into the house.

"Merissa!" he called out to her frantically. "Merissa!" He tried to wrench himself free but Vanessa was holding him in a deathly demented grip. "Get the hell off me!"

"Don't worry sweetheart. She's gone my love. You have me now," Vanessa soothed.

He heard his car rev up and screech out of the driveway.

He looked down at Vanessa in disgust. The woman was crazy. She had a funny unbalanced look in her eyes and he realized she could be capable of many things. He had no choice but to play along until he could get rid of her.

"Yes I have you now." He forced a smile to his lips.

She grinned and ran her hands up around his neck and lifted herself to kiss him.

"Not here," he said quickly and held her shoulders stiffly as he moved to go inside. She allowed herself to be pulled along, but she still didn't release him.

He'd gotten as far as the kitchen door when she pushed him against the door suddenly and tried to kiss him; her hands moving over the zipper of his jeans. Alex shoved her away violently. She fell to the ground. He stepped over her, ran through the front door, and jumped the fence to Toby's.

"Toby, lend me your car!" he yelled through the grill.

Toby came out tossing the car keys and looking puzzled.

"It's Meri, she took off!" Alex explained.

"Here," Toby put the keys in his hand.

"Thanks."

Alex drove around for hours looking for her. It was getting dark and he knew it was time to give up.

He was thankful to see Vanessa had left and Toby had put on his house lights for him when he arrived home.

"Toby!" he bellowed over the fence.

"Alex?" Cymone came to the grill. "She just called."

"Where is she?" He held his breath.

"Miami." She watched as he seemed to stagger. "She said your car is parked at the airport." She didn't tell him that she also said that she's not coming back.

He didn't say anything but looked out into the darkness solemnly.

"I'm sorry Alex," Cymone said quietly.

He shook his head, before walking slowly into his empty house, his heart in shreds.

Chapter Forty-Five

Round about that same time, Vanessa sat watching Roger Coombs take off his clothes. What a fat slob, she thought. Tonight would be the last time she would do this. Tonight she'd be going home and making her dear husband dinner. Then she'd make sweet love to him, running her fingers over his young, solid muscles.

As she thought about her husband, her hand trailed down to her breast.

"That's right my girl, get yourself all hot and ready for me," Roger Coombs said, chuckling as he walked over to the bed in his plaid underpants. "Come over here. I'm ready for you," he ordered.

She walked over to the bed and lay down beside him. She closed her eyes and thought of her husband. He had kissed her today.

Her husband was above her, inside her and she moaned and bit his shoulder.

He collapsed over her.

"I told you never to do that!" Roger Coombs accused angrily. "Do you want my wife to see your marks?" he remarked, looking at his shoulders.

Roger Coombs? Why was she with Roger Coombs and where was Alex?

He got up and went into the bathroom and looked at the rest of the marks she had left on his body. He marched back into the bedroom. Vanessa watched as he went over to his trousers and drew out the silver buckled leather belt he always wore with his brown suit. He began twisting it around his fat fist as he walked menacingly towards her.

She'd almost made it to the bathroom when he grabbed her and flung her down onto the bed and using her own tights, tied her down. He shoved a sock in her mouth. He raised his arm above his head and brought the buckle end of the belt down on her. Vanessa tried to scream out but the muffled sound was never heard. At some point after taking her again, he left.

He'd been beating her for what seemed like hours and when she slowly turned her head and saw the time, she realised it was much too late to cook her darling husband dinner tonight.

Two days later, Vanessa walked into her building. She knitted her brow as she stood waiting impatiently for the elevator. Everyone was looking at her. She consciously touched her face, where a large bruise had developed on her jaw. She turned around and realised they really were staring at her – the doorman, the security guards and even people who worked on different floors. What was going on? Turning her back on them, she waited for the elevator with her head held high. They can all go to hell. She didn't need them! She didn't need any of them! She had her darling Alex!

The elevator whisked her up to her floor. It was ten thirty and the place was busy, but everyone stopped what they were doing and watched as she walked towards her office. Her head still held high, she moved proudly to her door and stopped dead. Her name plate! Where was her name plate? She looked around wildly for her secretary.

"What's the meaning of this?" she asked her calmly, flicking a glance at the door.

"It was Mr. Hunter's orders, ma'am," her secretary answered with a smug expression.

Vanessa stormed into the older man's office. He wasn't there.

"Where is he?" she demanded.

"Speaking to Miss Webb," her secretary answered as she smiled with satisfaction.

"And who the hell is Miss Webb?"

"Your replacement." She smiled openly.

Vanessa slapped her. "Don't you talk to me in that tone of voice! Get back to work!"

She pushed pass the stunned crowd and went into her office.

"Get out," she told a young girl who was sitting in *her* chair and clearing out *her* desk.

"We've been expecting you Miss Powers," the girl said then reached for the phone. "Jennifer? Would you please call security, we have a slight problem."

"Where's Hunter?" Vanessa asked, walking menacingly towards the desk.

"Right here." The old man strode into the room and closed the door with a slam.

"You're fired Powers." She stood still.

"May I ask why?" she asked calmly. Too calmly.

"You messed up the Coombs account."

"I did everything you told me to do."

"Yes, but he's not satisfied. You have two seconds to leave the building."

"I'm not going. After all I've done for you? You can't do this!"

"Oh I can Powers. In fact I already have. Miss Webb, I'm sorry for all of this," he apologized, then turned to Vanessa.

"Miss Webb here went all the way through law school sitting up! This company needs a good mind and someone with integrity and honesty. You have neither of those qualities."

Just then the uniformed security guards came in.

"Please escort Miss Powers out of the building and make sure she never puts her foot back in it!" He turned to the other girl and began talking as though Vanessa was no longer there.

It was happening again! They were all using her. Just using her! Her uncle, Hunter, Roger Coombs…

Fuming with hatred, she grabbed a heavy brass owl paperweight and slammed it down on the back of his fat head.

She heard a scream. The old man turned to look at her with a stunned expression on his face, then his eyes glazed over and he fell to the floor. Miss Webb rushed around the desk, feeling for a pulse.

"He's dead," she confirmed.

Vanessa smiled and calmly allowed the guards to hold her.

Several weeks later, a clean and relaxed Jonas was sitting out on his brand new boat called the Rum Runner II, smoking a Cuban cigar. The wonders of money, he thought. All of a sudden he had all these friends and women vying for his attention. He hadn't paid for sex in weeks!

He chuckled. What a life! He didn't need to be out fishing, he was a rich man now. But he missed the big booms. Throwing a stick of dynamite over the side just for the hell of it, he watched it blow and waited. There was nothing like fishing, nothing like a good old explosion.

People at Jack's had told him that his family had left the area shortly after he had left. The house stood empty. He didn't care. He was staying at an all-inclusive resort in Negril. He looked over at the sight of the explosion. Nothing came up. Not that he was going to haul in any fish. He just wanted to see the blood. Sighing, he brought up anchor and motored further out. He could see Cousins Cove in the distance.

The police – it seemed – had given up their search and as time passed it became obvious the little coolie gal had never told them who he was. That was good, very good. When his money ran out he'd simply go back and get more.

He reached under his seat for his silver flask filled with white rum. What a glorious life, he thought again. He released the anchor again and took several sticks of dynamite out. He placed three on the floor carefully, whilst he lit a bustle and threw it out. He sat down and waited for the boom. None came. Disappointed, he re-lit his cigar, dropping the match.

Too late, he heard a sizzling sound. Hypnotically he watched the flames rapidly eat the fuse. He had nowhere to go. Surrendering, he watched the flame burn. He was going to miss the biggest boom of all.

From the beach at Cousins Cove fishermen stood from fixing their nets and watched the fantastic display of huge orange fireballs rolling into the blue sky. Loud explosions sounding like thunder broke the silence before everything settled and became still.

"Who was dat?" one toothless fisherman asked another.

"Jonas. Me did see im go out not so long back."

"Should we go an see?" another fisherman asked.

One of them laughed. "Fi wat? His eye balls an teet?" He was still laughing as he walked away, that was the fifth fisherman killed by dynamite this year. Why did they never learn? He shook his head.

Alex drove slowly along the highway deep in thought. It was late and he was miles behind. At this rate he wouldn't reach Negril until early tomorrow morning. He loved driving to Negril and looking at the beautiful scenery but tonight it was dark and dismal.

"Damn it!" he shouted aloud. It was starting to rain heavily. Maybe I might use the cottage after all, he thought to himself. Just yesterday he'd gone to say goodbye to Joseph who had insisted on giving him the spare key in case he got tired on the way down. Alex had told him he'd be fine, having driven down on a number of occasions for the past few weeks. What he hadn't admitted to Joseph was that he couldn't face the memories.

The last time he'd been there he was a happy, just married man, enjoying the time alone with his wife. Merissa had filed for divorce shortly after arriving in Miami, where she had gone into hiding.

He still hurt. Still loved her. They hadn't even been married a full year before…

Alex's mind trailed as he automatically turned left at the bottom of the hill and flipped the wipers into fast speed. It was pouring with rain and lightening was flashing. He still couldn't believe the day he'd been in a board meeting and Mary had called him out, saying something about it being urgent. A man was standing beside her desk in a bad fitting old fashioned suit. He'd had an envelope in his hand. Alex knew who he was without having to be told. He'd walked into his office in a daze, the envelope scorching his fingers. He'd felt as though he was in another dimension, another world and was watching from above, everything in hazy motion. The rough brown envelope sat on his desk for ten minutes before he could even pick it up and when he did, he'd died.

She was asking for a divorce.

He sat stunned for what seemed like forever. She hadn't even had the decency to phone him before hand. He'd been furious and hurt and he still was. For several days, he'd been trying to get a hold of her, until he drove up the hill and Joseph told him she was still away. She hadn't even given him a chance to explain.

In all his life – not even when his family had died – did he remember feeling like this. She was his life, his world, his everything.

Much later, being guided by a watery moon and sweet memories, Alex pulled into the driveway. It was dark and he had to leave his car lights on whilst he dashed through the rain to open the front door. A strong wind had picked up. All he could hear was the sound of the crashing waves mixing with the heavy sheets of rain and the clapping of thunder.

Running to his car once more, he grabbed his bags and briefcase and ran back to the house, slamming the door shut against the dark, angry elements.

Merissa woke up suddenly. She wasn't a light sleeper, but something had woken her.

Sitting up, she waited. Nothing. She lay against the pillows and tried to drift back off to sleep. Sleep was a luxury she missed. She hadn't had a good night's sleep in weeks. The nightmares had suddenly stopped a few weeks ago and the same quirky feeling of uneasiness had suddenly disappeared around the same time. She felt free, completely free of her past, the noose no longer around her neck. She seriously doubted Jonas would be back. She had a strong gut feeling.

Sighing again, she snuggled down and tried to make herself comfortable. The wind outside made an eerie sound and she was a little afraid. She'd only arrived from Miami this afternoon and had had all intentions of staying at the Treasure Beach Hotel, but on impulse, had stopped at the cottage first to see if anyone was staying there. It was empty. She decided to stay. She needed to tell her memories goodbye.

She planned to spend several days before heading back to Kingston to rebuild her life. She'd neglected it for so long. Thomas would have been ashamed of her. Alex, she thought, must have started his life with Vanessa by now. Merissa closed her eyes as a familiar shaft of pain shot through her. She couldn't bear to think of her husband with that evil woman; sleeping with her, caring for her.

One lonely tear slipped from her eye and she dashed it away with an unsteady hand. She had shed enough tears this past year. She was not going to cry again. She didn't want to hurt anymore.

The sound of a door closing made her sit up again suddenly. This was not her imagination. Gathering her wits about her, she wrapped her dressing gown around her securely and got out of bed as quickly and as noiselessly as she could. She picked up a wooden tennis racket from behind the bedroom door. Slowly, she steeled through the door and pressed her back against the cold wall of the dark corridor.

The kitchen and porch lights were on. She was sure she hadn't left them on. Or had she? She inched her way up, listening intently for any sound. The fridge was opened and then closed, and then she could have sworn she heard a soda bottle being opened. What kind of thief was this?

Letting out her breath, then holding it again, she glided over to the wall beside the kitchen door, the tennis racket posed way above her head and waited. She didn't have to wait long, the thief walked out casually as if he owned the place and she brought the racket down with all her strength, hitting him on the back of the head. He groaned then went down. Merissa raced pass his lifeless form and ran to the phone, dialling the emergency services with petrified hands.

The phone kept ringing, typical she thought. The one time she needed the police, they didn't answer the phone!

She turned and looked at the thief; she couldn't see his face but his body looked vaguely familiar. He was clad in black from head to toe.

"Oh yeah Merissa, a familiar thief!" she said out loud.

"Damn it! Pick up the phone," she yelled frantically into the mouth piece.

The thief groaned again and shifted.

"Oh God!"

Petrified he would wake, she put the phone down and went to stand over him. The tennis racket raised in position again, above her head.

"Oh my God...*Alex*?"

She was beside him in a flash, cradling his head in her lap.

"Alex? Come on wake up. Wake up!" She tapped his cheeks firmly. At least she hadn't killed him.

She gently released him again and went into the kitchen. She wet a towel and wiped his forehead with it while trying to wake him.

Alex thought he was hearing things. Someone was calling him but somehow he couldn't open his eyes. Then he was wet and a person... Merissa? Was it his Merissa calling him? No, she was overseas. She'd left him. God his mind was foggy!

"Alex, please I'm sorry, wake up," Merissa urged frantically and was back to tapping him on his face. What if he wouldn't regain consciousness?

Alex forced his eyes open and looked up and saw the face of his love inches from his. He reached up to touch her, just to make sure she was real. His finger tips came away wet with her tears.

"Meri?"

"Oh thank God. I thought I might have killed you!" She beamed down at him in relief. He moved to get up but she pushed him gently down again.

"Don't get up yet," she told him softly and stroked his hair.

"My head," Alex grimaced as he touched the back of his head, feeling a large lump.

After a time, he staggered over to the couch to lay down. He watched as Merissa poured him a glass of Brandy. All traces of gentleness gone to be replaced by watchful stoniness as she glared over at him.

"What are you doing here?" she asked coolly, one elegant eyebrow raised.

He looked at her and blinked several times before answering.

"I know this is your house, but Joseph said you were in Miami and as I needed to drive down to Negril he offered me this place."

"Well as you can see, I'm back and I'd appreciate it if you left."

Alex stiffened. Why did she hate him so much?

"It's almost two in the rass morning! There's a damn storm going on outside, you almost killed me and I'm not going anywhere!"

Merissa gave him a look of pure hatred then stood up stiffly, her chin raised, her eyes cold. "You go or I go."

"What the hell is this, you can't even be in the same room with me anymore? I'm still your husband and…"

"You haven't been in a long time," she shot back.

"What the hell is that supposed to mean?"

"I'm sure you can figure it out."

Merissa was close to tears. She didn't need this.

"You were the one who told me – in no uncertain terms – to get out of your life and leave you alone," he reminded angrily.

"What would you expect me to do or say to you? Kingston is a damn small place to have an affair in. I'd suffered more than enough humiliation on your behalf…flaunting Powers in my face everywhere I turn. Then to hear from the press – not from you – that you once had an affair with her years ago and you've rekindled the fire! What would you want me to do?" she seethed.

Alex was silent.

"Do you deny having an affair with her?" she asked as tears streamed down her face.

"It was a long time ago," he admitted simply. "It meant nothing to me."

"Is that right?" she drawled sarcastically. "Why didn't you tell me?"

"Oh rass," he swore loudly and stood up, grimacing as his head swam. "Why didn't you come to me?"

"Come to you! Come to you?" she laughed bitterly. "When I did go over to your house, do you know who answered the bloody door? Your mistress, and do you want to know what she said to me?" She didn't wait for him to respond. "That you've been sleeping with her from before we were married and after! You'd married me for my money Alex and that the two of you had planned it!" She was hysterical and she didn't care. It was past time she let all the anger out.

She looked around for something to throw and picked up a hand blown vase and sent it flying. He ducked and it crashed against the wall. Alex stared at it in shock. Never had he seen Merissa so angry and hurt. He'd kill Vanessa for this. That bitch! He'd kill her!

"She was lying."

"I don't believe you."

"She was lying damn it! I slept with her once. Once! The night I buried my family. I haven't touched her since!"

Merissa picked up an ashtray and sent it through the air followed by another ornament and yet another. She didn't wait to see if her missiles hit him, she just wanted to hurt him.

"Stop it!" Alex yelled angrily at her before ducking and grabbing her arms as she picked up a wooden elephant. "Drop it Merissa," he ordered softly. "I said drop it!" he repeated when she didn't release it.

It fell with a heavy thud to the floor. He let her go. Merissa threw a quick punch with her fist, catching him on the side of his face. "How could you do this to me? I loved you. I really loved you." She hit out at him with her fists and bare feet.

He let her hit him.

"Why didn't you just tell me Alex? I don't understand why you had to marry me because you obviously couldn't keep your hands off Powers to even give our marriage a chance. Or maybe you didn't want to."

She moved away, turning her back on him with rejection. She felt defeated, she looked dejected.

"I've been such a fool, such a fool." She threw at him over her shoulder as she turned to leave the room.

"It wasn't like that Merissa, you have to believe me," he begged, stopping her in her tracks.

She looked at him through large, pain-filled eyes.

"Why should I, you…"

"Because I love you."

"Don't make me look more stupid than I already feel."

"I love you. I always have. Vanessa was only ever a friend to me, I guess she had her own agenda Merissa, but I swear to you. It is only you I want."

Merissa steeled herself against the look of vulnerability on his lovely face. She wanted to believe him, she really did. But it wasn't just this thing with Vanessa. It was everything else as well. She needed time alone.

"Too late. I know you got the divorce papers."

The blood powered through his veins and stopped. "And that's another thing," he snarled. "Couldn't you have at least brought it to me yourself?"

"Why? I didn't want to see you then and I don't now. Just sign the papers and you can live your life any way you please."

"I won't sign them."

They glared at one another, both breathing heavily, neither giving in.

"You will sign them Alex," she warned softly through clenched teeth. Then flinging her arms in the air rounded on him again. "Because of you I can't have children!"

"No! How can you say such a thing?"

"You have more experience. You should have protected me!"

Her accusations blew his mind. "Don't say anything more Merissa. You just might regret it," he finished softly.

"Our marriage was a sham in your eyes in the first place. I don't want to be married to you!" she screamed.

"It's not what you want and we both know it. You want a divorce so that you can go off and see that James person!"

"Oh for God's sake! Don't you try and shift everything on my side. I have not been having an affair with James! Although now that you mention it I just might," she added with a spark of dreamy contemplation.

A rage like he'd never experienced burst through him. Alex grabbed her shoulders and raised his hand to strike her. He was shaking with the effort to control himself.

"Go on hit me!" she taunted. "Do it," she challenged.

Alex saw red, but let her go and stepped back, moving to the other side of the room, putting the brown suede couch between them.

"I don't want to hurt you."

"You already have," she snapped back.

He lost it, stalked over to her and pulled her roughly into his arms. There was nothing gentle about his mouth on hers. She struggled, pushed at him but still he wouldn't let her go. When she raked her nails down the side of his neck, he winced, picked her up and pushed her down onto the couch.

"Don't fight me," he told her as he held her arms above her head and moved lower, kissing the hollow of her neck and sucking at the tiny pulse fluttering madly there.

"Stop it Alex. Please don't do this," she begged as she tried to ignore the warmth spreading throughout her body. "I hate you. You're despic..."

He stopped her words with his mouth, his tongue moving inside, invading, coaxing and demanding all at once. She refused to kiss him back. His hand released her and she immediately began to fight again. He let her, holding her down with his full weight ignoring the pain she was causing with her nails. He wanted her and nothing could stop him from taking her.

He shifted slightly to look into her dark eyes.

"I've never slept with her since that time. I love *you*." His eyes glittered with tears and for a moment she softened. "I've always loved you."

He lowered his head to hers.

"No! Stop it! Stop it Alex!" She struggled beneath him. "Let me go."

"No."

"Let…me…go!" she screamed, raised her knee and kicked him in his most vulnerable spot.

He freed her and groaned.

Merissa scrambled to her feet and ran towards her bedroom; only he caught up with her and pulled her roughly to him again.

"I hate you," she spat.

"No you don't." He picked her up and slung her over his shoulder before dumping her on the bed.

Standing guard over her he flung his shirt off. His muscles flexed. Merissa jumped off the bed and almost made it to the bathroom but he grabbed her.

"Don't do this to me Alex!" She slapped his face with a stinging blow.

He winced and Merissa watched mesmerised as his eyes darkened to a terrifying deepness, and for the first time ever, she was afraid of him. He twisted her arm behind her back, pushed her down onto the bed and covered her body with his. He was everywhere at once. Merissa tried not to respond, she really did, but when his lips found her nipples and his hands went down to her centre, her hips rose to eagerly meet him. He made love to her for the rest of what was left of the night. Sometimes hard and fast as though he had to make up for lost time. Other times, slowly and ever so gently as though he knew he had the rest of his life to love her.

When he finally left her, he looked into her sleepy eyes.

"Tell me you don't love me and I'll sign the papers and leave you alone," he whispered.

She looked into his eyes. She loved him. Always had, probably always would.

"I don't love you."

He looked at her long and hard before kissing her softly and picking up his clothes. He quietly left the house.

Chapter Forty-Six

Merissa sat at the very edge of the shore, her naked feet caressed by the morning cool waves of the ocean. She looked out across the horizon as a burst of pink, gold, lavender and rust touched the earth with gentle subtleness; shades of dawn, she thought, her favourite time of day.

In another two hours her workmen would be busy finishing up the paint work and the first load of furniture would arrive.

Her hotel! She sighed with satisfying accomplishment. For six months she had been building on her father's land – her land. Thomas had bought it back before he died – his last gift. A beautiful carefully planned hotel stood proudly on the little raise of hill which overlooked the beach. It promised to attract tourists from all over the world and already it was booked solid for the next year!

It was only the tiny cove she had left untouched. It was her place.

Her mind drifted back to the very first time she had walked down the pathway and stepped onto the sand. None of the horrible memories raised their ugly heads. She had found peace at last.

She spent almost all her mornings down here, planning her future, thinking about the baby and Alex. He didn't know about the baby and like many times before, when she allowed herself to think of him, she felt guilty for keeping it to herself. Her hand automatically moved to her well-rounded stomach and she smiled as she felt a strong kick.

Her life was so full right now. The hotel almost finished, her name established as a designer, a healthy pregnancy, but yet she still felt a subtle emptiness.

Joseph and Mrs. Dobbson had finally married. Toby and Cymone were engaged to be married. Toby had insisted on a short engagement saying he'd waited for over two years for Cymone to even notice him. He wasn't waiting any longer. Already, he'd filed adoption papers for Nathan.

Merissa smiled when she remembered Toby's adamant determination. Alex had been like that once. Her smile faded.

That night, all those months ago he had walked out of her life, taking her happiness with him. She missed him and it was only now when she was alone bathed in the Jamaican sunrise that she allowed herself to think of him. They would have been married over two years by now. How had things gone so wrong? Her eyes filled and overflowed with an unexpected tear. She touched a finger to it and looked at the circle of wetness on her finger tip. It had been a long time since she had allowed herself to cry.

"I miss you," she whispered into the wind.

Alex looked down at the tiny beach below. He could see her sitting on the sand looking out to sea.

Merissa, my love.

He had summoned up the nerve to finally go to the hotel just to see her, even if it was from afar. They had parted on such bad terms. He needed to say sorry.

He'd been living in Negril for over two months and was running the new branch. He'd been glad to get away from Kingston and for a time, thought he was free of the memories and he could move on and rebuild his life without her coming into his thoughts every other second. He'd been wrong.

Living just half an hour away from her made him look into every passing car just to catch a glimpse. She was so very, very near, but yet so far.

He took a deep steadying breath before descending slowly down the steep pathway, his eyes never leaving her back. When he finally reached the bottom and he stopped, the feeling of uncertainty rose again. What was he doing? Why did he want to set himself up for rejection yet again?

Merissa felt, rather than saw a presence behind her and turned around. A man in pleated trousers, white shirt with a navy blazer casually flung over one shoulder stood watching her.

Two brown eyes met and held.

Merissa felt a wave of excited heat flood her lungs.

"Alex?" she whispered in shock and consciously wrapped her bulky jumper around herself.

He walked towards her, his gaze never leaving hers.

"Alex," she said again, not knowing what all the feelings inside her were saying.

He sat beside her and stared silently ahead. The sound of the rough sea crashing against the rocks was nothing compared to the loud heart beats the two of them were fighting to control.

"Hi, Meri," he said eventually.

She smiled. "Hi."

They were silent again and Alex watched as a lonesome seagull stood on a rock surrounded by the rough elements. That's how I feel, he thought to himself.

"Your hotel is beautiful."

"Thank you." Finally she could say something. "I tried not to spoil the natural beauty around it; I wanted it to blend in as much as possible," she explained nervously.

"You did a wonderful job. When will it be opened?"

"In three weeks."

Silence.

"What are you doing here...I mean here in Negril?" she corrected quickly. She wanted him here.

"I live this side now. We finally opened the new branch about two months ago. I've been living here permanently ever since."

Silence.

"You look good Merissa," he told her honestly. She'd cut her hair and had a flushed healthy look about her.

Her hand automatically went to her bump. He didn't notice. "Thanks. So do you. A bit underweight but you look well." Her eyes dropped to his body and little furnaces deep within her body switched on in rapid succession.

He shrugged, "Can we..." he cleared his tight throat. "Can we have dinner sometime?" he asked cautiously.

Blood pounded in her ears as she panicked. Her hand went to her bump again. He'd know! "I can't," she told him and watched the hope die in his eyes. He took a deep shaky breath and hauled himself up to his feet.

"I've...I've missed you Alex," she admitted softly and bit her lip nervously, tasting the sting of salt against them.

"I've missed you too," he told her sitting down again, encouraged. *At least she misses me. It's a start.*

"Alex, I didn't mean..."

"Meri, I didn't mean..."

They laughed.

"You go first," he told her.

"No you."

He took her hand.

"Meri...I didn't mean for any of this to happen." He looked sadly into her eyes. "I didn't mean to hurt you like I know I did. Since we've been apart, not a single minute has passed without you coming into my thoughts, it's driving me crazy. I miss you so much and I love you so much more."

He held up his hand when she started to interrupt him. "I really acted like a fool, a blind fool. I didn't see what Vanessa was up to, I really didn't know the woman had alternative plans about me and her." He shrugged. "Misguided loyalty to an old friend and all that. I didn't want to believe anyone, much less her, could be so malicious. I found out she was the one feeding the papers."

"We shared one night, one night, years ago," he stressed. "It was sex. It meant nothing to me." He squeezed Merissa's hand, willing her to believe him. "She's undergoing psychological evaluation at the moment to see if she's mentally fit to stand trial for the murder of her boss," he explained.

Merissa gasped. She had no idea!

"You're my whole life Merissa," he went on passionately, looking into her eyes. "I've been wandering around these past months feeling lost without you. I don't want to be lost anymore." His eyes shone with tears.

"I love you Alex, but I…"

He silenced her by gently putting his finger to her lips.

"That's all I wanted to hear." He looked at her tenderly, reached out and touched her cheek. Then he stood, turned and walked away.

Merissa sat up straight and watched him walk away.

He can't leave! I love him! I love him damn it!

She stood and ran after him.

"Alex wait! Wait!" she called up to him as he climbed the dark craggy rock.

He turned and looked down at her.

"I love you!" she yelled up to him, tears of happiness streaming down her cheeks. "I love you!"

"What?" he shouted back.

The wind carried her words across the sea. He couldn't hear her.

"I said I love you. I'm sorry!"

"What?"

Merissa looked at him in frustration.

"Come down." She signalled him with her arms to come back down and watched excitedly and impatiently as he picked his way down the rocky path.

When he finally reached the bottom she flung herself into his arms and hugged him tight before kissing him deeply. He was slow to respond but once he did, her heart took off and hit the heavens.

"I love you."

"I love you too," he said gruffly, stooping to recapture her lips once more. He couldn't believe she was in his arms again.

Slowly she stepped away from him.

"Will you marry us again?" she asked, biting the side of her lip. He thought he hadn't heard right and looked at her in confusion. "Will you marry us Alex?"

"Us?" He looked at her stomach as she touched it and turning sideways, pulled her jumper across the heavy roundness showing him his baby.

"Yes, us."

He grinned, and then laughed out loudly before taking her into his arms and kissing her with sensuous promise.

"Yes I'll marry you," he whispered as he touched her stomach and felt the baby kick. He grinned and looked down at his hand in wonder. The baby kicked again. "And you too!" He laughed then kissed her hands.

He looked around. "I can't make you a ring," he told her with a regrettable smile minutes later.

"That's ok. I have this." She reached into her jumper and pulled out a thin gold chain, attached was a tiny gold unicorn and a very brown, very dry circle of plaited palm leaf.

Alex's heart burst with love.

"I love you Merissa York," he told her, emotion making his voice deep.

"And I you, but now I need to be shown." She took his hand and pulled him down to the sand.

LaVergne, TN USA
04 December 2009
166013LV00004B/6/P